PHILLIMORE PLACE
LONDON

By Kim Hunter

Kim Hunter

Copyright © 2014 By Kim Hunter

The right of Kim Hunter to be identified as author of this work has been asserted in accordance with sections 77 and 78 of the Copyright, Designs and Patents Act 1988.

All rights Reserved

No reproduction, copy or transmission of this publication
may be made without written permission.
No paragraph of this publication may be reproduced,
Copied or transmitted save with the written permission of the author, or in
accordance with the provisions of the Copyright Act 1956 (as amended)

This is a work of fiction.
Names, places, characters and incidents originate from the writers imagination.
Any resemblance to actual persons, living or dead is purely coincidental.

Table of contents

Title Page
Copyright
Authors other works
Foreword
Prologue
Chapter one
Chapter two
Chapter three
Chapter four
Chapter five
Chapter six
Chapter seven
Chapter eight
Chapter nine
Chapter ten
Chapter eleven
Chapter twelve
Chapter thirteen
Chapter fourteen
Chapter fifteen
Chapter sixteen
Chapter seventeen
Chapter eighteen
Chapter nineteen

Chapter twenty
Chapter twenty-one
Chapter twenty-two
Chapter twenty-three
Chapter twenty-four
Epilogue

OTHER WORKS BY KIM HUNTER

WHATEVER IT TAKES
EAST END HONOUR
TRAFFICKED
BELL LANE LONDON E1
EAST END LEGACY
EAST END A FAMILY OF STEEL

Web site www.kimhunterauthor.com

FOREWORD

He had two lives; one open, seen and known by all who cared to know, full of relative truth and of relative falsehood, exactly like the lives of his friends and acquaintances; and another life running its course in secret. And through some strange, perhaps accidental, conjunction of circumstances, everything that was essential, of interest and of value to him, everything in which he was sincere and did not deceive himself, everything that made the kernel of his life, was hidden from other people.

Anton Chekhov 1896 - 1904

PROLOGUE
MI5 Headquarters
(Two months earlier)

The telephone in Silvia Gladman's office rang in the middle of her afternoon nap and she wasn't pleased at being disturbed. Due to working late the previous evening, which was common practice for her most days, she had taken to power napping every day after lunch. Sighing heavily she picked up the receiver.

"Yes!"

When she heard the voice on the other end, she quickly changed her tone and sat bolt upright.

"Yes Sir, right away Sir."

Being summoned to her boss's office was always a big deal and even though she was second in command, she rarely got to see the man as the majority of contact was usually carried out by email or telephone. Wracking her brains she couldn't think of anything shed done wrong and there were no terrorist threats on the horizon or none that she was aware of, now Silvia was very intrigued. Walking into her private bathroom she splashed her face with water and combed her hair. Happy with her appearance she smoothed down her skirt and made her way up to the top floor. The Director Generals office was situated at the far end of a long hallway. Knocking on the double oak doors she waited to be invited in. Unlike conventional offices, there was no reception area as anyone who was on the top floor were here by invitation only. When she heard the words enter, Silvia Gladman made sure she was standing straight and then went inside.

"Don't bother to sit Silvia, this won't take long. We have reason to believe that confidential information is being leaked from within the building. It may not be from this department but wherever it's from I'm determined to root it out and god help those responsible. Pick the best from you team and instruct them to follow these men. If they frequent any places out of the ordinary or meet any person that appears to be of a dubious nature then I want to know about it."

The Director General slid a piece of paper across his desk and motioned with his head for Silvia to pick it up.

"As you are only too aware, these people are very high profile and anything concerning them is strictly classified."

Her boss then picked up his phone and began to dial; it was an indication to Silvia that the meeting was at an end. Just as she was about to turn the door handle he spoke again.

"I don't need to remind you that everything must be carried out strictly by the book. We can't afford for any slip ups to occur."

"Yes Sir, of course Sir."

CHAPTER ONE
2012

Lucy Urquhart stretched out her arms, opened her mouth wide to yawn and then snuggled back down under the duvet. The Egyptian cotton sheets that covered her bed were the best that money could buy and so very soft to the touch. For her entire life Lucy had lived in total luxury and wanted for nothing. Even her time spent at university was cushioned when her father purchased a town house on one of Edinburgh's finest streets. The stone built three storey Victorian property boasted four bedrooms and three bathrooms. It was decorated with antique furniture and had a state of the art kitchen. Any ordinary person would have been over the moon to have such a beautiful place to stay in while they studied but not Lucy Urquhart. Lucy craved normality and had dreamed of spending her time in the halls of residence having fun with the other students. After several arguments, George Urquhart had finally relented when his daughter told him that the only way she would move into the property was if she was allowed to rent out the other three bedrooms to fellow students. George had been involved in politics since his early thirties and coupled with inheriting a vast fortune from his own father, wanted his daughter to mix in the right circles and marry into a family befitting his own. Lucy's mother had passed away when Lucy was just ten years old and being his only child, George was fiercely protective of her. He worried that her housemates wouldn't be as refined and could lead her down the wrong path but Lucy was adamant that she needed the company. Promising that she would thoroughly vet any applicants, he finally gave in to her demands. Unbeknown to George, the vetting never happened and Lucy had let anyone stay whenever they wanted. It wasn't a lie when Lucy said she needed company but she also wanted to party and the straight laced girls from her own social circle were definitely not the types she wished to share a house with. After sixth form and before going to university, Lucy Urquhart had spent two years in Switzerland. The finishing school was supposed to make a lady of her but Lucy rebelled at every opportunity. Leaving the grounds a couple of times each week, she would venture down to the village to buy alcohol and mix with the local girls. They often asked her to sneak them all into the school but they were so noisy Lucy knew they would be found out in an instant. She always seemed able to come up with an excuse for them to stay in the village, a village where there were lots of places to sit and get absolutely legless. Many times Lucy would only just make it home in time for breakfast and would have to climb through a window so she wasn't seen by the Matron. On the day she finally completed her course of improvement, Lucy actually saw the Head smile and clap as George's car left the estate grounds. At twenty years old she went on to win a place at Edinburgh University on a four year course in politics. As with most students partying became a regular occurrence but she did manage to knuckle down in her final year. Lucy Urquhart gained her master's degree and much to her father's pleasure achieved a good grade. One thing George hadn't been privy to was the fact that a year into her placement his daughter had added another subject to her curriculum, one that interested her far more. Psychology was now her passion, though Lucy hadn't yet plucked up the courage to tell her father. Finishing University and after taking a six month break to travel around Europe with her friend Olly, a friend George assumed was female and called Olivia but who was in fact very much male, Lucy was now living back at the family home. Manor Lodge on Abbotsbury Road was a magnificent three story Georgian villa and Holland Park was a fantastic area to live in. Neighbouring properties were also home to stars of stage and screen, not to mention the numerous premiership footballers. Young girls could often be seen walking the streets in the hope of catching a glimpse of their idols but to Lucy Urquhart it was nothing special, just the place shed called home for as long as she could remember. The expensive antique furniture that filled every room didn't impress her or the fact that they had a chauffeur and housekeeper as they had always been in her life and she never gave them any thought. Occasionally, when any of her University friends called to visit, Lucy would become embarrassed by the grandeur of their lives. Her friends were always overly impressed with the splendour and would ask lots of questions but she would cringe and try to play things down. Lucy Urquhart was not only physically beautiful, she had an inner beauty and kindness that couldn't help but endear her to anyone she met and her list of friends was vast. At Manor Lodge, her room which was actually the whole of the third floor, consisted of a lounge, small kitchenette, en suite and of course her sleeping area. The total square footage was larger than most suburban semis but Lucy thought little of it. It wasn't a case of taking what she had for granted or that she was spoilt, which she undoubtedly was but purely the fact that she really didn't care about it all. Lucy could have lived in a tent and it wouldn't have bothered her, what mattered to her was people, real people and the lives that they chose to live. Pulling on her dressing gown and after brushing her teeth, Lucy descended the fine Georgian staircase with a spring in her step. Her head was filled to bursting point with all that she wanted to do and she wasn't concentrating. When she reached the bottom step she almost bumped into Mrs Sanderson who had just walked through the door from the basement and was carrying a large armful of flowers. Norma

Sanderson was now in her early sixties and had been born and raised in the east end of London. Most would never know it by her polished accent as she had tried desperately hard to lose her cockney slang over the years and had almost managed to achieve it except when the odd word would escaped from her mouth in a way that only a true cockney would pronounce it. A plump woman with the soft warm face of a grandmother she was the only person Lucy ever turned to when she had a problem. Never having married, Norma had been employed as the Urquhart's housekeeper since before Lucy was born and she loved the family dearly. The day that Sonia Urquhart had carried her baby into the house, Norma instantly fell in love with the child. That feeling had only grown stronger over the years and she now loved the girl as if she was her own. Norma had been witness to all the pain and heartbreak that Lucy had gone through when her mother passed away. Many times in the early days she had been the only person able to calm the girl when she woke sobbing in the middle of the night. She had been witness to Mr Urquhart's struggle with his own grief while trying to console his child and it had broken her heart. It had taken several years for them both to get back on track but Norma had never doubted that they would. Now that Lucy had returned home, the house was again filled with laughter and energy, not to mention many many arguments.

"Morning Norma! Is he in the dining room?"
"And a good morning to you too Miss Lucy. Yes your father has just sat down to breakfast. Now what would you like to eat my darling?"
Lucy scratched at her unruly mop of blond hair as if she'd been asked to explain what the meaning of life was. Several seconds later and when Norma, through frustration, was about to walk away Lucy at last decided what she wanted.
"Oh just toast please, I'm not that hungry. Norma did you manage to get what I asked for?"
Norma Sanderson smiled as she handed over a copy of the Daily Mail. The girls head was permanently in the clouds and Norma wondered how she'd ever managed to do so well in her studies. Lucy slowly walked towards the dining room and at the same time she opened up the newspaper and began to scan the classified adverts section. When her eyes settled on her own advertisement she smiled from ear to ear. Folding up the paper, she placed it under her arm as she entered the formal dining room. A vast mahogany table stretched out and her father was seated at one end. As with most rich or titled families a place would have been set for Lucy at the opposite end but she wouldn't hear of it. She always made Norma set hers to the right hand side of her father so that she was close enough to touch him if she wanted to. Placing a kiss on the top of Georges head, she wrapped her arms around him and squeezed.

"Morning Daddy. Sleep well?"
George Urquhart lowered his copy of the Times and with his glasses still perched on the tip of his nose, looked up into his daughters face. She was the image of her mother and his heart would melt whenever he looked at her. Lucy was his entire world and without doubt he loved her unconditionally.
"Yes I did my darling thank you."
Taking a seat at the table she poured herself a cup of fresh coffee from the cafetiere. Not being able or wanting to hide her excitement didn't go unnoticed by her father and instead of returning to his paper he studied his daughters face trying to work out what she was thinking. The corners of her mouth were ever so slightly turned up and he could see she wanted to grin about something.
"You seem in a very good mood this morning darling?"
"I am. Daddy can we have a little chat while were eating?"
George sighed; he knew that Lucy was after something. Oh she always liked to chat but when she actually asked to speak to him, he knew trouble could be on the horizon. Folding up his paper he placed it onto the table and looked in his daughter's direction.
"Of course we can. I did actually want to talk to you regarding your future. Now as you achieved such fantastic results in your masters, well I was hoping

that you would consider going into politics. A minor post in the house will soon be available and I wondered if you would like me to put your name forward? It's only a formality really, after all it's who you know not what you know."

This wasn't what Lucy wanted to talk about and the idea of spending her days working in The Houses of Parliament filled her with utter dread. The day had gotten off to a good start but she sensed that it was all about to change.

"Look Daddy, I may as well get this off my chest once and for all."

George didn't like her tone and had a feeling he definitely wouldn't like what was coming next.

"I don't and never have wanted to work for the government and if I'm honest, I only chose politics to keep you happy. I love you dearly Daddy but the thought of spending my days in that dreary old building with all those dull pompous old men, well I think I'd rather become a nun!"

George Urquhart couldn't help but laugh at his daughter. He wouldn't deny he was disappointed but her happiness was more important to him than anything.

"So what do you want to do then?"

"Write a book."

Lucy often had scatter brained ideas and this was probably another one. His daughter was bright but she also got bored easily and he didn't think for one minute that she had the dedication to sit and write for hour upon hour. George desperately tried to stifle a laugh. He knew his daughter well and if she thought he was ridiculing her, she would storm out of the room in a temper.

"And what genre might this so called book come under?"

Lucy knew that with her next sentence the sparks would really start to fly. Her father had just taken a mouthful of coffee when she began to speak.

"It's about the sex industry, well not exactly the........."

Suddenly a fine mist of coffee showered the table. George began to splutter and cough, which made his face turn red and his eyes water. Lucy wanted to giggle but knew that it wouldn't be wise as it would only inflame the situation. Waiting for him to launch into one of his lectures she sat back in the chair and crossed her arms. As usual she would allow her father to rant on for a while and then when he'd calmed down she would begin to work on him.

"The sex industry! Now you listen to me young lady. I have not put you through some of the finest schools that money could buy just for you to write a smutty book and then there's my reputation! Good lord, the men I work with would have a field day if they got wind of this, let alone the tabloids. No, I'm sorry Lucy but I absolutely forbid it."

George Urquhart was a respectable upright man who adored his child but he also cared very deeply regarding how others saw him. He had raised his daughter well and had always known that her mother would have been proud of her but this latest idea of Lucy's was just shocking and unacceptable. On the other side of the door, Norma Sanderson had her ear pressed tightly against the woodwork. She smiled to herself when she heard George's authoritarian tone. Nothing ever changed in this household and arguments like this had taken place ever since Miss Lucy was able to talk. As yet Norma couldn't recall a single occasion when Mr Urquhart had won.

"Daddy in case you hadn't noticed I'm all grown up now and I'm not asking for your permission but if you would just hear me out, I think you might see it a little differently when you know the whole story." Georges face was now set like stone and Lucy thought to herself that at times he must put the fear of god into his fellow members of the government. It was never the case with her though; she knew that deep down he was just a pussy cat at heart.

"Take your best shot but I must warn you Lucy, I won't give in on this one."

Again she wanted to laugh at how absurd her father sounded but she didn't. Standing up from the table and uncrossing her arms, Lucy slowly walked around the room in a relaxed way. From the corner of her eye she glanced in her father's direction to make sure she still had his undivided attention and then she began to talk.

"While I was at university I saw a lot of things."
"Like what may I ask?"
"Please Daddy don't interrupt. There will be time for questions when I've finished talking but until then, will you for once just listen and not keep butting in. Now as I was saying, when I was at Uni I saw a lot of things. I always spent the weekends out and about on the streets of Edinburgh. The night life was, well a real eye opener I can tell you and I observed so many of the sex workers plying their trade."
"Good Lord!"
"Daddy please! What I witnessed, well it intrigued me so much that I decided to add another subject to my course work and a year into my Masters I enrolled in psychology. I find it fascinating and I just want to know why these people choose to do what they do. Oh I know some of them have no choice, not if they're mixed up with drugs or crime but those are not the ones I'm interested in. The people I want to look into are those who have actually chosen it as a profession, in particular high class prostitutes and dominatrix's. Now I've placed an advert in the Mail and asked for people to come forward and tell me their stories, for a fee of course."
She could see that her father had gone red in the face for a second time and was about to speak again but she raised her hand and instantly he was silenced. Lucy continued to walk around the room but she now added a slight swagger to her steps.

"I haven't and won't mention my name and I've also purchased a pay as you go mobile phone so no one will ever be able to trace me. If this works out Daddy it could be fantastic. If it isn't, then I wouldn't ever dream of trying to get it published. I know this is probably not what you hoped I would choose as a career and it's not the norm but haven't you always been the one to say that I'm far from normal?"

Lucy wanted to giggle at her own words but she held back, even when she saw the glimmer of a smile cross her father's lips.

"Now do I have your blessing or not?"

Deep down shed already made her mind up and seeking her father's permission, was in all honesty just being asked for out of politeness.

At the same time she hated disappointing him and really wanted his approval, she also knew the task she was about to undertake wouldn't be an easy one. With her father on board to provide moral support it would help her if things became difficult.

George Urquhart sighed heavily and at the same time shook his head.

"Lucy you never cease to amaze me but then I can remember seeing the same spirit in your mother when I first met her. No one could ever talk Sonia out of anything not when she'd made her mind up and I can see so much of her in you."

For a moment they were both silent, as they thought about the woman who had been so special and

instrumental in their lives and who was so terribly missed. Even after all these years just the mention of her name could still reduce George to tears. Finally and after a rather large sigh, George Urquhart nodded his head.
"Alright Lucy I will give you my blessing but you have to make me a few promises first."
This little ritual was always part of her getting her own way and Lucy would promise her father the moon if it would get her what she wanted. It was another matter when it actually came down to keeping the promises and they both knew that.
"Firstly you will not take any chances. You will meet these people, if any bother to reply to your strange advertisement, out in the open where you can be amongst others. Finally, you will not mention me or anything about our lives and this is nonnegotiable Lucy."
Lucy flung her arms lovingly around her father's neck. When she began to shower him with kisses he started to laugh and playfully acted as if he was fighting her off.
"Thank you Daddy and I promise I won't let you down."
"You had better not my girl! Now off with you, I have to finish getting ready before my car arrives."
Out in the hall Norma Sanderson smiled to herself before disappearing back down to the kitchen. Once more the little minx had gotten her own way but then she had never doubted Lucy's ability to

win over her father for a single moment. Norma knew that the girl would now set about her task with gusto and for the next few weeks at least, the house and everyone in it would be in a state of total chaos.

CHAPTER TWO

By ten am and when she thought that the house was empty, Norma Sanderson made her way back upstairs to clear the breakfast things away. Picking up the plates she saw the Daily Mail laying open on the table but never one to pry, she closed it and placed it onto the sideboard. Due to her ongoing bronchitis she coughed and the sound seemed to echo around the vast room. Even after all these years the house still seemed far too big for just the three of them and she had often wished Mr Urquhart would find himself a new wife. Norma had loved Sophie dearly but even she knew there had to come a point when it was time to move on. When Lucy had reached her teens, Norma had begun to occasionally drop subtle hints to her employer but he either hadn't picked up on what she was saying or he just didn't want to hear. Either way she now accepted that George Urquhart would spend the rest of his life alone and it saddened her. After her father left for the office, Lucy had gone straight up to her room. Removing the mobile from her bedside cabinet, she switched it on and sat for the next hour willing it to ring but the screen remained blank. Starting to doubt that anyone would even bother to phone her she decided to give up waiting around. Placing the phone into her shoulder bag, Lucy pulled on her coat and made her way downstairs. Carrying a large tray of crockery, Norma had just walked out of the dining room as Lucy crossed the hall.

"Hello love! I thought you'd already gone out."

"I was just about to."

Almost at the door, Lucy Urquhart stopped and turned to face the woman.

"She wouldn't mind about all this, would she Norma?"

"Who darling?"

"My Mum."

The question took Norma Sanderson by surprise and she could feel a lump instantly form in her throat. Putting the tray down onto a chair, Norma walked over to Lucy and placed her hands on the girl's shoulders.

"Of course she wouldn't."

Lucy Urquhart smiled and the housekeeper could see the pool of tears that had begun to form in Lucy's eyes.

"You know something? Sometimes I can hardly remember what she looked like and it hurts me so much. I feel like I'm betraying her but I'm not, honestly I'm not."

"Darling we all struggle with things like that, if I want to remember my parents I have to get all my old photos out as it was so long ago and memories fade fast sweetheart. Remember one thing, you have her love in your heart and that you will never forget. I only have to look at you and I see her, I

suppose it's the same for your father too. She would have been so proud of you Lucy and don't you ever forget that. Whether she would have agreed with this latest little escapade of yours I'm not so sure but I do know that she would have been glad that you were doing what you wanted no matter what anyone else says."
"Thanks Norma, I needed to hear that."
Norma Sanderson resumed her usual brisk manner in order to stop herself from crying.
"Right then young lady, now where are you off to?"
"To the shops. A spot of retail therapy always cheers me up and I definitely need cheering up at the minute."
"Then best you get yourself off and if you're planning to stay out all day don't be late back for dinner, you know how your father worries. Goodness me look at the time, I can't be standing here nattering all day with you young lady."
With that Norma turned and walked towards the basement door and the sanctuary of her warm kitchen. Smiling, Lucy stepped out into the fresh morning air. It took her fifteen minutes to reach Kensington High Street and just as she was about to enter Musa boutique, her phone finally started to ring. Desperately she delved into her bag to retrieve it but it had already switched over to answer phone and just as Lucy suspected, there was no message left. Now even more depressed, she deciding to grab a coffee and think things over.

Making her way to Pret A Manger, Lucy took a seat at one of the outside tables. When the waitress approached she ordered a latte and the whole time, even as she placed her order, her eyes never once left the screen of her phone. Five minutes later and as if by magic it suddenly began to ring and almost knocking over her coffee, Lucy grinned widely as she snatched it up from the table.
"Hello?"
To begin with there was only the sound of heavy breathing and she thought there must be a bad connection. Nervously she repeated herself.
"Hello?"
"I'm phoning about your advert and I want some information."
Lucy was instantly excited and smiled as she spoke.
"Of course Sir and thank you so much for calling. Now what would you like to know?"
"Tell me what you're wearing?"
The smile disappeared from Lucy Urquhart's face and her brow furrowed with confusion.
"I beg your pardon? I'm sorry but I don't quite understand what you mean can you......"
"I said what are you wearing? Do you have crotchless knickers on you dirty bitch?"
Lucy instantly thought back to the conversation shed had with her father over breakfast and knew that if she was to succeed in this then she had to be strong but at the same time could feel her face begin to flush.

"Why don't you just fuck off you disgusting pervert." Suddenly the conversation was no longer private, passersby and other customers stopped in their tracks to hear more. It wasn't usual to hear such language on Kensington High Street but Lucy didn't indulge the nosy parkers any further. With her cheeks now glowing a deep shade of red, she pressed the cancel button and threw the mobile into her bag. The rest of the morning and into the early afternoon dragged by slowly but there were no more calls. She browsed the shops for a few hours and every once in a while would check her phone but still there was nothing. Lucy was now wondering if it might have been a bad idea placing the advertisement if she was only going to attract weirdoes. Finally deciding that it had all been a useless exercise she decided to give up and make her way home to Abbotsbury Road. There really was only one person she could talk to, though how that person would feel about discussing such matters was another thing. Norma had always been her rock and Lucy knew she would try her hardest to help, even though the subject might turn out to be a bit embarrassing for them both. Climbing the front steps and after closing the imposing front door, Lucy went downstairs into the kitchen. The old stone steps were noisy but she didn't bother to call out and let Norma know who was about to enter. Norma Sanderson was standing over the Aga and stirring one of her famous stews and swiftly turned when she heard Lucy's footsteps clack across the stone floor.

"Goodness me you gave me a fright."

"Sorry Norma."

"You're forgiven, now shall we start again? Hello love and how did it all go today?"

Lucy removed her coat and scarf and Norma could see the young woman was deflated.

"Not so good I'm afraid. It seems that no one's interested in the two hundred and fifty pounds a time that I'm offering."

Laying down her wooden spoon and after wiping her hands down the front of her apron, Norma walked over to where Lucy now stood.

"Let me have a look at the ad you've placed."

Norma studied the advertisement for a few seconds and then smiled. Turning to Lucy she handed back her copy of The Mail and made her way over to the Aga.

"Love, you've put your ad in the wrong paper, if you don't mind me saying."

Lucy looked quizzically in Norma's direction but the woman had her back to Lucy so she couldn't see her face. Still the look said whatever would you know about such things.

"How do you mean?"

Still facing in the opposite direction Norma smiled to herself and once more set down the spoon as she turned to look at Lucy. Together the women took a seat at the table and Norma poured them both a cup of earl grey tea.

"Well for what it's worth and it's only my opinion, not that I know anything about such things, you're targeting the wrong market. The type of people you are after wouldn't read The Mail, The Times or any other upmarket tabloid. They may entertain high flying clients and dine in fancy restaurants now and again but most, I would imagine, would come from a more working class background."

"Why do you say that?"

"Miss Lucy sometimes you do come across as a bit naive, I really think you need to get more streetwise if you're to succeed with this. Sweetheart have you ever heard of a lady or anyone from a wealthy family come to that, choosing to go into the sex industry by choice? The kind of women who opt to do that for a living, do it solely for the money and if you don't mind me saying, your class of people definitely don't need any extra cash."

"So?"

"Well I imagine The Evening Standard would attract the sort of women you would be looking for. It is women you're interested in I take it?"

Lucy began to laugh, Norma could be so comical at times and the best part was she didn't even know it.

"Of course its women Norma but thanks for your input and I think you might be right. I'm starting to realise you really can be a wise old bird sometimes."

"Don't be so bloody cheeky young lady!"

Lucy giggled as she scooped up her coat and placed a kiss lovingly on Norma's cheek.
"I'm going to place a fresh Ad right now."
"Then best you go and do it and get out of my kitchen I do have a dinner to prepare you know. I don't know, whatever is this world coming to when I have to spend all my time talking about such things as adverts for the sex industry. My word whatever next?"
Lucy Urquhart laughed again and almost skipped out of the kitchen with excitement but at the same time chastised herself for being so stupid in the first place. In the quiet of her bedroom she dialled the telephone number of the Evening Standard and waited with baited breath. Placing the advert was easier than it had been with The Mail. The Standard didn't ask any personal questions, whereas The Mail had treated her as if she was a prostitute. It had taken several minutes of explaining and not before shed been put through to the editor, before they had accepted she was genuinely doing research. When the telephone was picked up by the Standard it was a different matter altogether.
"Hello, Evening Standard classifieds."
"Oh yes hello, I'd like to place a wanted advertisement please."
"Its fifty pence a word but that's only a line above and below. If you want a box that's another seven fifty."
Lucy was a little taken aback. She hadn't been

asked what the advert was concerning, in fact the young man on the other end of the telephone really didn't seem that interested in anything. Choosing a box for the most impact, she began to nervously repeat word for word the same advert that shed placed in the Mail. When she finished the young man simply read back her wording, asked for a card payment and then thanked her for her custom. Lying back on her bed, Lucy stared at the ceiling and could once more feel the excitement begin to build. Good old Norma always seemed to come to the rescue. Thinking about it all now, it seemed ridiculous not to have known what was staring her straight in the face. Problems always had a way of turning out to be far simpler than you first thought they were, if you only took the time to think about them. Still she did feel like a bit of a fool for imagining that a sex worker would be so upmarket but then Lucy Urquhart hadn't bargained on the woman she was soon to meet.

CHAPTER THREE
1966

Liam Flanagan arrived in England on March the seventeenth nineteen sixty six. The troubles in Northern Ireland were getting worse by the day and Liam could see that it would soon escalate out of control. Even though he'd been raised in the catholic faith he wasn't particularly religious, that said he had great respect for his brothers in arms and would do anything asked of him if ever called on by the provisional IRA. Reluctantly he knew it was time to leave his homeland if he was to stop himself getting in too deep regarding the politics of his country. The morning he set foot on English soil just happened to be St Patricks day and just eight days after the Kray's had shot dead George Cornell in the Blind Beggar pub. The whole of London seemed to be talking about the murder and Liam was intrigued. Making his way over to Whitechapel, he stood on the opposite side of the road and looked across at the building. Flowers were lying on the pavement outside and Liam wondered what it would feel like to have such a reputation that just the mention of your name instilled fear into people. He was desperate to go inside The Blind Beggar but at fifteen years old, knew he would be told to sling his hook as soon as he walked through the door. For now he would have to make do with reading about this particular crime and others just like it in the local paper. The sixties was a growing time of gangster culture in the East End and everyone knew someone who was related to, was friends with or even worked for one of the firms. After weeks of lifting and carrying on market stalls and doing the odd delivery job, Liam finally managed to gain regular work on a building site. At The Britannic Tower, which is now known as City Point he was taken on as a labourer. His Irish accent led him to be called Murphy, Paddy, Mick, Michael and any other derogatory name that referred to the Irish but Liam ignored them all. He was there to learn all that he could and none of it concerned the building trade. He saw how the heavies would come onto site every Friday for their pay offs and he noted everything from the protection rackets to the building materials that disappeared from the site at an alarming rate. By the time the structure was completed a year later, Liam Flanagan was ready to move up a step. He was confident and cocky to boot and seeking out the Richardson gang, he blagged his way into a job as a gofer. It wasn't what he had hoped for but at just seventeen he wasn't in a position to complain. Charlie Richardson had just been sent down on a twenty five stretch and the Kray's would be indefinitely caged two years later for the murder of George Cornell and Frank the hat McVitie. Freddie Butcher had taken over the reins since Charlie's departure but in Liam's eyes he was weak and it was just a matter of time before someone bigger muscled in. That really wasn't any of Liam Flanagan's concern as he was only interested in learning the ropes, ropes that would include extortion, long hauling, running the brasses, pornography and setting up businesses with the gaming machines. By nineteen seventy six and with his twenty fifth birthday fast approaching Liam knew he was at last ready to go it alone. For the past couple of months he'd been procuring a few loyal men he worked closely with and they were all now happy to jump ship. Things had changed since Charlie's incarceration and they saw Freddie as nothing more than a prize prat. A prat, who had in the last few years, let things slip to such a degree, that there wasn't much of a firm left to take over. What the men wanted and needed was a new leader, someone who was strong and could take them forward into the future and all that it had to offer. Liam had the sense not to go overboard when it came to stepping on another firm's toes. Charlie still had contacts on the outside and Liam didn't want any unnecessary conflict at such an early stage in his career. Walking away from the failing Richardson Empire meant Liam had to start from scratch but with all of his contacts the Flanagan firm was profitable within the first couple of weeks. Unlike the Kray's, who had run their operation from the front room of their family home, business for

Liam was carried out at The Nags Head over in Holloway. Over the years he had purposely lost his Irish accent and now spoke with a real cockney twang. He had quickly realised that he wouldn't be taken seriously and would even be ridiculed if he sounded like a paddy, not to mention the fact that he could also be branded as a terrorist. His reinvention allowed Liam to rule the area with an iron rod and no one dared to cross him. He lived and breathed business and there was never any time for women. In truth they did little for him and the girls who hung around the firm, to Liam at least, were whores pure and simple. He was particular where he dipped his wick or that was the excuse he used to his men. In reality he never wanted a woman, especially one that would try and control him. Back in Belfast he had spent his childhood in one care home after another and had also been subjected to abuse by the local priests. Luckily for Liam the abuse he suffered hadn't been anywhere near as severe as it could have been. Other boys in the homes had been raped and beaten to within an inch of their lives and it wasn't much of a shock when details emerged of several boys committing suicide. As much as Liam had hated the men pawing him, it wasn't anything that troubled him now and it certainly hadn't turned him gay. At school the girls had always been ready for a kiss and a cuddle round the back yard alleys but Liam just hadn't been interested. Now years later and as his porn empire grew, he had started to take more than a casual interest in the magazines that he was shipping over from Holland and America. Some were hard core and it certainly made for interesting reading. Finding a like minded woman to feed his sexual desires was a different matter but over the ensuing years Liam did manage to fulfil his needs a few times. He could have gotten his kicks on a daily basis with any of the Brass's that worked for him but he saw them as slag's. What Liam Flanagan wanted was a good clean but dirty girl and even he realised it was a contradiction in terms. As time passed he had to admit that the chance of finding such a woman was almost impossible. He didn't dwell on it too much and instead concentrated his efforts on business. By the time he reached thirty he was known as the enforcer, a name he inherited from the original hit man of the time Jimmy Moody. Moody had worked freelance for all the major firms in the smoke but when he was jailed in seventy nine the position immediately became vacant. Too mean to pay another body to carry out his unsavoury work Liam decided to do it himself but whereas others were in it solely for the money, Liam Flanagan was sadistic and enjoyed every minute of inflicting pain. Beatings occurred on a regular basis and one such occasion which occurred by chance resulted in a man being tortured so badly that he ended up a crippled vegetable who was unable to even feed himself. It happened in the back yard shed of the Nags Head. It wasn't anything to do with another gang member but a small time thief who had been helping himself to cash from one of Liam's gaming arcades. Desmond McKeon had found a way of opening up the backs of the slot machines. A pick pocket by trade, he was quick and left no trace that the machines had been tampered with but one day his luck just ran out. Bobby Henson the arcade manager had returned early from his tea break and caught Desmond red handed. Bobby was a large man and easily able to frogmarch Des round to the Nags Head. Desmond McKeon had always been a chancer and even though he knew who owned the arcade he had decided to take that risk. Sadly this would turn out to be the worst day of his life and when he felt a hand roughly grasp his shoulder, knew well enough where he was being taken to. Desmond McKeon began to sweat profusely and his words were pleading.

"Aye ye caught me red handed Pal but come on, giz a break. What say we split the cash?"

Desmond's Scottish accent was so strong that Bobby had difficulty understanding the man but it wouldn't have made any difference either way. Someone had to pay for the money that had gone missing over the last couple of weeks and Bobby Henson was damn sure it wasn't going to be him. Liam Flanagan had taken up his usual morning residence and was holding court with three of his men when the door flew open and Bobby almost threw Desmond inside.

"Found out why the machines have been light Gov. This tosser has only been getting his hand in round the back!"

For a moment Liam studied the man but he didn't speak. You always had to be careful that you weren't being set up by the Old Bill. Desmond's clothes were dirty and his hands and fingernails were stained through heavy smoking. When Liam was happy that everything was as it should be he stood up.

"You little cunt! So you're the fucking problem are you? I've been wracking me fucking brains as to why those machines weren't producing much and now I find out that some cunts had the audacity to rob me. Bobby, take him out the back to me workshop."

Liam's workshop was in fact the old brick beer store that was no longer used. The firm had taken over the whole of the rear yard, much to the disgust of the landlord but he knew better than to voice an opinion. Brian Mason, who ran most of the girls in Soho and who had been in the middle of talking to Liam, suddenly piped up.

"You want me to sort him out Boss?"

"Nah you're alright son, I like to keep me hand in from time to time. You boys get off now, me and Bobby can handle things from here."

Bobby Henson grabbed Desmond by the scruff of

the neck and frogmarched him outside. The little Scotchman was so frightened that his resistance was only verbal as he pleaded with his captors.
"Please Mr Flanagan, I'll pay you back. I promise I will, please don't hurt me."
"Pay me back? Indeed you will my son, indeed you fucking will and as for hurting you? What I'm going to do goes way beyond hurt sunshine."
Desmond again started to plead and now through fear, he actually began to cry. The pathetic sound instantly grated on Liam Flannigan's nerves.
"What the fucks he on about Bobby, I can't understand a word of that scotch fucking lingo?"
As the rest of Liam's men disappeared through the rear gate, Bobby Henson started to laugh at the absurdity of his Boss's words but he couldn't resist having a joke.
"I think he said something about a kilt Boss."
Now it was Liam's turn to laugh at Bobby's remark and for a moment Desmond had a raised hope that he would be let go but it turned out to be futile. As Desmond McKeon was hauled into the workshop, he could see by the equipment that it was or had been used to carry out some kind of engineering work. There were all types of machines from drills to lathes and even welding paraphernalia.
"Right then, where were we? Bobby lift his leg up."
When Desmond McKeon started to struggle Bobby and Liam roughly grabbed him and wrestled his right leg up onto the bench. Liam forced

Desmond's ankle into a large open vice and without being asked, Bobby quickly spun the handle and closed it up tight. Desmond was desperate not to get hurt and hopped on one leg in the hope of avoiding it. It didn't work and within seconds a searing pain shot through his body. As his free foot made contact with the concrete for a third time it slipped and went under him and his body fell to the floor. His foot, which was securely clamped in the vice, now twisted and all in the room could hear the sound as his ankle snapped.

"Arrrgh arrrrrgh!!

"Listen to him cry Bobby, it's like music to me ears."

Walking over to the oxy acetylene bottles, Liam turned on the gas and flipping open his lighter, proceeded to ignite the torch. The flame burned yellow until he switched on the accompanying oxygen. As it turned to a bright blue, Liam adjusted the heat setting and the fierce roar of the power could be heard. With some effort he dragged the equipment nearer to Desmond and the poor little Scotchman began to scream out.

"Please Mr Flanagan noooo. Oh please God no pleaseeeeeeee!!!!"

Liam was oblivious to the begging and pleading. Placing the torch on the sole of Desmond's shoe, he grinned as he set about the task. In seconds the oxy acetylene had cut through the plastic sole of the trainer and made contact with the man's skin. Now the screams were blood curdling but Liam Flanagan

didn't even flinch. He wasn't worried about anyone hearing the screams, people in this neck of the woods kept themselves to themselves and they were all well aware of who ran the manor and what would happen if they ever crossed the Irishman.
"I can't watch anymore of this boss."
"Don't be a fucking wimp Bobby and for fucks sake shut him up will you, he's doing me fucking head in."
"Please Mr Flanagan no, oh no pleaseeeeee nooooooooooooo."
With his Boss's order and desperate not to hear the man's begging again Bobby picked up a against Desmond's temple. The Scotchman went out like a light and in all honesty it was probably a good thing. Bobby Henson threw the hammer to the floor and started to wretch uncontrollably. The look of disgust on Liam's face made Bobby walk out of the workshop and into the yard. As he held onto the wall to steady himself, the contents of his stomach splashed down onto the cement floor. He didn't know if it was due to the scene he'd just been hammer from the bench and swiftly cracked it witness to, or the horrific smell of burning flesh which mixed with the toxic rubber from Desmond's shoes and now filled both of his nostrils. Maybe it was a combination of the two but either way he had no stomach for it. Back inside Liam Flanagan released the vice and Desmond's twisted crippled leg fell to the floor. It had been a while since Liam

had flexed his muscles and to be honest he was really starting to enjoy it. Thankfully Desmond was still out cold but it didn't stop his assailant from continuing his assault. Liam Flanagan was still angry and set about causing the same damage to the man's other foot. It couldn't have come at a worse time as Desmond was just beginning to come round. Unbeknown to anyone, the blow to the head had caused damage beyond repair and probably should have killed him. Unluckily for Desmond it hadn't and he would now have to endure even more torture. Once again he began to scream out in pain but the sound was muffled and incoherent due to the brain damage he had just received.

"Naaaaa ye barrrrrstardsssssss!"

Liam called out for help.

"Bobby get your arse back in here now you lily livered cunt!"

As Bobby Henson entered the workshop, he spied Desmond trying to crawl towards the door and looking in his Boss's direction saw that Liam was meticulously replacing the equipment back on the racks.

"Get rid of him out the back gates and then take the gas bottles round to Charlie Newham's, just in case some cunt contacts the Old Bill. I doubt very much it will come to that but you never know."

Even to Bobby Henson the sight was pitiful. He couldn't argue with his Boss, wouldn't dare but he hated this side of things. For god's sake, he was the manager of an arcade not Al Capone. Sighing heavily, Bobby tried to lift Desmond McKeon to his feet but the man again screamed out in pain. With no alternative, Bobby grabbed Desmond under his arms and dragged him outside. Pulling Desmond's dead weight, he had to stop a couple of times to catch his breath. Finally he made it out of the gate and when he reached the opposite side of the road he released his hold on Desmond. The man's body hit the pavement with a thud. Luckily no one was around but Bobby still looked up and down the street to make sure. As far as he was concerned Liam had well and truly overstepped the mark but like everyone else he knew better than to voice his opinion. He stood and watched for a few seconds as a horrifically damaged Desmond pathetically tried to crawl away but with his shoes still smouldering, it was only a few yards before the man passed out and slumped face down on to the pavement. Bobby Henson felt guilt beyond belief but there was nothing he could or dared do. With a heavy heart he crossed the road, walked back inside and closed the rear gates. Sometime later Desmond was at last found by a woman out walking her dog but by then he was too far gone to offer up any explanation. Liam Flanagan and Bobby Henson were both in the back room as the ambulance screeched to a halt but when Bobby looked in his Boss's direction, Liam just shrugged his shoulders and said "Serves the thieving little cunt right!"

Word of Desmond McKeon's terrible fate rapidly spread around the manor and because of this the firm began to coin in the money. Anyone who had gone only a couple of days over with their repayments miraculously turned up the following day to settle their accounts. Business was so good and would continue to be so through the eighties and nineties, that Liam Flanagan was at last able to enjoy the fruits of his labours. Unbeknown to anyone, a large slice of the firm's profits were being sent back to Ireland to fund the cause. In many North London pubs that were frequented by the Irish it was common place for a glass to be handed round. It wasn't compulsory to donate but all knew it was in their best interests to do so. It wasn't a way that Liam championed but whenever he was in a particular pub that did, he would donate heavily. Robert Gerard Sands, better known as Bobby Sands, had now been dead for ten years but Liam Flanagan was still angry. Bobby had been the leader of the nineteen eighty one hunger strikes at the Maze Prison. Along with nine others he began the anti H block campaign and wanted privileges not afforded to other inmates. Bobby saw himself and the rest of his comrades as political and not criminal prisoners. They fought to be reclassified but it was something the British government would never allow and resulted in Bobby's demise sixty six days later. The news of his death caused angry shock waves around the world and none more so than in Ireland.

Liam hadn't personally known the man or his family but he had been close friends with Pat Doherty back when he lived on the Falls Road. Pat was a fierce supporter of the IRA and whenever he came to visit Liam in London, which had been several times over the years, he would always tell Liam about his friend Bobby and all that he was doing for the fight. Liam Flanagan didn't feel guilty about leaving Ireland but he did feel it was his duty, now that he had money, to give a little back to his fellow countrymen. Of course none of his own men were ever privy to the fact, he knew only too well that if they ever got the slightest hint of what he was doing then they would down arms and walk away without a second thought. Liam didn't caught trouble and he liked to keep his political views private, not only from his men but also from the government and when the troubles had really escalated there were plenty ready to grass up a Paddy if they got the chance. Just before the Flanagan firm had been forced to move from The Nags Head; Liam met Jess the woman of his dreams. Jess Metcalf was everything he had ever hoped for and he couldn't have been happier. Their relationship was strange but suited them both for different reasons. Deep down, though he wouldn't admit it to anyone, Liam Flanagan had fallen head over heels in love with her but it was a love that wasn't and never would be reciprocated. When the Nags Head closed its doors for the last time in two thousand and four, business was moved to the backroom of a pub called The Head. Of all the places that they had used as a base, Liam liked The Head best of all. He really like the name and saw it as fitting for the boss of a firm. When the brewery, much to Liam's disgust, sold it off to a developer seven years later, the Flanagan firm was forced to move for a third and final time. The Hercules Tavern wouldn't have been Liam's first choice of venue but he needed somewhere to trade. From the outside the little corner pub was rough looking and a place you didn't venture into unless you were a regular or had purposely come to see Mr Flanagan. It wasn't ideal and to begin with Liam hated it but at the end of the day it served a purpose and that was all that mattered. The landlord Mickey Jones was well aware of just who had taken residence in his back room. He did without question, everything he was told to do and his orders definitely didn't come from the brewery. As long as the bills were paid at the end of the month, then the company had little or no interest in the place and Mickey was too scared to try and get out. Once again the pub had a brick built building in the rear yard and Liam though disappointed with the interior decor couldn't have been more pleased with the pubs outside space and facilities. Luckily for Bobby Henson he didn't have to personally witness anymore atrocities but there would still be plenty that took place. It had taken years but Liam

Flanagan had finally built up his firm and come into his own. He was stronger and more feared than any other crime Boss and was, at least as far as his men were concerned, a legend in his own lifetime.

CHAPTER FOUR
2012 Early Autumn

When the black cab came to a stop at the top of Horton Road in Hackney, the driver couldn't help but admire his passenger through the rear view mirror. For the whole of the journey he had done nothing but stare although his fare had totally ignored the man's gaze. She was drop dead gorgeous and if it hadn't have been for his wife; he would have chanced his arm and asked the woman out on a date. The door swung open and a set of long slender legs, wearing a pair of six inch heel Louboutin thigh boots, stepped out onto the pavement. After paying her fare and telling the driver to keep the change, Jess Metcalf began the short walk to her parents house. Her full length leather coat was just the right weight to keep her warm on this cool but sunny day and her makeup was meticulously applied. Jess knew she looked good and the cabbies admiring glances hadn't gone unnoticed but it was something she saw and felt on a daily basis. Her slender body mirrored that of a model and her long dark hair was vibrant and shiny but the thing that struck most people was her beauty. Her looks could have been mistaken for someone of Mediterranean decent as Jess had the most enormous hazel eyes, olive skin and perfect gleaming white teeth.

Today's ritual was the same as it had been every Sunday for the last ten years. Sometimes it felt like a bind but none the less she would never stop it, never stop coming to see her poor old mum. Jess could have asked the driver to drop her right outside of the house; he had to pass it to get out of the street but as always, she preferred to walk the few hundred yards to her old home. Horton Road wasn't upmarket, in fact it could be said that the area was more than a little rundown. It contained a row of Edwardian terraces on either side that were mostly in need of a total revamp. The houses were predominantly owned by the local council and her parents had occupied the same two up two down for the last thirty five years. The road was now quiet and cars were parked bumper to bumper on either side but Jess could remember a time when hardly any family in the road owned a vehicle. A time when every occupant knew their neighbour on both sides, the entire road come to that, and they were all on first name terms. Back then families intended to stay for the whole of their lives but now the properties had different tenants on a yearly basis, or that's how it seemed. Jess strolled along and in one hand she carried her black Hermes Birkin bag, a gift from a grateful client who had since passed away. In the other she held a vintage shopping basket. The previous day she had popped into the deli at Fortnum and Masons and asked the young girl on the counter to fill it full of luxuries.

The old man, as she referred to her father and that was only if she was feeling charitable had always kept her mum short of housekeeping and Jess loved to bring her mother something special on her weekly visits. When she reached the house Jess Metcalf rapped loudly on the brass knocker that her mother always kept gleaming. Her father had forced her to hand back her key when he'd found out what her new line of work entailed. From that day onwards he'd had to dig deep within just to acknowledge his only child. A few seconds later Jess could see her mother's silhouette as she seemed too shuffle along the hallway. Annie Metcalf was only in her early fifties but to look at her she appeared far older. Her hair, which was now a premature silver grey, was always pulled back into an unflattering style. Her clothes all came from the local market or second hand shops and for some reason; Annie's stockings were always rolled down to her ankles and nestled on the top of her slippers. Opening the front door, Annie Metcalf's face broke into a broad smile when she saw her girl.
"Hello my darling how are you?"
Jess stepped inside and planting a kiss lovingly on her mother's cheek, hugged her tightly.
"Hi Mum. I'm fine thanks."
Taking her daughters arm, Annie attempted to twirl Jess round.
"Let me have a look at you. Oh darling you look beautiful real beautiful just like a model."

Jess smiled and shook her head. Her mother could always make her laugh but suddenly she stopped when her mind switched to something more serious.

"Is the old bastard here or down the pub?"

Annie Metcalf sneered her mouth up on one side as she answered her daughters question.

"He's here worse luck. Come on sweetheart well go through to the back room."

The house was a typical terrace with two small reception rooms and a kitchen at the back. A ground floor bathroom had been added in the late seventies just before the Metcalf's had taken over the tenancy. As a teenager Jess hated having to walk through the kitchen after she'd had a bath but then most of her school friends had experienced the same so it wasn't anything out of the ordinary. In her own home she had the luxury of an en suite, though her mother still hadn't plucked up the courage to visit the place. Jess knew that if her old man ever found out her mother was planning a visit he'd go up the wall and make the poor woman's life even more unbearable than he usually did. As they walked along the hall and passed the front room Jess could see through the door which was slightly ajar. Her father was asleep in the chair with the Evening Standard newspaper covering his face. Thankful for small mercies, she continued into the next room. The place was cold and she knew that was down to her father hardly ever allowing

her mother to have the heating on. While Annie busied herself with the tea Jess took a seat at the table and looked around at the sparse room, a room Annie was forced to spend most of her time in. The walls were still decorated with the wallpaper Bob Metcalf had hung back in nineteen seventy seven. It amused Jess as shed seen a similar patterned paper on her last visit to Liberties a couple of weeks ago, fashion really did repeat itself. The only furnishings were a single wall unit and square wooden table and four hard chairs which Jess guessed must have been made just after the last war. Her father purchased everything second hand and his saying of they don't make them like that anymore had always grated on her nerves. The one thing that always brought a smile to her face was the seventies teak wall unit as the only thing in it was a photograph of Jess in her school uniform. A few minutes later and Annie appeared with two mugs of tea. Her own cup had a large chip on the rim but she'd made sure that her girls was perfect.
"Here you go my darling."
"Thanks mum."
After taking a sip Jess placed the mug back down and then lifted the basket onto the table. The sight made her mother's eyes open wide with happiness.
"I got you a few bits yesterday when I was in Fortnum's."
"Oh darling you shouldn't have."
Before she had even finished protesting Annie was

rummaging about inside and Jess smiled to herself when all she could hear was Ooooos and Arghhhhhs. Annie looked a little thinner this week and Jess couldn't help but be concerned.
"Mum you are eating alright?"
Annie Metcalf smiled but grabbed hold of her daughters hand and squeezed it hard as she did so. As she spoke her words were almost a whisper.
"That old bastard has gone and cut me housekeeping again. Lord knows it was hard enough feeding the two of us before but now the tight bastard has knocked another tenner off."
"Mum how much does that old sod give you a week?"
"Well, now it's down to twenty five quid. Sometimes less if he's got the nark which is most of the time."
"What!"
"Shush Jess hell hear you. Look it aint so bad, I get scraps for myself from Tony the butcher. He knows the score and always helps me out bless him. Besides, you'd be surprised how far a stew will go if you keep adding a little bit of water. It wouldn't be so bad if the old twat didn't insist on proper meat every day. Its chops on a Tuesday, sausages on Wednesday and by far the most expensive, steak on a Friday. In between I manage to get away with mince but it means me going without. I shouldn't moan girl, I mean there's plenty worse off than me. The poor buggers sleeping rough round Victoria are

the ones we should be worrying about."
"I do care about all the others but there isn't much I can do for them, on the other hand you are my mum and I can help you."
Jess pulled her purse from her handbag and taking out two crisp fifty pound notes laid them on the table. Annie instantly grabbed her daughters hand as she shook her head.
"Thanks but no thanks. You keep your money darling, you never know when you might need it."
Jess knew that she had to be firm with her mother if she was ever going to get her to accept some help. Annie Metcalf had lived a shit life, most of which Jess had been witness to and she knew that the only thing her mother had been able to hold onto was her dignity. Annie was proud and hell would freeze over before she accepted charity from Jess or anyone else.
"Now you listen to me. I want you to hide that away somewhere and you're not to spend it on food for him! I can well afford it and more besides but I didn't bring a lot out with me today. Next week I'm really going to see you alright. Mum I want you to have an escape fund, so that if a day ever comes when you can't
put up with that sorry excuse for a husband anymore, then you'll at least have a bit put by. There's always a bed at my place Mum, you know that."
"Sweetheart I'd never intrude, you've got your own

life to live and you don't want an old woman like me cramping your style."
"Old woman! You're my mother and Id do anything for you if you'd only let me."
Grabbing her daughters hand, Annie's eyes were full of tears as she thanked her girl over and again. Out of the corner of her eye she saw the door handle begin to turn and Annie snatched up the money from the table and stuffed it down her top. Bob Metcalf walked into the room but he didn't speak to Jess or acknowledge her in any way. The one thing he did do was fart loudly and then burp as he passed by his daughters chair. He didn't say pardon or excuse me and Jess knew that he'd actually done it on purpose. Laying his paper down onto the table he stared daggers at his wife and almost shouted as he spoke.
"Get me a cup of tea woman!"
Annie was instantly on her feet and scurrying into the kitchen. The room was silent for what felt like an age but in reality was only a couple of minutes. You could cut the atmosphere with a knife as Annie re-entered the room and handed her husband a steaming hot mug of tea. He took a sip and then spat the liquid from his mouth back into the cup.
"Tastes like fucking dish water! What's wrong with you woman, can't you even make a decent cuppa now? Get me another one and don't take long about it!"
His wife duly obliged and while she waited for her

mother to return Jess could feel her blood begin to boil. Annie handed her husband a second cup and then stood with her head hung low waiting for his seal of approval. He took another mouthful and thankfully this time he didn't spit it out, neither did he say thank you and leaning over the table he began to have a poke about in the basket. Bob Metcalf's eyes lit up as his hand settled on a packet of the finest Belgium chocolate biscuits but as he pulled them out Jess slapped his wrist hard.
"Get your fucking hands off! I brought those for Mum not you."
Bob Metcalf was sarcastically smirking as he spoke.
"I don't know what you're making such a Bleeding fuss about, aint as if you had to work for them. Well not unless you count spreading your legs for all and sundry as work. How are tricks these days? Old Reg from down the Railway Tavern said he might have a crack at you sometime."
Jess knew her father was just being spiteful and that he would never discuss his private affairs openly with anyone. Still he knew his words would hurt her and somehow that made it all the worse.
"Why are you such an arsehole Dad? I know you don't agree with what I do but when will you get it into that thick fucking scull of yours that it's my life and not yours. Who I do or do not choose to have sex with is my business and for your information I'm high class but you'll never see it like that will you? Fuck me, if I went out every Saturday night

and had a one night stand that would be fine wouldn't it, as long as I didn't get paid. You really are a tosser Dad."
"Oh listen to Miss high and fucking mighty. Do you think I came off the last bleeding banana boat or what? I've been down the Cross enough times and seen them for myself, plying their trade the dirty whores. You aint no bleeding different girl, you just aint got the guts to admit it."
Suddenly and without warning Bob Metcalf shouted at the top of his voice.
"Annie!"
Jess's mother flinched when she heard her name.
"Make sure you give that chair a good scrub when the tarts gone home. We don't want to be catching anything nasty now do we?"
Jess bit down hard on her bottom lip. His last words had cut more deeply than any before but she wouldn't let him see that. She knew it was useless to argue and as her father walked back out into the hall, she could only grit her teeth and shove two fingers into the air. Jess spent another ten minutes with her mother but as usual the visit had been spoiled and now she couldn't wait to get out of the place. Standing up from the table she pushed her chair back under and looked down at her mother.
"I think I'll get off now Mum."
Annie Metcalf's face showed sadness and hurt and for a moment guilt engulfed Jess. How could she leave her mum here alone with that pig. God she

felt like going into the next room and strangling the old bastard. She knew deep down that if she could have gotten away with it there was a real chance that she would have carried it out without any remorse. Jess wished with all her heart that her mother would just get up and leave but she knew it would never happen. Annie was institutionalised and fetching and carrying for a man who treated her like a dog was all that she had ever know or understood. As she stood beside the table looking at her mother something made her look down. Spying her father's copy of the Evening Standard something made her pick it up and place it into her bag. Jess didn't know why shed done it as she hadn't read a copy for years; maybe it was just to wind him up when he looked for it later. As they walked back along the hall both women noticed that the door to the front room was now firmly closed, which told them in no uncertain terms that he was well pissed off with both of them. At the street door Annie kissed her daughter goodbye but she held onto her hand for a few seconds longer than was necessary and Jess noticed.
"What's wrong Mum? I know living with that pig is a nightmare but you would tell me if it was something more than that wouldn't you?"
"My darling I'm fine. It's the highlight of my week when you visit and I'm already looking forward to seeing you again soon. If we're lucky, that old bastard will be out and we can have a real long chat

just like we used to when you lived at home."
"With any luck he might just croak it in the night! Now that really would be nice, better than winning the bleeding lottery."
"Oh Jess don't say that, he is still your Dad."
"And don't I know it! Anyway Mum let's not talk about that wanker anymore. Now you take care do you hear and phone me if you need anything alright?"
Jess Metcalf kissed her mother again and then set off up the street; she didn't look back but knew Annie wouldn't go inside until Jess was out of sight. Not one to ever bother about boyfriends even though she did sometimes get lonely, Jess only had to think of the life her mother had to endure and she would once more be glad that she hadn't married. Annie Metcalf closed the front door and lent back against the wood and glass. She now wouldn't see her daughter for another week and as always, the time would pass slowly until she heard her daughter knock on the door again. Trying hard to hold back a tear she breathed in deeply and made her way along the hall. The door to the front room was still closed and she prayed that her husband wouldn't hear her. Entering the kitchen she removed a small tin box that years ago held oxo cubes but was now her secret hiding place where she put anything she didn't want Bob to find. The man never lifted a finger to help her so there was little chance of him preparing any food. Placing the cash Jess had given

her inside, Annie gently replaced the tin just as the back room door opened.   Annie was frozen with fear as she knew what was about to happen. It was always the same after one of Jess's visits but it was something she would never share with her daughter.

"I see the whores gone then?"

Annie turned to face her husband and she could feel the rage begin to build up inside but she knew better than to ever try and vent it as she was no match for a man like Bob Metcalf.

"Please don't talk about her like that; she is still your daughter."

With one swift movement, the palm of Bob Metcalf's hand made contact with the side of his wife's head and she fell to the floor. He kicked out at Annie striking her thighs and back and she screamed out in pain.

"When will you get it into that thick fucking head of yours that I don't want that dirty fucking bitch in my house?"

Finally when Bobs rage had subsided he stormed off leaving his wife in a crumpled mess on the floor. It took several attempts but finally Annie managed to stand. Shakily she made her way upstairs to the bedroom and lifting up her skirt examined her thighs. The bruises were already starting to show but thankfully she would be able to hide them when Jess next came to visit.

It would be a good few minutes' walk before Jess

would be able to hail a cab and that was only if luck was on her side. It wasn't and after she turned onto Richmond Road she walked for a further five minutes. When the road merged with Mare Street Jess decided to give up for a while and take a rest. Spying Cuatro Cafe on the other side of the road she quickly crossed and went inside. The place was quiet, really quiet and she was in fact the only customer. Expecting trade to be slow on a Sunday afternoon even Jess had to admit that it was overly strange but she didn't mind and secretly relished the solitude. Taking a seat by the front window she tried to order a latte but was soon informed by the young waitress, a girl who appeared to be in her early twenties, that they only did Nescafe. Jess smiled and told the girl that would do just fine. As she waited for her order she looked into her hand bag to check her phone calls and her eyes fell upon the Evening Standard. Casually she removed her father's newspaper and as it was yesterday's edition, was about to hand it to the waitress and ask her to put it into the bin, when she suddenly had a change of heart. Opening it up Jess flicked from front to back and after a couple of pages wasn't overly impressed with what she saw. The numerous adverts for estate agents and household products bored her and she now remembered why she preferred The Daily Mail. Reaching the classifieds she was suddenly stopped when her eyes settled on something of interest. As the waitress brought over her coffee in a retro clear glass cup and saucer Jess was deep in thought.

"I hope there's something in there worth having a butchers at for a change?"

Jess quickly closed the paper and hoped that the young woman hadn't seen what she was reading. She wasn't one to get embarrassed easily but she still didn't like strangers knowing her business.

"Just the same old rubbish I'm afraid."

Jess willed the girl to go away but she seemed to be loitering for some reason and definitely couldn't stop staring at the Birkin handbag that sat beside Jess's chair.

"Did you want something darling?"

"Nah not really, I was just admiring your bag. Is it real or a snide one? Only I was down the Lane early this morning and saw one just like it. I tell you, some of them copies are better than the real thing. My names Mandy by the way, Mandy Drew."

Jess wanted to laugh at Mandy's words but refrained for fear of embarrassing the girl.

"Nice to meet you Mandy and no it's not snide as you so eloquently put it."

Jess struggled to hold a laugh inside as she didn't want to appear rude. As politely as she could she informed the waitress that the bag had been a gift from a friend. She hoped that would be the end of the conversation and turned back to her newspaper but still the girl stood at her side. Finally Jess gave Mandy a stern look that told her in no uncertain

terms to go away and leave her in peace.
"Sorry, it's just that this place has been like a bleeding morgue all day and it's nice to see another face. If you want me to clear off just say so, I don't mind."
"Well in all honest love I've got a bit of a headache, so I wouldn't mind being left alone. I don't want to seem rude or anything but you know what it's like?"
"Yeah I do. Get migraines myself sometimes, especially when me old man wants a little fiddle if you know what I mean."
Jess didn't continue the conversation but did sigh heavily and at last Mandy took the hint.
"No sweat, enjoy your coffee."
As soon as the waitress was back behind the counter Jess once more opened up the paper and scanned her eyes down the column.

WANTED

Individuals who work in the sex trade. People that are willing to provide information to a budding novelist. Females preferred and in particular the role of a dominatrix but will consider anyone that is involved in the industry if their lifestyle is relevant. £250 paid for each story used. 100% discretion assured. Please call 0789564269.

A smile began to form on Jess's face and she wondered if she should give it a go. Savouring her coffee, that for an instant blend was surprisingly good, she decided to think it over for a few minutes.

Jess tried to weigh up the pros and cons of confiding in a stranger but she couldn't really come up with a reason why not to get involved either way. If she took the plunge then it certainly wouldn't be for the money but there was still something about the Advert that intrigued her. Jess supposed she was bored and possibly unburdening her problems would help but then again that might not really be what the person wanted to hear.
For all Jess knew they could have been some kind of pervert who just wanted a sexual kick. Drinking the last of her coffee she decided to just go for it and retrieving her mobile from her bag dialled the number. Lucy Urquhart, after one of Norma's large Sunday roasts, was lying on the bed flicking through this month's copy of Marie Claire. Her father was enjoying an afternoon nap in his study and as usual Norma had gone over to Bermondsey to visit her sister. The house was as quiet as a graveyard and Lucy jumped when her pay as you go mobile started to ring. Excitedly but still a little apprehensive after her earlier altercation, she snatched it up but there was no number showing. Swinging her legs over the side of the bed so she was sitting up straight Lucy patted down her hair and wanted to laugh at the absurdity of her action.
"Hello?"
"Hi! I'm calling regarding the advertisement in the Standard."
The woman sounded polite and Lucy punched the

air, euphoric that someone had at last contacted her.
"Oh I'm so pleased you have called. Obviously
by reading the advertisement you know what I'm
looking for. Is there any chance we could meet up?"
The woman on the other end of the phone sounded
a bit pushy and to begin with it put Jess off.
Deciding she needed to find out a little more
information before she committed herself to
anything, Jess began to speak.
"Can we just back track a little love? Only I need to
know more about the set up before I arrange
anything like a meeting."
Lucy was stunned. She thought that it would all be
simple once someone had contacted her and she
was now slightly embarrassed.
"I'm so sorry, please forgive me and of course you
need some information. I get a little carried away at
times but it's only because I'm enthusiastic about it
all."
Jess smiled to herself.
"Well what exactly are you enthusiastic about
Miss?"
"Lucy, please call me Lucy. Well, I want to write a
book about why people do what they do for a
living. It's predominantly about sex workers and in
particular the role of a dominatrix. I find it
fascinating and....."
Jess stopped Lucy mid flow. The woman or girl
sounded very young and Jess was starting to have
doubts about it all. She was wondering how a

young girl could possibly understand her life and be able to portray it fairly.

"Can I stop you there a minute. I need to ask a few questions myself before we continue. Is this for real or are you just out for kicks, only if you are I really don't want to waste my time."

"Oh no not at all Miss?"

"Jess."

"Not at all Jess. You see my father wants......"

Lucy Urquhart stopped talking when she recalled the promise she had made to her father. For some reason, this time she really wanted to honour that promise and she took a deep breath before she continued.

"Well basically I did my Masters in psychology and now I would like to write articles on the sex trade and somehow collate them into a book. I don't know how it will all turn out but I do know that I need help on the subject. I swear that anything said to me will remain strictly confidential."

Lucy Urquhart waited with baited breath for her callers reply.

"Well ok then. I suppose we could meet up and have a chat about it but I'm not making any promises though. We'll just see how it goes. I have a free couple of hours tomorrow at about eleven if that's any good to you?"

"That sounds great! Any preference as to where we meet?"

"Do you know Covent Garden well?"

"Oh yes I know it very well. Actually I love to roam the streets there whenever I'm at a loose end."
Jess could already tell that the girl was a talker and she rolled her eyes upwards at the thought of it all. Jess Metcalf was able to converse on any level but talking for the sake of it had always been a pet hate of hers.
"Well if you get to Long Acre and then turn left onto Arne Street there's a small cake shop come cafe it's called Patisserie Valerie, I don't know if you've heard of it?"
"Why yes, I've had a coffee there many times. So I'll see you there at about eleven tomorrow then?"
"Ok, well bye for now."
"Thank you so much for calling I ...."
Jess had already hung up but it didn't bother Lucy. As she pressed the end call button on her telephone she couldn't have been happier. It wasn't the same for Jess who now wasn't so sure shed done the right thing. For a start the girl sounded so young and Jess wasn't sure she was going to get along with her. Still shed made an arrangement and would see it through. She consoled herself with the fact that if they didn't hit it off then she would immediately call it a day. Quickly finishing her drink, Jess decided not to dwell on the matter anymore and leaving the cafe once more set out in her hunt to find a taxi.

CHAPTER FIVE

Lucy was up with the larks. She was so excited about her meeting that she'd had difficulty in sleeping and had been awake on and off for most of the night. Even the lack of sleep couldn't dampen her enthusiasm and as soon as the first rays of sunlight had filtered through her blinds she was out of her bed in a flash. Bounding down the stairs she reached the dining room ten minutes before her father and was tucking into bacon and egg as he entered. George Urquhart was more than a little surprised to see his daughter; Lucy was so fond of her bed that she often wouldn't surface until after ten, much to the annoyance of Norma Sanderson.
"Goodness Lucy, couldn't you sleep?"
Lucy smiled up at her father as he bent down and placed a kiss on her forehead.
"Morning Daddy, no not really."
"Is there anything bothering you sweetheart?"
Just then Norma entered carrying Mr Urquhart's porridge and as she looked in Lucy's direction the young woman winked and smiled.
"Nothing at all Daddy. Actually, things couldn't be better I've got my first interview this morning and I'm so excited. I know it's not what you want to hear but I really feel like things are starting to happen and life couldn't be any better at the moment."

George frowned as he took a seat and it didn't go unnoticed by Norma. Even though she'd helped Miss Lucy out with the advert she still had a feeling that there was trouble brewing. Still she knew it wasn't her place to say anything so she set the bowl of porridge down in front of her employer and left them both to it.

"Now I hope you've remembered my conditions young lady and the promises you made to me?"

"Daddy I'm meeting someone in a cafe over in Covent garden. I would imagine that we will be surrounded by several hundred other people, well outside anyway, so I will be quite safe. Now please will you just stop worrying?"

"Ok Ok! And I'm glad to hear that you're being sensible. One more thing, it is a woman isn't it?"

"For goodness sake Daddy! Yes of course it's a woman."

"Well at least that's one thing I'm pleased about, now can I give you a lift?

"Thanks but I think I'd like to walk. It's a nice day and it shouldn't take me more than thirty minutes. Besides it will give me time to work out exactly what I'm going to ask her. I've got all these questions buzzing around in my head and I really don't know where to start."

George wasn't happy with her reply but he wouldn't push the matter even though he had an ulterior motive. He wanted to see who this person was and to make sure that his daughter was safe but he knew better than to try and force Lucy into doing something she didn't want to. If he did it would only end up in an argument and Lucy could argue like a politician if she had a mind to. George left for work at around nine thirty but not before kissing his daughter goodbye and reiterating his conditions. Nodding goodbye in Norma's direction he then told Lucy he would see her for dinner that evening. Running up the stairs Lucy was on a real high, her whole being was tingling with excitement and she couldn't wait to get started. Filling her bag with note pads and pens, she was about to leave when she remembered her Dictaphone. Snatching it up she ran from the house and even though there was plenty of time to spare, Lucy was desperate not to be late.

Over in Kensington, Jess Metcalf had begun her day more calmly. She hadn't entertained a client the previous evening and had managed an early night for once, not to mention a lie in this morning. Sitting at the breakfast table in front of the floor to ceiling window of her apartment, she ran over everything from yesterday. Thoughts of her mother and how she looked were still weighing heavily but what bothered her most was the telephone conversation shed had with the young woman. Now the countdown had begun and she had just over an hour and a half to her first meeting. For a moment she toyed with the idea of not turning up but Jess was an honourable person and she didn't like to let people down. Deciding that she would go as she could always say she'd changed her mind if she didn't like the look of the woman, Jess made her way to the bedroom and started to get ready. After showering she chose a smart navy two piece Versace suit and matching high heel courts. Jess turned from side to side as she admired herself in the full length mirror and just for good measure smoothed down the nonexistent creases on her skirt. Smiling to herself at the result, even she had to admit that she looked good. Checking her watch, Jess knew that it would take her about twenty five minutes so at ten thirty she left her flat on Phillimore Place and began the walk over to Covent Garden. Reaching Shaftesbury Avenue Jess could feel the tension begin to build in the pit of her stomach. She was normally a very confident woman and not much bothered her but today it was different, today she would have to open up to a complete stranger. Sharing intimate private details about her life wasn't going to be easy. Turning onto Long Acre her destination was almost in sight and when she saw the signpost for Arne Street Jess knew there was no going back. Patisserie Valerie was a traditional continental cafe that had been trading in London since the nineteen twenties. The delicious cakes and pastries were to die for and Jess loved to pop in whenever she was in the area. The staff only knew her on nodding terms but they were always very welcoming. Many times over the years she had shared a table with a star or two who had popped in from the Theatre Royal on Drury Lane during a break in rehearsals. She wasn't a star spotter, quite the opposite and looked upon everyone as equal. It was probably the reason why most were happy to share a table with her and make idle chit chat. The morning was chilly, so rather than opt for her usual table outside on the pavement Jess went inside and taking a seat by the window removed her coat. Suddenly she realised that she hadn't a clue what the woman she was supposed to be meeting looked like. Glancing round she saw there were all manner of people sitting at the tables, most were in pairs which ruled them out but there were one or two who sat alone. Studying them she didn't think they looked the type to be doing research but then again, in London you could never really tell. Jess decided to order a coffee and then wait and see what happened. Ten minutes later and the door flew open and Lucy Urquhart came bounding in. Dressed in a blue anorak and pink bobble hat that was pulled down low around her ears she looked the epitome of a student. She was flustered and red in the face and Jess quietly laughed to herself. Now in no doubt, that this was the person shed been waiting for Jess waved her hand motioning for the girl to join her. Lucy pulled her hat off as she neared the table and revealed her mop of unruly blond hair that was in desperate need of a brush.

"I take it you're the young lady I spoke to on the telephone?"
Lucy nodded her head vigorously and as she did so thought to herself that she must have resembled the kind of nodding dog people sometimes have on the parcel shelves of their cars. Her cheeks again flushed and were now an even deeper shade of red with the thought. Standing in front of the table Lucy stared at Jess but didn't utter a single word.
"Well you'd better sit down then."
Lucy was seated in seconds and immediately began to rummage in her bag, a bag that seemed to Jess to be bottomless. Removing the pads, pens and Dictaphone she suddenly felt Jess's hand on her arm.
"I'm more than happy for you to make notes but it's a definite no when it comes to recording things. I am a very private person as you will find out and my client list is to a degree also private. If it got into the wrong hands not that I'm saying you would let that happen, but I can't risk anyone ever hearing me talk about very personal matters that have been put onto tape. I'm giving this information willingly, as long as it's understood that no names will ever be mentioned. Now what say we have a coffee and get to know each other a bit before we get down to the nitty gritty stuff?"
Lucy realised that as usual she had been like a bull at a gate and had handled things all wrong. She was worried that the woman sitting opposite her

would get up and walk away and all because of her energetic approach. That didn't happen and a few minutes later the women sat looking at each other over two steaming hot cappuccinos. After eyeing the girl up Jess decided that she had to take the lead and lay down a few ground rules before she revealed anything.

"Right you know my name is Jess. Now I'm sorry and I know it appears terribly rude but I can't for the life of me remember what you said yours was?"

"Lucy."

"Well Lucy it's nice to meet you but I think that's about as much as either of us need to know regarding private details, don't you? I will give you names for my clients but they will mostly be pseudonyms. For obvious reasons I don't think it's right or proper for me to expose their true identities and in some cases I really don't know who they are anyway. People have a fear of being found out and you wouldn't believe what some choose to call themselves. Now where would you like me to start?"

Lucy placed her oversized cup back onto the saucer and Jess tried to hold inside a giggle that was desperate to escape as she pointed to the girls mouth. A frothy white coffee moustache covered Lucy Urquhart's top lip and her face once more became crimson. After wiping it away with a serviette and when Jess had told her that her face was now clean, she began to speak.

"Could I know a little about you and why you chose this line of work and how you got into it in the first place?"

"Well, when I left school I seemed to drift from one job to another but then I managed to get a placement at Selfridges on the makeup counter. To a teenager, back then at least, it was classed as a dream job and my school friends were all dead jealous. I actually worked there for just over four years, the pay was good and I suppose even now it would be looked upon as a bit of a status job for a working class girl from the East End. The other girls I worked with were nice enough if a bit snooty but it didn't stop us going out most Saturday nights for a drink together after work. After a lengthy session in the pubs up west we usually ended up in Stringfellow's or somewhere similar, maybe Ruby Blues. Two of the girls, Susie and Pam who also worked at Selfridges and who happened to be two of the biggest trollops to ever walk this earth, always seemed to pull at the end of the night. Don't get me wrong, anyone that has a one night stand though I won't ever be able to understand why they do it, well they're welcome to it. Each to his own and all that. I'm not judging them in any way but it was a bit different for me as I always believed you should get to know a man first, so I usually went home alone not that I minded. After a few months I at last met a bloke and in all honesty I was more than a bit sweet on him. Things began to get serious and when he invited me round to his flat because he had a question to ask me, well as you can imagine I was thinking it might be a proposal and even brought a couple of wedding magazines. After a nice meal he suddenly asked if I'd do something for him. Sure I said what is it? His face went red and he said it was a bit embarrassing. I was desperate for him to spit it out thinking he would then get down on one knee."

Lucy hung on Jess's every word and couldn't wait to hear what was coming next.

"What was it? What did he ask you?"

"He wanted me to pee on him."

"What!"

"Straight up, that's what he said. It changed my opinion of him straight away I can tell you and he could see that from the look on my face but there was just one problem, he'd shown his true colours and was committed so to speak. I told him in no uncertain terms that I wasn't into kinky fucking acts. Until that point our sex life had been good, or so I thought."

"What did he say?"

"He pleaded with me like a baby, saying that it wasn't that bad and that it would really turn him on. He also said he would give me five hundred quid if I did it."

"No! What did you do?"

"I did what any self respecting London girl would do of course. There and then I whipped off my

knickers, pushed him to the ground, squatted over him and pissed for England. That night as I lay in bed it got me thinking and the next morning after counting the money again I placed an advert in the newspaper. The rest so they say is history."
"And what about the man, I mean your boyfriend?"
"Well it didn't take much for me to realise that he didn't respect me and to tell the truth I couldn't respect him after that so it ended. I soon had a steady stream of clients and do you know something?"
"What?"
"That bloke is still one of my regulars today!"
Lucy burst out laughing and now that the atmosphere had relaxed Jess continued to talk. Already the two women were warming to each other. It was just one of those times when people just seem to click and everything feels right.
"Anyway, when the job at Selfridges started to get a bit boring as all jobs do, I handed in my notice. I don't really know why I stayed for as long as I did; my sideline was going well so it certainly wasn't for the money. I was making a decent living by anyone's standards but it wasn't a fortune and I had to work damn hard I can tell you. Over the next few months I saved as much as I could and when Id managed to get together a few grand I rented a small flat. Of course I've upgraded since then and now have a very desirable residence, not too far from here actually. Once I got my own premises

and because it was in a different area of London I had to start all over again. It was slow to begin with; well that's a bit of and understatement really. You see Lucy, it's easy to have an idea about how to earn money but actually making it happen is another story all together and believe you me it wasn't easy. I started off by placing cards in the shops and phone box's but that brought me all sorts of aggro not to mention weirdoes. I then decided to advertise in the more upmarket tabloids and things quickly changed, almost overnight in fact."

It instantly crossed Lucy's mind that maybe Norma had been wrong after all. As she scribbled away Lucy didn't make any comment and her silence was Jess's cue to continue.

"Most of my clients are men but there are I might add, also the occasional women. All of them tend to be city types and have plenty of money."

"So what exactly do you class yourself as and how long have you been doing it?"

"I suppose if I had to label my profession which I really don't like to do, I would say I'm a high class prostitute but then I also offer my services as a dominatrix as well. That's where you can make some real money if you've got the guts to do it. Anyway, it's been just over ten years now and there isn't much more you could teach me about it either. I've entertained stars from the stage and screen, a couple of high profile chefs and sports personalities, not to mention numerous government officials.

I really should have had a to do chart and crossed them off as I made my way through the list."

Jess giggled out loud but Lucy didn't see the funny side.

"Can you tell me a few stories?"

"A few? Darling I could fill several books with the tales I've got in here."

Jess Metcalf tapped the side of her head and winked in Lucy's direction as she did so.

"What happens when you meet a new client for the first time and let's say, they want to be dominated."

"Well like I said, I now have a very upmarket apartment in Kensington and the client will visit me at home. When I initially greet them, for the first time at least, I'm dressed in a twinset and skirt. Real yuppie style clothes you know? Oh and I forgot to mention, that my accent is so polished you wouldn't be able to tell I wasn't educated at a public school. Anyway we sit and have tea..."

"Tea!"

"Oh yes it's all very civilised. I ask questions about why they want my services and the reason they feel that I can give them what they want, more than let's say a brass off of the street. When I'm satisfied that they've told me the truth and I feel safe we go into the dungeon. It's a spare room that I have set aside and which houses many weird and wonderful objects. Not going too fast for you am I?"

Lucy shook her head but in all honesty she could hardly keep up as she furiously scribbled away.

"Over tea we will have already discussed what they would like in terms of sex or pain and degradation. Some are really hardcore and some are very tame in comparison. Others, well you'll find out as you hear their stories, are just plain heartbroken wrecks."
"Do you look upon them as perverts?"
Jess laughed and at the same time beckoned to the waitress for a refill of coffee. Glancing at her watch she could see that they had already been talking for over an hour. At this rate it would take weeks for the girl to gather her information. Jess supposed if that's what it took then that's what it took, after all she hadn't really got much else to do with her free time, well not unless you counted shopping but of late she had begun to find that boring.
"Darling I don't see any of them as perverts, not in the sense you mean anyway. Some just haven't been able to get any sex for a while and are desperate. Others have been so dreadfully hurt or let down by life that they need a little extra help, the kind of help that most of society would see as weird. They hurt no one but themselves so I can't see what the problem is can you?"
Lucy Urquhart placed her pen down onto the table and thought for a moment. She supposed she couldn't see anything wrong with it in the least. Back when shed been at University her friends had told her stories regarding what their parents got up to, now some of those really had been weird.
"So can you describe your dungeon for me?"

Placing her finger to her lips Jess refrained from speaking until the waitress placed their drinks onto the table and had walked back over to the counter. Although Jess wasn't ashamed of what she did, she didn't want all and sundry knowing her private business.

"I personally refer to it as the dungeon but using that term would mortify some of my clients. It's just an average sized room I suppose, a room where different sexual practices are carried out. As you can imagine I needed to have it totally soundproofed. It cost me a small fortune but I couldn't have the neighbouring flats banging on the door when they heard some of the screams that come out of that room."

Jess giggled again but Lucy still didn't see it as funny and only stared at Jess.

"The walls, floor and ceiling are all painted in a deep scarlet red. High gloss paint of course, so that it can be wiped down easily. On one wall I have a set of purpose built racks which house dildos, whips, clamps and anything else you can think of including most items you can purchase in any sex shop on the high street. There are also things that you would never think of in a million years. I even had use for a cheese grater once but that's another story for another day. Now back to the dungeon. The other side wall houses a wardrobe that is full to the brim with costumes. At the bottom of the room is a large oak custom built cross with shackles.

A dear carpenter friend of mine made it and at the touch of a lever it smoothly rotates, actually I'm quite proud of it. Last but not least there's a large double bed on the other wall which is self explanatory."

"Why did you want me to be quiet when the waitress came over?"

"Because Sweetheart, I don't want anyone to hear things regarding other peoples affairs."

"Do you mean your clients affairs or you own?"

"Only theirs darling. Now my outfits are all custom made and hang in my private wardrobe. I wear only the highest quality leather or rubber. Personally I prefer the leather but for a lot of my clients only the feel of rubber will do. I want to give them what they want so I allow them to choose what I should wear. After that I am the only one doing the telling even if it's only for straight sex. A lot of my clients like to dress up themselves in various costumes which are again all catered for by me."

"You said about a carpenter friend?"

Jess smiled when she thought of him.

"That would be Felix but I'd rather save him for another day. Now what else do you want to know?"

"You mentioned that women come to you, how many and can you tell me some more about them?"

"There are only a few at the moment but if I go into too much detail before you know the facts, you might get the wrong impression of me. When I explain things properly, you'll get a better understanding of what I'm all about."

Lucy once more placed her pencil onto the table. "You know I really didn't expect you to mention females. I somehow thought, oh I don't know, that they wouldn't need to be degraded in that way. I mean most women are degraded every single day of their lives don't you think?"

Jess studied the girl and for a moment didn't say anything. Lucy was pretty enough and from the way she spoke Jess could tell that she'd had a marvellous education. It seemed strange that she appeared to be so naive about what really went on in the world. Normally Jess Metcalf was polite to the point where she would agree with someone just so it didn't cause an argument but today was different. If she was going to tell her story then today she would be honest, even if it seemed as if she was being blunt.

"Actually love I don't. Oh I'm not saying there aren't women out there who are degraded through sexual or physical abuse every day. Putting those poor cows in that category aside, any woman who willingly allows a man to do that to her when there's no threat to her safety or she isn't getting paid for the service is nothing more than a stupid bitch."

As soon as the words had left her mouth Jess wished she could have taken them back. She hadn't intended to include her own mother in her last statement but now thinking about it, her poor old Mum was one of the stupid bitches shed just referred to but then Jess wasn't aware that Annie was being physically abused. To Lucy Jess's words were brutal but honest and inwardly Lucy smiled. She liked this woman, liked her directness and no nonsense attitude.

Lucy Urquhart had a feeling that they were going to get along really well. Once again she picked up her pen. The clock on the wall was now showing one o'clock and she was starting to get hungry. There was only one problem, she didn't want to risk Jess clamming up if they stopped for a while to eat.

"So what story shall we start with?"

Jess took a few seconds to think about it and Lucy could see that she was mentally trying to work out which tale she was going to tell. When she at last smiled Lucy knew she had made up her mind and she bit down hard on her pencil in anticipation of what she was going to hear.

"I think the Trainer is as good a place to start as any as he's one of my newer clients."

"Trainer?"

"Horses love. I first met him when I went to the races at Ascot a few weeks ago. This year has been really hectic work wise and I decided that I needed a little change. I love the races but I always have to go alone so that takes away a bit of the fun, anyway......"

"Why do you go alone?"
"Darling you'll seldom find a woman in my line of work with a full dance card."
"Dance card? I don't understand what..."
"Let me put it another way. A woman that does what I do for a living will never have many friends, if any come to that. I mean, imagine if you had a friend like me and then you go and get yourself a fella. Well you'd be worrying all the time that he would want to try out what I'm offering. The same goes for most other women in the sex trade I suppose."
Lucy looked horrified at what she'd just heard.
"I wouldn't Jess, really I wouldn't. I would like to think that I would never be so narrow minded."
"Of course you do sweetheart, we all like to think like that but when it actually comes down to it human beings are too quick to judge and when they get insecure they always jump to the wrong conclusions. I learned early on, through firsthand experience I might add, that it's the way things are so you just have to live with it. People only see what they want to see and there's no changing them believe me. Getting back to the story, apart from my previous boyfriend it was one of the few occasions that a client has met me on a personal basis first. I was having a good day, well winning wise at least.
The sun was shining and it was starting to get a bit hot outside. The night before one of my clients had

given me a hot tip as he liked to put it and there aren't any sexual connotations when I say that." Jess giggled but when Lucy didn't join in with the laughter, Jess continued.
"I was feeling lucky so placed a bet of a hundred quid at ten to one on it. The horse romped home and as you can imagine I was well chuffed to be in profit to the tune of a grand. After making my way inside I was just about to order a bottle of champagne when out of the blue this man walks over and starts chatting to me. Now remember Id gone to Ascot alone and after several hours of not talking to anyone it becomes a bit boring. I never like to appear rude so I answered his questions but it was obvious he was interested in getting to know me a bit better. I don't usually bother with blokes on a personal level, more trouble than they're worth most of the time but I though why not, there's no harm in having a bit of fun. Anyway, he ended up buying the champagne and we took a seat and made ourselves more comfortable. He introduced himself and we must have talked for a good hour as we relaxed and sipped a fair few champers. He was witty and good company and it was nice, nice to have a conversation that didn't revolve around someone's sexual preferences. For a short while I wasn't anyone's mistress or a whore earning her living from the sex trade, I was just Jess and I liked it. Well, this is his story so far..."

CHAPTER SIX

As he walked into the stable yard, Nicky Brent was on a professional high. For months he'd been working on the Sultan in a desperate bid to train some of the man's expensive young thoroughbreds. He had wined and dined the Sultan and his agents, not to mention the numerous strip clubs and prostitutes Nicky had supplied for them at considerable personal expense. When he had all but given up, the telephone call he'd been waiting for had come through that very morning. When the Sultans aide had informed him that a delivery of three of the best two year olds available would be arriving at his yard the following day, Nicky had punched the air in happiness. Now with each footstep he took on the cobbles, the high was starting to rapidly diminish. He had a deflated feeling and recently nothing seemed to satisfy him for very long. Now at the top of his game the thought that there was little more to achieve troubled him. Nicky had worked hard to reach all of his goals, Tumbles stable yard and stud, a grand house, flash cars and more money than he could poke a stick at. It had only taken a few years and he now had in his collection several major horse racing accolades. There didn't seem much more to aspire to and the thought had crossed his mind that maybe he should look outside of the racing fraternity but to what he didn't quite know. It wasn't that he no longer loved the horses, they were and always would be his number one passion but Nicky Brent was a man who needed new experiences to thrive on. A thrill seeker who now wanted to try anything and everything no matter what that involved. Situated in Brentford, Tumbles yard was within a comfortable travelling distance for Kempton and Epsom race courses. Horseshoe in shape and not a small setup by any standards, it was renowned for its efficiency and cleanliness. This was all down to the many stable hands who worked exhausting hours for little money. Nicky wasn't the best boss in the world but the hands stayed on in the hope that one day they would be rewarded with a ride that would set them on the road to a professional career. The yard office was situated to the left of the horseshoe and standing inside was Shamus O'Dowd, Nicky's right hand man and manager. Shamus had been at Tumbles from day one and had seen the place go from strength to strength, which had been down to his own personal hard work and nothing to do with the yards owner. Now fifteen years later the two men's once close friendship was almost nonexistent. For the last two years and with total disregard for his friend, Nicky had been having an affair with Shamus's wife Rhea. Beautiful, tall and an ex model to boot, Rhea O'Dowd had been a challenge for Nicky and it had taken him weeks to get her into bed. No one was supposed to know about the affair but the couple did little to hide things and with rumours rife around the yard, it had finally reached the ears of Shamus O'Dowd. Shamus loved Rhea with all his heart and he had never been able to understand why she had married him in the first place. Now his fears had come home to roost and he was a broken man. Disappearing for several days, he had only reappeared when his wife tracked him down and begged him to come home. Rhea promised that it would never happen again and that she really did love her husband, something he found hard to believe but he would rather live a lie than not have her in his life. Now one week on and it was his first day back at the yard. Shamus was in the middle of a conversation with one of the stable girls and didn't see his boss enter. It wasn't until Nicky coughed loudly that he turned around. Nicky held out his hand and Shamus O'Dowd, for the sake of holding onto his job, accepted it. Inside he felt like ripping Nicky's head off but the only thing that stopped him was the fact that he knew the trainer had no deep feelings for Rhea. To end up in clink would accomplish nothing and besides at his age he would never get a job that paid so well. Nicky Brent was a lot of things and sneaky and manipulative were among them but the one thing he wasn't was mean when it came down to money.

"Shamus!"

"Mr Brent!"

The men had always been on first name terms but now Shamus couldn't bring himself to say his boss's first name. He would only be able to cope with seeing Brent if any dealings with the man were on a professional level and nothing more. It didn't go unnoticed by Nicky but he didn't want to upset the applecart any further, well not for a while at least. Glaring at the young stable hand and shifting his head to one side, told her in no uncertain terms to get lost. The girl quickly retreated to the safety of the yard, jobs were hard to find and Emma wanted to keep hers. Her boss was known to sack a person just for looking at him in the wrong way and today Nicky Brent didn't seem in the best of moods.

"I wanted to apologise for this little hiccup and all the trouble that its caused. I never meant to hurt you but you know how it is Shamus, it all just got out of hand buddy. I hope that we can carry on working together because you and I go back a long way and we make a good team."

Nicky waited for his old friend to embrace him or at the very least shake his hand so that they could draw a line under everything but there was nothing. The office was silent for a few seconds too long and the atmosphere was now uncomfortable for them both. Shamus O'Dowd knew exactly what he was doing, it would bother his boss that he couldn't get his own way and Nicky Brent always had to get his way. Well this time Shamus would make sure that he didn't.

"Not a problem Mr Brent. Now if you will excuse me I have a lot to do. I've only just learnt that the new horses will be here tomorrow and we still haven't cleaned out the allotted stables."
With that Shamus walked outside and his face wore just the glimmer of a smile. Nicky was left standing alone in the office and he could feel the anger beginning to grow deep inside. The only problem was he had no way of venting it, at least not at the moment. He now realised that from here on in things would become increasingly more difficult. If it wasn't for the fact that Shamus was such a good manager, the best in the business in fact, then Nicky would have fired him for all the aggro he'd had to put up with. Admittedly Rhea O'Dowd was a good shag but he hadn't been getting such a buzz out of it lately and he'd been about to dump her anyway. The yard was always full of idle gossip and for the life of him he couldn't work out why so much fuss had been made. It wasn't as if he was trying to steal the dirty little bitch away, he would have been content to just share her but Nicky knew Shamus would never have been that accommodating. He was glad he'd never married if this was what happened when you had a bit of slap and tickle outside the marital bed. For a second he gave it some thought and felt better when he consoled himself with the fact that when it came down to brass tacks, women were only good for one thing. Closing the door he took a seat at the desk and

after switching on the computer, logged onto the web. Searching through numerous porn sites he stopped on one that introduced the surfer to the dominatrix scene. Sitting up in his seat Nicky leaned in close so that he could study the images on the screen. Fleetingly and it was only that, he considered subscribing there and then. The women looked pretty good and he was about to log onto the site when he thought better of it, though the idea wasn't totally dismissed out of hand. Logging off he entered the yards private information file and studied the performance charts in readiness for Thursdays big race. One mare had stood out of late and the ground was coming just right for this little beauty. Picking up the telephone he called the owners and asked them if they would be happy to supplement the mare. When they agreed, Nicky was over the moon at the prospect of a decent earner. Shamus wouldn't like it but then it wasn't up to him, Nicky was the boss and he now felt like reinforcing that fact. For all concerned, from the jockeys right down to the stable hands, Ascot was one of the highlights on the racing calendar. It had always been a favourite of Nicky's long before he'd even had a yard of his own. He was a real social climber which was probably the reason his yard had done so well in the first place but the reason he loved Ascot the most was the fact that he got to ogle all the beautiful women who attended the race meeting. A regular gambler, Nicky always seemed to be lucky at this particular venue and on Ladies day he would experience his biggest win to date. The following couple of days passed without event and by the time the big day arrived Nicky was chaffing at the bit. He could feel the adrenalin as it cursed through his body and he loved the feeling. Driving down the previous night he had booked into the De Vere hotel. It was situated close to the course and had the benefit of a health suite and pool, though keeping fit was the last thing on Nicky Brent's mind. At precisely three pm the following afternoon and after checking on his horse, he told Emma the stable hand to accompany him down to the members enclosure beside the track. The pair walked towards the on course bookmakers but stopped before they reached the numerous rows of stalls. There were many to choose from but for Nicky it was always the pitch of Big Barry Denton. The man was loud and obnoxious and if Nicky was going to fleece one of the bookies it would be all the more enjoyable if it was Barry who bore the brunt. It was frowned upon for a trainer to be seen openly betting and Emma knew she was being used but she didn't dare say a word to her boss. Nicky removed several bundles of cash from his jacket pockets and placed them into Emma's hands. Nicky repeated what he wanted her to do and then gave her a gentle shove in the direction of Barry Denton. As she approached the man's pitch to place the bet Nicky could see Barry perched on his box and lording it to anyone that passed by. As usual he was overly rude and as one young girl struggled to remove two pound coins from her purse Barry Denton told her he hadn't got time to wait around and to fuck off out of it. Nicky Brent didn't like what he heard but he didn't defend the girl either, there was no point. The crowds were too big and noisy and when it boiled down to it he didn't really care. It was purely down to the fact that he hated Barry, hated him with a vengeance. When Emma reached the front of the queue she removed the money shed been given and proceeded to tell the bookie that she wanted twenty thousand pounds placed on Colour Vision. Normally Nicky only ever placed bets on horses from his own stables but he had a good feeling about this one. Big Barry's eyes opened wide when he saw all the notes. It wasn't that unusual for him to take large bets but this girl looked so young. He eyed Emma suspiciously but then greed got the better of him and he snatched the money from her and shoved a slip into her hand. Seeing her walking back towards Nicky, Barry snarled his lip back in anger. He knew he'd been tucked up but could do nothing about it. Nicky stared back at the man but didn't gloat as he wanted to save that until he collected his winnings. The pleasure and fear of laying down so much money wasn't only to do with the bet but also down to the fact that he had withdrawn the funds from the yards account. If he didn't win it would cause all manner of problems with the investors but the chance of getting caught out gave him a real buzz. The race started on time at precisely three twenty five and the crowds were tense as the horse hit the front and just managed to hang on. The adrenalin was pumping and Nicky thought his heart was going to pop right out of his chest. As it crossed the line and took first place he let out a gasp of relief but his euphoria was short lived as seconds later it was announced that there would be a stewards inquiry. On the run in, bumping and interference had occurred between Colour Vision and its stable mate Opinion Poll. The next few minutes were extremely stressful and once again Nicky's nerves were in tatters. Finally the call came over the tannoy system that Colour Vision had been declared the winner and Nicky Brent beamed from ear to ear. When he went to collect his return of one hundred and forty thousand pounds Barry's face was set in stone as he counted out the notes. No words passed between the two men, they didn't need to. Nicky Brent knew that he along with many other punters had ruined Big Barry's day and that was enough. Walking back into the bar, Nicky ordered a bottle of champagne to celebrate and as he did so his eyes glanced upon the woman standing next to him who was tall and slender and dressed up to the nines. Knowing he had time to spare as the horse from his own yard wasn't running until the last race and that Shamus and Emma could sort things out if he got delayed, Nicky decided to try his luck and talk to her. By anyone's standards she was a real stunner but with so much cash to splash around he thought that not many women would turn him down.

"Fancy sharing a glass with me?"

Jess Metcalf smiled and nodded her head. They stood together at the bar for a while but after a few minutes of awkward conversation, Nicky nodded his head in the direction of the plush sofas and they walked over and took a seat. For a moment he contemplated giving her a false name but it wouldn't have mattered either way to Jess as very few of the men she met ever gave their real names. The conversation now flowed easily and Nicky Brent talked at length about himself. It was a further hour before he actually got round to asking Jess what she did for a living.

"I work in the hospitality industry."

Nicky found the subject boring but out of politeness he smiled and asked more.

"Some five star hotel I take it?"

"No. Actually I'm a dominatrix."

Nicky Brent had just taken a swig from his glass, the liquid went down his throat the wrong way and he began to cough. Her words hadn't really shocked him it was simply that she was so up market looking and he couldn't have envisioned meeting a dominatrix at Royal Ascot. He wasn't disappointed; in fact he was desperate to ask more regarding her line of work. Putting aside the money he had just

won from Big Barry, Nicky felt as though he'd also won the lottery.
"Sorry, did I shock you?"
"Not at all, in fact I think it was fate that we met today. I really would like to ask you more about what you do and it's not in a perverted way. Obviously we can't talk in depth about it today, but if you give me your number before we leave I can contact you if that's alright?"
Jess smiled to herself at the prospect of a new client. A week after their initial meeting saw the first of many sessions that would take place at Jess's flat. The obligatory cup of tea had resulted in Nicky Brent revealing all about his life. He explained that he didn't feel a need to be punished in anyway, he already knew that he was a bastard through and through and he couldn't care less who else knew it. Nicky bragged for a while about all that he had achieved but when he saw that she wasn't impressed he soon stopped. This woman was special, she made him feel alive and the feeling was new to him.
"So exactly why do you want to use the services of a dominatrix Mr Brent?"
"Please call me Nicky and I'm out for the thrill pure and simple!"
"You do know that what I offer can sometimes be extremely painful?"
Her words, come to that just the sound of her voice excited him and he couldn't wait for the fun to start.

"Of course I do!"
"Well then, can you tell me what sort of things you are into?"
"I haven't got a clue to be honest. I want to try it all!"
"I think you may come to regret that Mr Brent but we'll just have to wait and see. Shall we get started?"
Nicky was standing in seconds and leading him through to the dungeon she instructed him to choose something to wear and informed him that on her return he would address her as Mistress. Nicky pointed to the cross at the far end of the room.
"Out of curiosity, what's that?"
"That beautiful creation Mr Brent is used for only the best of my clients. Satisfy your Mistress today and I may indulge you on a future visit."
When Jess left the room Nicky opened up the wardrobe and was momentarily taken back by the array of costumes. He slowly touched the rubber shorts and trousers before his eyes settled upon something that had always excited him. Removing it he made his way over to the racks and inspected the array of whips, dildos and other items, items that he hadn't a clue what their use was. The smell of the room, or at least he thought it was the smell, excited him. It wasn't dirty, far from it but there was just something about the place and the atmosphere. Maybe it was purely down to the fact that he could envisage all that had previously gone

on in this space that was aptly named the dungeon. Nicky could feel the onset of excitement and he smiled to himself as he donned his chosen attire. Jess was in her bedroom and had opted for a black leather all in one cat suit topped off with eight inch high patent boots. Her hair was now scraped back into a pony tail and a cat woman style mask covered her eyes. Crimson red lipstick had been neatly applied which gave her lips a fuller sexier look. Deciding to give her newest client a little extra time she sat down on the edge of the bed and digested all that he had confided to her. Jess didn't know if she liked the man but then it wasn't her business to like someone. The five hundred pounds an hour he was paying was all that mattered. Ten minutes later she at last opened the door. Nicky Brent stood naked before her; the outfit he'd chosen was a gimp mask with zippered mouth, rubber cuffs and a dog collar complete with attached chain lead. Eyeing him up she mentally noted that his penis was only average in size and that there was as yet no real sign of an erection, something she hoped to quickly rectify. Walking over to him she grabbed hold of his manhood and squeezed hard. Because of the mask Jess wasn't able to see his reaction but the soft whimper that emitted from his mouth and his eyes moving quickly from side to side, told her all that she needed to know. Still tightly holding his now erect penis she led him over to the rack to select her implement of torture. Opting for a standard riding crop, which was more than appropriate for this particular client, Jess stood legs apart in front of him and released her grip.

"On your knees! You are my slave now and will do all that I command."

Nicky did as he was told and Jess could already see that his erection was now even harder. Raising the crop, she thrust it back and forth through the air so that it made a whipping sound. Glaring down at her client she pouted her lips seductively as she spoke.

"Lick my boots Slave!"

Nicky instantly took to the task like a duck to water but it wasn't good enough for his mistress and he would soon learn that nothing would ever be good enough for her. Jess raised the whip and with one swift movement of her wrist the tip made contact with Nicky Brent's bare buttocks. He let out a howl in pain and Jess inwardly smiled, they were all such babies when it came down to pain. Nicky continued to obey her command but now he seemed to be licking as if he was desperate to please, desperate not to feel the crop make contact with his skin again but at the same time willing it to happen. Just as he'd hoped his initiation into the world of the dominatrix had been pure ecstasy and within a very short time and after he'd felt a little more pain he was harder than he'd ever been in his life before. Just as he was beginning to feel a strong urge in his penis, Jess took a step backwards and stopped all contact. For a few seconds Nicky stared up in disbelief as he was desperate for her to repeat the act. It was a common scenario but Jess wouldn't give in, it was always best to leave them wanting more.

"You sorry excuse for a slave."

"But Jess I..."

Nicky instantly felt pain as the crop once more lashed against his buttocks.

"Sorry Mistress but can we carry on, I feel as if I'm only just getting started."

Jess pushed him to the floor and as he lay on his back she pressed the spiked heel of her boot into his groin and Nicky Brent howled out in pain. Removing her foot, Jess ordered Nicky to get up and grabbing his hard penis with her gloved hand she slowly pulled it backwards and forwards. Gradually she speeded up the motion and at the same time let fly with the crop against his buttocks. Nicky Brent groaned out loud as he violently ejaculated. Jess knew exactly what she was doing and revelled in the power that she felt. This was all so professionally carried out and Nicky Brent couldn't believe his luck. With one final act of domination Jess grabbed hold of his bollocks and squeezed them firmly as Nicky whimpered.

"When I say enough, then it's enough! Only ever refer to me as Mistress, do you understand slave?"

"Yes Mistress."

Jess left the room so that her client could clean

himself up and get changed. Usually a new client felt shame and needed a little time to compose themselves after their first session. Somehow she didn't thing that would be the case with Nicky Brent. Five minutes later and he appeared in the kitchen to find his host once more dressed in her twinset and pearls and pouring them both tea from a fine china pot.

"So Mr Brent, how did you find it?"

"Absolutely brilliant thanks; actually I have an Arab friend who might be interested in your services. Is it alright if I tell him about you?"

"Certainly."

"I was also wondering if we could move things on a bit. Maybe go to the next level if that's ok with you?"

Jess pondered his request for a moment as it was highly unusual to move on so quickly but the money he was paying was the deciding factor in her decision.

"What exactly do you have in mind?"

"I'd like to heighten the level of my orgasm."

"Well that's something we can do I suppose but I don't quite understand, you said you enjoyed it today wasn't that enough for you?"

"Like I said, it was brilliant but I want to try everything."

After this, each session became more and more intense and his requests got closer to the point where Jess wasn't comfortable with the situation.

Nicky kept bringing new ideas to her and the sadistic nature of these ideas was growing. After their last session Nicky had taken a seat at the table and looking in Jess's direction seemed to be leering at her. His action unnerved Jess and sent a shiver down her spine but he didn't seem to notice as he spoke.

"I've been investigating web sites for new ideas."

"And?"

"I'd rather not say until I've looked into them further, I don't want to spoil the surprise but if it's what I want then Ill text you with the details. They do look really interesting though."

Against her better judgement Jess decided to let him visit again, after that if she still wasn't comfortable then that would be it. They made the next appointment for one weeks time and Nicky Brent left the Kensington apartment with a spring in his step. Until his first meeting with Jess he had never experienced orgasms so powerful and with every session since, they had seemed to grown in intensity. If things carried on this way then he knew that for a while at least, his thrills would be guaranteed. For the entire journey back to the yard, he mentally relived every single moment of his evening and he couldn't wait until his next visit.

Alone in her flat Jess immediately washed herself, washed far more thoroughly than usual and then put on her onesie. There was something comforting in the childlike costume that made her feel safe and after this evenings visitor that was a feeling she desperately needed. Although she hadn't had sex she somehow felt dirty and it wasn't how she liked to feel after a visit from one of her clients. It was strange but for some reason Jess didn't feel in control and control was the one thing she had to have in her line of business. It was a routine of hers to put on some music, open a bottle of wine and relax but she just wasn't in the mood tonight. Her life felt as though it was spiralling if only in an emotional way, downwards. Her confidence wasn't as high as it usually was and things seemed to be changing but she didn't know why. Jess couldn't put the blame at Nicky Brent's door because the way she was feeling had begun before shed even met the man. Pouring herself a sizable brandy she curled up on the sofa and pulled a large fur throw over her legs. Maybe it was time to find a new career, something that she could sink her teeth into and also possibly get her mum on board. Trying to think of anything other than the horse trainer became increasingly difficult and no matter how hard she tried her thoughts would return to him. There was something about Mr Brent that she really wasn't sure about but no matter how hard she wracked her brains she just couldn't put her finger on what it was. Jess decided to call it a night, maybe tomorrow she would feel differently. For Nicky Brent there had been no such doubts. He had never felt so alive and for the next seven days he would surf the net for new ideas that he could share with his mistress. Time seemed to drag by as he eagerly awaited their meeting. Everything was running smoothly at Tumbles and even Shamus had entered into a couple of conversations with him. For once he could keep work and his private life separate while still seeking out new pleasures and he felt as though at long last his personal life was starting to take a turn for the better.

CHAPTER SEVEN

Jess woke with the mother of all headaches. She had slept badly and all the tossing and turning throughout the night only ended when she had finally drifted off at around five am. Having laid in an awkward position her neck was now painful and she had no doubt that it was the main cause for her headache. Making her way into the kitchen she swallowed two paracetamol and guzzled down a large glass of water to refresh her mouth. Glancing up at the clock made her groan out loud when she saw that it was just after nine. Jess was due to see Lucy this morning for their second meeting but there was no way she was going to make it. Picking up her mobile from the kitchen table she slipped it into her dressing gown pocket and went back to bed. Deciding to reschedule rather than cancel Jess sent a message to Lucy telling her that she couldn't make it until two that afternoon. Switching the phone off so that she wouldn't be disturbed, Jess lay her aching head back down on the pillow and drifted back to sleep.

Lucy Urquhart was about to leave the house when she received the text. At first she was disappointed but Lucy soon realised that a delay was still better than a cancelation. Making her way down to the kitchen she decided to spend some time with Norma and bring her up to speed with all that had

been happening. Norma Sanderson had just finished loading the dishwasher with crockery when Lucy entered the kitchen. Expecting to be asked for something, she was surprised when the young woman walked over and took a seat at the table. Lucy didn't speak and Norma knew this was her signal for a chat. It had been the same since Lucy was a child. If there was ever a problem at school she would come in and sit down in silence and Norma had quickly come to recognise the look.
"I thought you were going out today Miss Lucy?"
Lucy Urquhart sighed heavily.
"I was but my new friend has just cancelled, well not cancelled exactly but she can't make it until this afternoon. I'm really disappointed Norma its really messed up my whole schedule. I had a lot I wanted to get through today and this will put me back considerably."
Never having children of her own, Norma Sanderson loved the girl deeply. She also saw Lucy's faults and always wanting her own way was one of them. It was a trait Norma didn't particularly like.
"Maybe this woman had something she couldn't get out of. I hate to tell you this Lucy but it's not all about you, you know? People do have lives of their own and sometimes they have to let people down. Anyway I've been waiting for you to tell me how it's all going. I was telling my sister all about it the other day and she..."

"Oh Norma please tell me you didn't? Daddy will have a fit if he finds out; I mean what if your sister tells someone?"

Suddenly Norma Sanderson was angry, more than angry she was livid and she did nothing to stop it showing on her face. For all the years she'd served this family and served them well, not once had she ever let them down or betrayed them and it hurt that she was now possibly being accused of that very thing. Throwing down her tea towel, she turned to face Lucy and the next sentence to come from her mouth was not spoken in a soft tone.

"Now you listen to me young lady! My sister is the most honest and discreet woman I know and when I tell her never to repeat anything then she doesn't. It hurts me to even hear that accusation, especially when it comes from you."

Norma quickly turned her back on Lucy and busied herself at the sink as she didn't want the girl to see that she had tears in her eyes. Usually she would take anything Lucy said with a pinch of salt but today the girl had overstepped the mark. She began to hum away to some tune that was playing low on the radio. It was her sign to Lucy that as far as she was concerned the conversation was now well and truly over. Lucy Urquhart was thick skinned at times but even she could see that shed hurt Norma. Getting up from the table she walked over to the sink and wrapped her arms around Norma's neck. It usually did the trick but not this time. When

Lucy began to talk in a babyish voice and said I'm sowey Normy Norma dried her hands and turning around pulled the girls arms away.

"Lucy you really must start to think before you speak. Normally it doesn't matter when you run off at the mouth and your father certainly doesn't scold you but you've got to start growing up love and thinking about other people's feelings. Lord knows you've got a fantastic brain in there but tact is something you have very little of. Now sit down at that table and I'll make us some tea and then we can start again."

Like a child Lucy did as she was told. She didn't mind being told off by Norma as it was something that rarely happened so she knew when it did she deserved it. The women spent the next hour talking about what was happening with Lucy's research. Norma found out that Jess was beautiful and intelligent and she wanted to laugh at the picture she had in her own head of what Lucy had imagined the woman was going to be like. After sharing a quick bite to eat at lunchtime it was soon time for Lucy to head off for the rescheduled meeting. At around noon Jess woke for the second time that day. Her headache had eased and she tentatively got out of bed, scared that if she made any sudden moves it would return. After making herself a light lunch she switched on the radio and knew that everything was going to be alright. Taking her time she washed and dressed but today

Jess Metcalf wore old jeans, a sloppy oversized jumper and no makeup. It wasn't her usual attire but today she felt like taking it easy and the last thing she wanted was to strut about in high heels. Pulling on her trusted old parka she began the walk to Covent Garden. Even though the weather was chilly she was enjoying the fresh air and it really was helping to clear her head. Usually dressed up to the nines, it made a refreshing change not to be noticed and stared at by the other people on the street. Reaching Patisserie Valerie Jess peered in through the window and spotted a frantically waving Lucy gazing back at her. The girls enthusiasm seemed never ending and even though she smiled, Jess thought to herself that she really could be doing without this today. Grinning broadly she made her way inside to find a cappuccino already waiting for her at the table.
"Hello Love and before we start I would like to apologise for this morning. My head has been pounding like a drum. I really felt like crap and to be honest I just wasn't up to it."
Lucy squeezed her on the arm and taking a pad and pencil from her bag, didn't even give Jess time to take her coat off.
"That's alright. We all have off days from time to time, now shall we get started? I've been thinking that maybe a question and answer session might be good and then perhaps end with a client story if that's ok?"

"That sounds fine love but can we take it slowly as I don't fancy another headache like the one I had this morning."

"Ok, well I've made a list of questions that I feel most people would like to know about but as yet I don't know how I'm going to use them. Anyway I won't worry about that for the moment so here goes. Do you have penetrative sex with your clients as I've heard some dominatrix's don't?"

"Remember Lucy that I don't only carry out the roll of a dominatrix, I'm also a good old fashioned whore but getting back to your question. I can only speak for myself as it depends on the individual I suppose. On the whole when I'm supplying the services of a dominatrix then I don't often have intercourse with my clients. Of course I do make exceptions when there's a physical attraction and I feel comfortable and in control. After all I am only human and get turned on the same as most other women."

"On a typical day, how many would there be?"

"Sweetheart, there's no such thing as a typical day in my line of work. I may only have one client but then again it could be as many as five or six."

"So are you talking about the number of clients or the amount of times you have sex?"

"Clients but if you want to know how many times I've had sex in one day I would probably say no more than three. I know the girls working out of the massage parlours or down the Cross have a lot

more but then they have to. The amount of money I charge I can afford to be choosey and there's no need to flog my arse off like they do, bless them."
"Bless them? You sound as if you really feel for them?"
"Of course I do, don't you?"
"Well I suppose I do think about it a lot. When I was in Edinburgh I tried to talk to some of the street workers but they always seemed so aloof. No matter how hard I tried to get inside their minds they wouldn't let me, it was almost as if they were hardened to the life they lead and had built up these invisible barriers."
"It's understandable. There but for god's grace go I."
There was a moment's pause as both women reflected on Jess's words.
"So what is the greatest number of dominatrix sessions you've had in one day?"
"Probably six or seven but that's rare. Its less physically demanding than intercourse though no less tiring but it can also be more fun."
"Fun?"
"Yes of course, I love it. My clients can be real characters when it comes down to the nitty gritty and I can find myself having a right laugh sometimes."
Jess smiled when she mentally recalled some of the escapades but she didn't feel like sharing them with Lucy.
"Getting back to the dominatrix sessions, I find it

difficult to understand how you switch so easily from that to straight sex."

Jess Metcalf casually shrugged her shoulders. "Were all different darling. All I can say is it works for me and like I've said before if I don't like someone then I don't have to oblige them. Shall we have some more coffee? All this talking is making my throat dry."

Lucy just waved her hand in dismissal which made Jess want to laugh. The girl was so engrossed in her research that she couldn't be bothered with anything else. Jess nodded in the direction of the waitress and when she turned back to face Lucy saw that the young woman looked put out by the delay. Jess smiled and Lucy Urquhart once more consulted her notes.

"How many clients would you say that you have on your books at any one time?"

"That's a difficult one to answer. I could see someone once in a blue moon and then there are others who visit me weekly. If I'm really pushed on a number then I'd have to say in the region of one hundred."

"So what activities do they request, you know what sort of things do you do?"

"It all depends on what they want. In some cases we just talk, in other cases it might be just cuddles. There's one client who only wants to shower me with expensive gifts. He even sent me to the Bahamas for an all expenses paid holiday just so

that he could pay for me. It's a whole different world Lucy and not the one that's often portrayed in documentaries. The media seem to like showing a dominatrix as hard core and depraved and while it can be like that sometimes, it's not always the case. There is one man who I see once a month for afternoon tea. I dress in a French maids outfit and serve him earl grey and fondant fancies. He pays me to wait on him for one hour and that's all."
Lucy laid her pen onto the table and turned to look at Jess.
"Do you ever think you're exploiting them?"
"No."
"Is that it, just no? No other answer?"
"None needed."
"Fair enough I suppose. Now regarding the role of the dominatrix and your sex sessions, within those boundaries can you explain how they receive their punishment and the pleasure they get from it?"
Finally Jess had been asked a question that she was looking forward to answering and she also wanted to set Lucy Urquhart straight on a few things.
"I'm glad you've asked me that Lucy. You often find heterosexual men who outwardly condemn homosexuality in a big way, like to take it up the arse. When it's being dished out by a dominatrix they love it. So in one way they're screaming from the roof tops that it's a despicable act but in my company they're begging for more of the same. Now wouldn't you say that's a contradiction in

terms? It's something they wouldn't choose to do with their wives or girlfriends for fear of appearing unmanly. I've actually had conversations with the butchest of men before a session who actually say that they hate all queers. After their first experience of anal they leave my flat meek and feeling awkward. Strange don't you think?"

Lucy started to giggle, she was really getting into it all and found Jess's answers riveting.

"Well I think I've got enough for a good start. Oh I forgot to ask, how did you get on with the trainer?"

"I don't really want to go into that for now but I'm really not sure about him. There's something that I can't quite put my finger on, then again maybe it's just me. Anyway would you like me to tell you about a woman?"

Jess proceeded to tell Lucy Sharon Russell's story but changed the ending. She didn't feel good about it but this way there was less chance of Lucy finding out Sharon's true identity if she decided to do some digging. If she'd repeated the story word for word then it would have been easy to track her down as there couldn't be many policewomen who had been shot in the city. When it came down to sex, Jess had stretched the truth. Well in all honesty shed actually told the story of two different women and mixed their two lives into one but she wasn't about to admit it. True Sharon's story was real for the most part but it never involved sex in any way shape or form. The two were actually best friends and Jess hoped that Sharon wouldn't mind about what she'd said. The girl had wanted a woman to feature in her books but there wasn't one worth elaborating on, so Jess Metcalf had partially fabricated a story that she knew well. When she reached the end Lucy Urquhart had tears in her eyes and it was clear to Jess that the tale had touched the young girl deeply.

"Oh how sad. I know you told me that there would be some heartbreaking stories but still I didn't expect anything like that!"

Jess tenderly touched her biographer and friend, which was how she was starting to look upon Lucy.

"Darling you haven't heard anything yet but I think we should take it one step at a time, for your sake at least. If you're the girl I think you are, then too many sad recounts will play heavily on your mind. Lord knows they have on mine over the years."

"So what about the carpenter, you said you would tell me about him."

Jess was starting to get tired but she also found that she enjoyed recalling the tales and as the girl was showing so much enthusiasm she didn't have the heart to refuse her.

"Felix? Oh he's really special to me and I don't mean in a sexual way. I first met Felix many years ago while I was still at school."

Without being asked, Jess went into further detail but Lucy soon became bored. The story wasn't gritty and there was no sex involved. There was no way that it would ever feature in her book but she still tried to look interested. When Lucy yawned twice within as many minutes Jess quickly got the message.

"Anyway that's about it for today. My how the time flies, look its already getting dark outside."

"Do you have any clients tonight?"

As she spoke Lucy removed five fifty pound notes from her purse and placed them on the table.

"No but as it happens I do have one tomorrow night. A nice little dwarf who travels up by train from Brighton once a fortnight."

"What, I mean pardon, did I hear you right? What did you say?"

"That's right a dwarf and please don't think I'm being nasty when I call him that. I'm well aware of the politically correct term but he actually prefers to be called a dwarf. I tell you, for a little one he hasn't half got some stamina and believe you me he isn't that small either if you know what I mean!"

Lucy didn't laugh and for a second but only that Jess felt a little mean. The two women had been talking for over four hours. Luckily they were not asked to vacate the premises as the Patisserie stayed open late in the hope of attracting some of the theatre goers. Lucy again tried to pay Jess for talking to her just as she had on their previous meeting but once again Jess told Lucy to keep her money.

"Now I really must get going Lucy but I'll ring you

soon to arrange our next meeting."
Jess Metcalf was the first to leave the cafe and pulling her coat up tight around her neck she said her goodbyes and set off for home. The weather had turned chilly and there was a fine mist in the air so she didn't hang about. The thought of getting back to her nice warm flat spurred her to walk faster. By the time she reached Kensington High Street Jess was becoming increasingly aware that someone was following her. The shops had begun to close and even though there were still a few people milling about, they were quickly diminishing. It was still difficult to hear individual sounds but call it a woman's intuition, she was sure that things were not right. Somehow in the cold darkness and with mist coming down onto the street things seemed eerie. Jess Metcalf had walked along this road for years and thought nothing of it but tonight for some reason it felt different. Stopping to see who would pass her by, she browsed in a few of the shop windows but when nothing out of the ordinary happened she chastised herself for being so silly. Just to be on the safe side she made her way into the centre of the pavement. Continuing her journey home it was only a few steps later that she again had a feeling someone was following her. When she first thought that she'd heard the footsteps she didn't think too deeply about it but now a short while later when she could again hear them she stopped. Her sense and

awareness was now heightened and there were definitely footsteps and they started and stopped at the same pace and rhythm as her own. Jess glanced in all directions but apart from a young woman pushing a pram that was directly behind her, it could have been anyone of the tourists or locals alike. The mist had quickly turned to fog and she could just make out the forms of people heading in her direction but it was difficult and besides it wasn't their feet that she could hear. Suddenly the idea seemed ridiculous and continuing on her way Jess tried to think of other things but within seconds the sound could be heard again. Listening hard, the footsteps were pummelling the ground and following the exact same path as her. She tried to work out if they were female steps, perhaps Lucy had attempted to follow her. Pulling the hood of her coat down she tried to block out any passing traffic and focus entirely on the steps. They definitely weren't female as they were too heavy and when she realised that, a shiver ran down her spine. Wracking her brains she tried to think of anyone who would want to scare her but she really didn't have a clue and wasn't about to hang around to find out. Jess quickened her walk but still she heard the footsteps and their rate of speed increased with her own. Turning every few seconds to glance backwards, all she could see was silhouettes in the fog. As each figure came into view she mentally discarded them but even so they all seemed to be staring at her when she looked in their direction. Stopping again she stood completely still and scanned the shops, the doorways, anywhere that someone could hide but there was no one. As soon as she began to walk again, the sound of footsteps could once more be heard as they followed her. Turning into Argyll Road Jess was really beginning to get frightened. Suddenly she did something she hadn't done in years, Jess began to run. Glad that she'd decided to dress down today the trainers now came into their own as her feet rapidly hit the pavement. With each step she took her breath became more and more laboured until the sound of her own breathing drowned out anything else. She continued to turn around and look over her shoulder but every time she did there was still no one that she could pick out. Jess could feel her heart racing and her mouth was dry through fear. In the cold damp air her breath now came out in a visible vapour and intensified as her heart pounded. As she struggled with every breath she desperately tried to swallow but with all the will in the world she wasn't able to muster up any saliva. The parka was making her hot, more than hot; she was actually sweating intensely and by the time she reached Phillimore Place she was totally exhausted and ready to drop. With no alternative Jess was forced to stop for a moment and bending over panted in a desperate attempt to get air into her lungs. Slowly she stood up but as she did so felt a firm hand as it gripped her shoulder from behind. With every ounce of energy left in her Jess tried to scream but try as she might nothing came out. Deciding to face her assailant full on she spun round and was stunned when she came face to face with Felix Abbott, her long time friend and carpenter. Through pure relief Jess fell sobbing into his arms.

"Hey hey! Whatever's the matter?"

As she sobbed and shook uncontrollably, Jess Metcalf tried to relay all that had happened.

"Some some someone's been following me!"

"Who?"

"I don't know but if they're trying to scare me, then they're doing a fucking good job!"

Felix Abbott placed his arm on Jess's shoulder and turning her around, guided her in the direction of her flat.

"Come on sweetheart let's get you inside. Bleeding hell Jess you're shaking like a leaf."

She allowed him to take control; she had no choice as her nerves were in shreds. Jess was just thankful that he was here but as a thought entered her head she suddenly stopped and turned towards him.

"It wasn't you was it?"

"Wasn't me what?"

"Trying to scare me. You wouldn't do that to me Felix would you?"

Felix dropped his arm from her shoulder and by the look of horror that now filled his face Jess knew that

she had hurt him deeply.
"No it bloody wasn't and I'm offended that you could even think such a thing. You're my friend and I would never do anything to hurt you."
Jess now felt embarrassed.
"I'm sorry alright! It's just that you appeared out of nowhere and well, oh I don't know."
Felix pointed his hand in the direction they had just come from. His works van was visibly parked on the other side of the road.
"Fuck me Jess! Just take a look over there will you?"
Doing as she was asked, she instantly felt ashamed.
"That happens to be my van and I was just going to pop in and see how you were. I saw you running and as I crossed the road you stopped, that's when I touched your shoulder. What on earth did you think I was going to do, mug you?"
Jess frantically rubbed at her brow. Today was turning into a nightmare and she just wished that she had never gotten out of her bed.
"I'm sorry alright, I'm sorry!"
She placed her key in the lock and invited Felix inside.
"Please come in Felix and I'll make you a drink. I'm sorry I thought, well you know..."
Jess really wanted to be alone but it was the least she could do after almost accusing him. Placing the kettle onto the hob she removed the parka and surveyed her armpits that were soaked through with sweat.

"Sorry but I really need to get out of these clothes. Would you mind making the tea?"

He smiled his answer and Jess could see that there wasn't an ounce of malice in the man. How could she have gotten things so wrong? As she made her way to the bathroom she began to wonder if she was losing her mind. Turning on the shower Jess undressed and stepped inside. For several minutes she stood motionless as the hot water ran over her skin. Applying a liberal amount of shower gel Jess covered her body and with each foamy caress she began to feel the tension subside. Finally after she had washed every drop of sweat away she stepped from the cubicle and for a split second thought she saw Felix in the doorway watching her. The idea that he had seen her naked made her feel strange but as the bathroom was so steamy and she wasn't sure exactly what she had seen, knew that she couldn't challenge him. Pushing the thought from her mind Jess quickly pulled on her comforting fleecy dressing gown. Slowly she walked along the hall and as she entered the kitchen found her guest seated at the table with two steaming hot mugs of tea in front of him. Felix had switched on the under unit lighting, drawn the curtains and the radio was playing a gentle tune which instantly relaxed her.

"Better?"

"Ummmm."

"Good! Now I've put a liberal tot of brandy in yours and I want you to sit down and tell me what the hell has been going on."

For once Jess Metcalf didn't mind being told what to do, for once she was glad that someone else was taking charge and making her feel safe. Totally out of character as she was always such a private person when it came down to her personal life, she relayed all the worries about her mother and how horrible her father had been.

"So do you think he's the one trying to frighten you?"

Jess raised her hands and the gesture told Felix that she really didn't have a clue.

"Do you want me to call the Old Bill?"

Instantly Jess banged her cup on the table and her answer was almost a shout.

"Definitely not!!!"

"Ok Ok I was only asking sweetheart, no need to bite me bleeding head off."

Jess held her head in her hands as she hunched over the table.

"I know you were and I'm sorry. God that's all I seem to be saying tonight. Look Felix, you know as well as I do that the law wouldn't be the least Bit interested not once they know what I do for a living and there's no way I could hide it from them. One look in my spare room would give it away in an instant. I mean there's no easy way to hide a fucking seven foot high cross and a selection of dildos and equipment that would put the best shops in Soho to shame."

Suddenly they were both laughing and as Felix took her hand Jess didn't see the look in his eyes, or if she did then she chose to ignore it. After another liberally laced tea Jess yawned out loud. She really was ready for her bed but wouldn't dream of saying anything, not when Felix Abbott had turned out to be her Knight in shining armour. Luckily she didn't have to as her yawn hadn't gone unnoticed.
"Look at you you're dead on your feet. I should get going now anyway as I've got a full day's work ahead of me. You're not the only dominatrix on me books Jess Metcalf."
They were still laughing as she showed him to the door and as Felix leant in to kiss Jess full on the lips she sharply pulled away. Now it was his turn to feel embarrassed.
"I'm sorry I don't know what came over me."
"It's ok Felix, it's been a long night and maybe were both just tired."
Jess watched him walk to the lift before she closed the front door. A smitten carpenter was all she needed but she wasn't about to lose any sleep over it. Tonight had been more than eventful and worrying about anything else would be just too much. Turning out the light she crawled into bed and wouldn't know another thing until the morning.
Standing outside in the cold damp air Felix Abbott watched as she switched her lights out. Walking along the street he made his way back to his van

and decided to sleep there for the night. It wasn't that warm but he had a couple of blankets in the back and he couldn't take the chance of going home, not if someone really had been following her. Felix certainly hadn't seen anyone and wondered if it was just some silly female hysteria but then he'd known Jess a long time and silly she definitely wasn't. The trouble was, Felix knew that in her line of work you couldn't be off meeting weirdo's and sometimes those weirdo's wanted to take things a step too far. Unseen and unbeknown to Felix, in the doorway to the vacant block of flats that was situated opposite Jess's apartment, a lone man struck a match and lit up a cigarette as he let himself inside. He wore a dark trilby hat and the collar of his coat was turned up high making identification almost impossible. The man's assignment was turning out to be more complicated by the minute. He had been watching the woman for some time but now with the added aggravation of a guardian angel looking out for her from his van, keeping tabs on Jessica Metcalf and finding out exactly what she was up to was going to be far more difficult than he'd first thought.

CHAPTER EIGHT

At seven the next evening Jess was dressed and seated at the table ready to entertain Morris Granger. He had been a regular caller for the past couple of years and even though Jess didn't like to get personal with any of her clients, she had to admit that he was one of her favourites. When the door bell rang she sauntered along the hall and peered through the spy hole before opening up. Morris Grangers face was obscured by the large bouquet of roses that he had purchased in the hope of pleasing her. He always brought along a gift but Jess never thanked him, it was all part of the game. Panting and out of breath he didn't speak and Jess knew to let him gain back his composure. The scenario was always the same as the poor little man couldn't reach the top button in the lift and had to walk up the three flights of stairs. Fortunately due to the button for the ground floor being lower he didn't have the same problem when it came to going back down. It was just as well as he always seemed to overdo things in the dungeon and end up totally worn out by the time he went home. Morris was a kind, polite and not unattractive man who had never married. Initially Jess would have put his dwarfism as the reason he was still single but it didn't take her long to learn that nothing could have been further from the truth. When it came down to it his sexual preferences they were just a bit peculiar, or at least they would seem that way to a prospective wife. On his initial visit he explained that he'd had a couple of girlfriends but nothing that had lasted beyond a few weeks. After their first session Jess quickly realised why he was and always would be a bachelor. Morris liked to wear a small modified tight pink leotard. For obvious reasons the groin area had been removed and a small flap of material was held in place by Velcro. It covered his modesty until he was ready to perform which as usual with Morris could be quite some time. His costume was topped off with a Porky Pig mask that made Jess want to giggle every time she saw it. As foreplay Morris Grangers passion was to wrestle and with his unusual choice of outfit Jess could now see why any young girl would run a mile. As Morris prepared himself in the dungeon Jess dressed in her own room. Her scarlet see through bra and panties along with a latex mask of a wolfs head had all been gifts from her client. Thigh high boots and a red riding style cloak completed her outfit. All in all the session could only be described as fairytale porn but whatever Morris Granger wanted he could have without question. Entering the dungeon she stepped over the imaginary rope that was marked out by four pieces of duct tape stuck to the dungeon floor to form a ring. On a small table stood a shiny brass bell, the kind that could be found on many hotel reception desks. Jess

slapped the bell signalling the start of the bout.
Morris Granger went straight into action and diving
onto Jess's legs tackled her to the ground. She was
well aware what was coming as he always started
like this but he was so quick that she could do little
about it. Morris now had his head between the top
of Jess's legs and was forcing his face complete with
Porky Pig mask into her groin. Again she knew
what was coming but as Morris started to rootle and
grunt like a pig searching for truffles she couldn't
help herself and burst into a fit of giggles. As her
uncontrollable laughter continued she felt every
ounce of her energy disappear but still Morris
wouldn't stop. The more she laughed and wriggled
the more he rootled and grunted. Stretching out her
arm as far as she could Jess at last managed to
pound her hand down onto the bell and Morris
instantly stopped and allowed Jess to get to her feet.
"Oh my god Morris you really crack me up!"
Puffing and panting Morris walked over to his
imaginary corner. Jess was having so much fun and
still laughing but stopped when she could feel his
eyes upon her. Morris took the whole thing very
seriously and besides she had to compose herself in
readiness for round two. Morris Granger jogged on
the spot like a seasoned veteran and his eyes stared
at her in anticipation for the bout to continue. As
Jess rung the bell Morris ran at her but this time she
took a step sideways. As he passed her she
playfully slapped him on the head like a mini

forearm smash seen in professional matches. Morris's legs went from under him and he landed flat on his back. For a split second he was stunned and it gave Jess an opportunity. Moving like greased lightening she dropped to the floor and straddled the little man. Pinning his arms to the floor she began to count and just as she was about to say three, Morris Granger screamed out it pain.
"Arrrgghhh. It's my back; I think I've put it out again."
Jess started to panic and getting off of her client stood up.
"Oh Morris I'm so sorry, are you alright?"
"I don't know Mistress I'm in so much pain."
Slowly Morris got to his feet but miraculously the pain had disappeared and he dived on Jess. Grabbing the back of her knickers he forced her to the floor. In seconds his masked face was once again in her groin and the rootling and grunting continued. Jess was laughing uncontrollably and trying to speak at the same time.
"You little bugger Morris you conned me."
Her laughter was infectious and soon Morris Granger had joined in. Reaching for the bell she managed to call time and the match was over.
As Jess got to her feet she could clearly see a large bulge fighting for release against the Velcro.
"Now get on that bed and fuck me from behind you cheating little dwarf."
"Yes Mistress."

"And you had better please me do you hear?"
"Yes Mistress."
"And take that stupid Porky mask off."
"Yes Mistress."
Fifteen minutes later and after Morris Granger had given it his all in more ways than one he was finally finished and totally exhausted.

With the session now over and as Morris exited the building with a broad grin on his face, Jess Metcalf had already changed into her pyjamas and fleecy dressing gown. Standing at the large window she watched her client as he disappeared down the street. Jess stretched up her arms and rolled her neck to relieve any tension. She was about to close the curtains when out of the corner of her eye she spied something odd in one of the windows in the building opposite. The premises had been vacant for some time and yet there was just the glimmer of a light on in one of the rooms. Turning off her own lights, Jess pressed her nose to the glass as she peered long and hard but she still couldn't make out what it was or if there was anyone in the room. One thing was for sure, there shouldn't be anyone in the building and for a second she worried that whoever it was might be looking back at her. Jess quickly pulled the heavy fabric drapes across the window but at the same time a shiver ran down her spine. Was her mind playing tricks on her, she was very tired and what with entertaining Morris Granger this evening it had felt like a long day. Deep in thought for a few minutes, she then went and double checked that shed locked the front door securely. Everything was as it should be but she couldn't help but have another look out of the window. Whoever had been there must have left and much to her relief the place was once more in darkness. Jess decided to turn in for the night. She also made up her mind to phone her friend Sharon in the morning. It wasn't directly to do with the trouble shed been having recently but it was always good to have someone in your corner and besides it had been ages since the two had got together. Also a little reassurance from her only female friend wouldn't go a miss at the moment. It turned out to be a restless night of tossing and turning as dreams of someone following her invaded Jess's mind. The next day and totally out of character as it wasn't a Sunday, she decided to pay her mother a visit. Once more dressed to the nines Jess got out of the taxi and began the short walk to her old family home. About to knock she stopped when she heard her father ranting and raving at the top of his voice. There could only be one person he was venting his anger on and when an image entered her head of what was going on inside, Jess felt like breaking down the door. Instead she knocked extra hard in the hope that it would defuse the situation. It did and seconds later Annie Metcalf could be heard shuffling along the hallway. When she opened the door her face looked so sad and her eyes were red

from crying. The sight tore at Jess's heart.
Normally she beamed when she saw her daughter but now the best she could muster was a weak smile. Taking the woman in her arms Jess tightly embraced her mother.

"Whatever's going on Mum are you Ok? Has that bastard been having a go at you again?"

Annie nodded her head as more tears began to well up in her eyes. She was about to tell her daughter all that had happened when Bob Metcalf walked into the hall from the back room. His appearance instantly silenced Annie and when Bob saw that their visitor was his daughter he gritted his teeth and shook his head in a show of disgust.

"I thought there was a bad fucking stink in here."

Jess tenderly took hold of her mother's elbow and led her along the hall. As she passed her father she sneered in his direction and her old east end slang spilled from her mouth with a vengeance.

"Why don't you just fuck off Dad? My mother must have the patience of a fucking saint because if I was married to you Id have fucking knifed you by now you bastard!"

"Likewise you dirty bitch. If I thought I'd get away with it Id strangle the life out of you right here in this hallway. You've brought nothing but fucking shame to this house."

For a second all the problems shed been having of late entered her thoughts but she instantly made them disappear when she looked at her mother and

realised that she had to put her personal issues to one side and concentrate on helping the one person who really needed her. Slowly they walked into the back room and Jess closed the door so that her father couldn't hear them. After settling her mother at the table Jess made them both a hot drink. Now sitting down herself, she took Annie's hands in hers. "Please come back with me mum! You can't carry on like this; he's nothing but a bleeding great bully." Annie looked deep into her daughters eyes. She was so proud of her girl, proud that Jess had the guts to get out of this shit hole and make a life for herself. At the same time she felt like a complete coward, one who would live this godforsaken life until the day she died. When she thought back to when she was a young girl, a time when shed had youth on her side and was full of confidence, it broke her heart. Meeting Bob had seemed like a dream come true and he had wooed her with gifts and treated her like a princess. His manipulative and browbeating ways had started slowly to begin with but by the time baby Jessica had arrived Annie was completely down trodden. Now all these years later she hated the very ground he walked on. It would have been easy for Annie Metcalf to just get up and walk out with her daughter but she wouldn't be a burden on Jess no matter what.
"My darling, we are all dealt different hands in life and this one is mine. I've never expected much from life and life gave me exactly that! You on the

other hand, well you are strong and confident. I know you want me to go with you but you have your own life to live and you don't want an old woman cramping your style."

"But Mum I..."

Annie still had her hands in Jess's but now it was she who was doing the holding. Jess felt her mother's grip tighten as she spoke.

"Now you listen to me Jessica Metcalf! I am so very proud of you and it's the highlight of my week when you come to visit. It's enough, honestly it is. With a bit of luck I will outlive that old bastard and then it will be my turn for fun, my turn to shine. On the other hand if he outlives me, then I guess I'll win anyway because I won't have to put up with him anymore. I don't want to hear another word about it, alright? Come on; tell your old mum what you've been up to this week?"

Jess knew when she was banging her head up against a brick wall and decided not to push her mother any further, for today at least. She may have lost this battle but definitely not the war and if it was the last thing she did she would get her mother out of this hovel of a house and away from her father. The two women talked about shopping and the new curtains Jess had bought for her flat, in fact they talked about anything but the things that were troubling them both. An hour later and it was time for Jess to reluctantly leave but not before she had left her mother a parting gift. Removing her purse she handed a large wad of twenty pound notes and winked.

"Just in case Mum, just in case."

Unlike on her last visit there was no forcing required as Annie Metcalf readily accepted the money. Even she could see that things were coming to a head and before very long she was going to need some cash. As usual, when the front door closed Annie knew that the assault would soon begin. Walking towards the stairs, she hoped that if she could just make it up to the bedroom her husband might leave her alone for once but there was no such luck. Annie only managed to place her foot on the second step when he roughly grabbed a handful of her hair and yanked her backwards. Her head hit the tiled hallway with a crack and curling herself in a ball Annie prayed to god that it would soon be over. Seconds passed and when she didn't feel any pain she lifted her head off of the floor and looked behind to where her husband stood. Bob Metcalf was staring at her and his lip was curled back in disgust as he spoke.

"You really are a pathetic fucking excuse for a woman. Look at you with your dirty hair and scruffy clothes, fuck me whatever did I do to deserve ending up with a cunt like you?"

For once Bob didn't put the boot in but as he turned to walk away he hawked up as much phlegm as he could and spat it directly into Annie's face. She didn't dare move and lying on the cold hall floor she pulled the cuff of her cardigan over her hand and wiped the slimy mess from her cheek. Annie didn't get up and instead she again curled herself into a tight ball. Her husband spitting at her somehow seemed far worse than the kicks and punches she usually received, now she felt totally humiliated and knew that any fight she still had inside had just vanished. Jess was able to hail a cab easily and was soon standing on Kensington high street. Slowly strolling past the shops she recounted all that had happened just a short while ago at her parents. When visions of her father entered her head she felt totally and utterly helpless. The feeling was alien to her and she didn't like it one bit, it actually made her angry and as her blood began to boil she suddenly stopped walking.

Delving into her bag she smiled when her hand settled on her mobile phone. Now she felt strong again and would once more take charge of her own destiny. Scrolling down she pressed connect when Nicky Brent's phone number appeared. Knowing that her decision had been made after seeing her mother today, Jess was not going to allow any man to threaten her or make her feel scared. Discussing Nicky Brent with Lucy had been one thing but deep down she knew if it hadn't have been for what happened at her mother's she would probably have allowed his visits to continue, well not anymore.

"Hello?"

"Hi Nicky."

For a moment there was silence. It was normally the client who made contact and not the other way round and Nicky Brent was speechless but it was short lived.

"Mistress! How lovely to hear from you. I was actually going to give you a ring later today. I've found some fantastic web sites on the internet, just the thing I've been looking for. You remember what I spoke to you about last time we met, well I......."

"I need to stop you there Nicky! I'm not calling you out of business. In fact the reason I'm ringing is to tell you that you are no longer a client of mine. I've thought long and hard about the matter but I feel that over the last few sessions things have been going in the wrong

direction, for me at least. I'm sorry but from now on you will have to find your thrills elsewhere."

Jess heard the man gasp on the other end of the line and was momentarily taken aback.

"But why Mistress? Whatever have I done wrong? Oh please don't stop me visiting, I've never experienced anything like it before."

"Maybe you haven't Nicky and it's not because you've done anything wrong in particular. Nicky I no longer feel comfortable in your company and its a strict rule of mine that if this situation should ever arise, then without question I sever all contact."

"Whatever I've said or done then I'm sorry but please give me another chance. I don't know what I will do if you won't see me again."

Jess knew she obviously wasn't being strong enough and changing her tone she became very authoritarian as she spoke.

"I said no!!! Now just accept my decision and let us part on friendly terms, alright?"

Out of the blue and as though someone had flicked a switch, Nicky Brent began to rant and rave. His voice had risen by several octaves as he called Jess all the dirty whores under the sun. He sounded menacing and she knew that if she had actually been with him in person when she ended the relationship, then she would have been very scared.

"Goodbye Nicky."

"You fucking bitch! I'll make sure you pay for this you stinking fucking whore! You'll be sorry you ever messed with....."

Now totally convinced that she had done the right thing, Jess hung up while he was still shouting obscenities at her. Somewhat relieved but at the same time physically shaking she scrolled down her phone list and pressed connect when Sharon Russell's number appeared. The call was answered in a second when her friend recognised who was ringing.

"Hello Jess darling, I was just thinking about you! How you doing?"

"Not so good Shaz and I could do with a bit of support."

"You at home?"

"No but I will be in about five minutes."

"As soon as you get in put the kettle on and I'll be over before its boiled."

With that the two women hung up and Jess felt as if her spirits had been lifted already.

CHAPTER NINE

By the time she reached her flat, Jess had calmed down and felt better about things. She was really glad that shed ended all contact with Nicky Brent and she tried not to dwell on the subject any longer as any thought of him made her skin crawl. The phone call earlier had actually frightened her but now she was getting her confidence back and it felt good. Placing the kettle on to boil she removed a couple of mugs from the cupboard just as the intercom buzzer went off. Viewing the screen she smiled when she saw it was her old friend. Jess opened up the front door and left it ajar before heading back to make the coffee. She was just in the middle of preparing them both a quick bite to eat when Sharon Russell entered the kitchen. The two women embraced and Sharon noticed how her friend held on for a little longer than she usually did. Releasing her hold Sharon took a seat at the table.
"So honey, what's all this about needing some support."
Jess placed the coffee and sandwiches onto the table then sat down. Slowly she told her friend all that had happened over the last couple of weeks and Sharon could see the worry in her friends face when she got to the telephone conversation with Nicky Brent.

"Why don't you make a formal complaint? I can make sure its handled in a delicate way but it will tell that bloke in no uncertain terms that you have friends in high places."

"You're a good mate Shaz but the law and my line of work don't mix too well. I think everything will be alright now, you know what it's like when you get a bit frightened it kind of knocks your confidence. Anyway enough about me, what have you been up to now that you're a high flying policewoman?"

"Its Deputy Chief Inspector if you don't mind but you can call me Ma'am."

"And you can call me Mistress."

They both started to laugh at the absurdity of it all.

"Oh Jess it still makes me smile when I think back to our days at Haggerston school. I remember several occasions when the teachers told me I would never amount to anything. I was over the moon just to be accepted into the Met but when the promotions kept coming, well I wasn't about to complain. I have to admit that this latest one shocked me more than a bit though."

"No one deserves it more than you sweetheart and that's the truth. God when I think about how it could have gone well..."

Suddenly the room was silent as they both remembered a time when things were very different, a time when Sharon had first joined the force and had thought she was invincible."

Sharon Russell's story

"Now you take care Sharon love!"
Closing the front gate Sharon Russell took one last look at the place shed called home, a place she couldn't wait to see the back of.
"I will Mum and don't be worrying. I promise as soon as I'm settled Ill phone you alright?"
When Sharon finished her education the family had moved out to Essex and adapting to a new area hadn't come easy to the girl. Gladys Russell now knew that she probably wouldn't ever see her daughter again let alone hear from her. Oh, she'd done the best she could when it came down to raising the girl but her Sharon had always wanted more. She couldn't blame her, God above knew if given her time over Gladys would have run a hundred miles if she'd have know she would end up stuck here in this flea pit of a home but beggars couldn't be choosers and she just hoped that her girl would make something of her life. Wearily she turned and made her way back inside the house to the four other hungry mouths that she struggled on a daily basis to feed and who would probably end up on the wrong side of the law. Sharon made her way from Basildon train station to the city of London, a journey that would take just over an hour and would change her life forever. She knew that her mother hadn't wanted her to leave but it wasn't out of any love for her daughter. Gladys Russell only ever thought of Gladys no matter how much

she said otherwise to friends and sometimes even to herself. Sharon had been born the year her mother turned seventeen and Gladys had immediately been given a council flat. To begin with shed been a good parent but the novelty had worn off within a year and by the time Sharon started school she was taking care of most things for herself. When Gladys was invited to the benefits office and informed that there was no reason why she couldn't seek out employment, a sibling for Sharon became a reality in her mother's gut within a matter of weeks. Gladys went on to have another child every eighteen months or so and by the time her eldest reached fifteen there were two younger brothers and two sisters to look after. This ensured her mother would never have to worry about going out to work again but she would also never climb out of the poverty trap that was now her life. Gladys spent all day lounging around the house and her eldest was expected to cook and clean, change nappies, read bedtime stories, in fact anything that constituted being a mother. It was no surprise when the girl rebelled and turned into a troublesome teenager. Sharon had been mixed up with the wrong crowd since the day she'd left school and moved to Essex but when she reached seventeen things suddenly changed. It wasn't down to having her collar felt by the Old Bill, though in all honesty that had been more down to luck than judgement. It was down to the mundane existence she was living and knowing that if she didn't do something now, then she would end up just like her mother. All of her friends were either pregnant or trying to get that way and all in the hope of obtaining a council flat. The boys that hung around the estate were all having a whale of a time and it was mostly with one of the girls that wanted a flat. Sharon Russell was adamant that she didn't want to become just another statistic, just another unmarried mother pushing a pram. Shoplifting a set of false eyelashes from Boots, she was stopped by a police officer but instead of arresting Sharon he sat her down and had a conversation. To begin with things had been difficult as she was full of attitude but something he said struck a chord and she started to listen to the man, the only man who had ever tried to help her. By the end of their little chat and when the officer had decided not to take her to the police station, Sharon had made a life changing decision. Enrolling at night school she knuckled down and studied hard. At times it was a struggle as she still had the little ones to care for but somehow she managed and the end result was four A levels. They were exactly what she needed to secure her future but she received no praise from her mother. It had taken her just two years to change her attitude, get her exams and her dream could finally become a reality. When she thought back, her bad ways now seemed like a lifetime ago and sometimes she couldn't believe how much her life had altered.

Instead of wondering what she could rob or who she could mug, Sharon was on her way to a whole new life.

There was no longer a cadet school for the police, it was all on job training but Sharon didn't care. A career was all that she was interested in and it didn't matter what it took to get that. Arriving at Whitechapel police station for her first day on the job she was full of nerves but strangely excited. As luck would have it Neville Foster was on duty and being a sergeant for over twenty years he was used to dealing with the new recruits. His warm smile instantly relaxed Sharon and when he introduced her to Mary Murphy the two had hit it off immediately. Arrangements were made for them both to stay at the same B & B on Grove Road over in Acton. It would be a bit of a trek each day to get to the station but the girls weren't in a position to complain and besides they were in agreement that a little distance from their place of work wouldn't be a bad thing.

Mary Murphy had been educated at a convent school in Dublin. She had only ever wanted to be a policewoman and everything she was experiencing felt fantastic like a dream come true in fact. Eileen Murphy, Marys mother, had been dead set against it but Mary was determined to follow her dreams. A staunch catholic, Eileen saw England as the enemy and a place where girls acted like whores and all ended up pregnant or on drugs. For a start

she couldn't understand why Mary didn't just stay in Ireland and join the Garda. After a fierce argument Eileen told her daughter that if she left then she wouldn't be welcome back into the house. The ultimatum backfired and the very same day Mary packed her bags and moved temporarily into a friend's house. There was now no choice and she knew that whatever it took she had to succeed.
The next few months passed in a blur as both Mary and Sharon worked their way through each and every department of the station. There was a small amount of rivalry between friends but it only spurred them both on to be as good as they could be. It didn't stop them seeking out fun on their days off and Mary, much to her friends amazement, had taken to Vodka like a duck to water. Finally their trial period was over and they were both invited to join the Metropolitan Police force. The girls had made such an impact on everyone they'd come into contact with and none more so than Neville Foster, that they were both offered places at the Whitechapel station and also partnered up together. Sharon and Mary couldn't have been happier; they got on really well and hadn't had a cross word since their first meeting. Renting a flat together they were hardly ever apart and before they knew it two happy years had passed and they had completed their probationary period. In the next few months things would drastically change.
Night patrol work was something that neither of the

WPCs liked but at least they were together and like all young women they would chat away about fashion and men as they walked the beat. The night that everything went wrong was a cold and frosty evening in February. Sharon and Mary had thought that they'd gotten off lightly when they were given the suburban patrol. Unlike the city centre, where they had to deal with drunks and men wanting to fight for no reason, things should have been quiet and uneventful. The streets seemed deserted as most people were tucked up in the warmth of their homes and didn't want to venture out unless it was absolutely necessary.

"So Mary, are you up for a night out or what? It's been ages since we let our hair down."

Mary Murphy laughed and thought long and hard for all of a few seconds before she answered. Her mother would go mad if she knew the kind of life her daughter had been living over the last few months. What with all the drinking and hangovers, the old woman would have had a heart attack if she'd ever found out but still Mary reasoned that it didn't really matter what her mother knew, she would never allow Mary back into the house again anyway.

"Is the pope catholic?"

Sharon burst out laughing as she patted her friend on the back.

"You crack me up Mary, honest you do."

Once again the two girls began to laugh but were

momentarily stopped when Sharon's radio suddenly began to crackle as it burst into life.
"Attention all units! Burglary in progress on Plumbers Row possibly armed. Any officers in the vicinity please advise."
Sharon couldn't wait to respond. The pair of them had long since wanted something to get their teeth into and if they were lucky, possibly receive a promotion. Smiling to her friend, Sharon pressed to respond.
"Two minutes away. Show Papa Victor 225 attending."
It was the first time that Sharon had used her unique code name for attending a serious crime and adrenalin was now pumping through her body.
"Received, backup on way."
The girls ran the whole length of the street and turned right when they reached the junction. In reality they were more than five minutes away but hadn't wanted to lose out on the call. Both were fit and they gave it their all reaching the address in record time. Sharon was on a high with the anticipation of an arrest and they only slowed down when the garden gate was within sight. As quietly as she could she lifted the steel latch but her anticipation was instantly halted. About to approach the property they were met by two men exiting. Suddenly one produced a gun and aimed it directly at Mary. She didn't scream, in fact she was surprisingly calm.

"Now come on love don't be silly. You know you'll never get away with this so why don't you hand me the gun and we can sort this mess out."
"Fuck off pig!"
Steeping forward Mary held out her hand and smiled at the man. Tommy Deacon, a small time burglar and renowned drug addict took a step back. Mary could see that he was sweating profusely and was obviously in need of a fix. The situation wasn't good but Mary knew that she had to keep trying, had to get the gun away from him at all costs.
"Look, this is all getting out of hand. I'm sure you don't want to end up doing a long stretch in prison and all because of a stupid botched up robbery. Come on now; let me have the gun before things go too far."
Her partners calmness wasn't reflected in Sharon Russell. As soon as she saw the weapon and heard her friends heroic speech Sharon turned and ran, ran as if her life depended on it and without a second thought for her partners safety. Fear wasn't an emotion shed felt before, well at least not on the force but then she'd never been faced with a live firearm being pointed directly at her, well at Mary anyway. In hindsight her running wouldn't have made a difference but on reflection Sharon Russell knew that she should have at least tried to save her friend. She had only got about fifty or so yards away when she heard the first gunshot and a single scream from her colleague. Turning she saw a

neighbour from across the road run over and then there was a second shot. The two men ran off in the opposite direction and Sharon didn't give chase. For a moment she was rooted to the spot and it seemed like forever before she found the courage to return. What greeted her was nothing short of a blood bath, the neighbour had taken a direct hit to the head and had been killed instantly but it was a slightly different matter for Mary Murphy. As she clutched her stomach her eyes pleaded with her partner and kneeling on the floor Sharon cradled her friends head in her lap as she called for help on her radio.

"Officer down! Officer down! Oh god in heaven help us pleeeeeeese!"

Tenderly she tried to whisper soothing words to her partner but as naive as she was even Sharon knew that it was far too late for her friend. Witness to Marys agony, she prayed that it would end as soon as possible. With her partners dying breath and as blood seeped from the side of Marys mouth, she stared at Sharon and said.

"Why did you leave me, why?"

Backup was on the scene in minutes but it was too late, Mary Murphy had died in Sharon Russell's arms within a couple of minutes of the gun being fired. All attention was now on Sharon, even the chief was in attendance and offering his condolences. The media became involved and television crews and reporters seemed to appear in

no time at all. As they jostled her for information all Sharon could see was a vision of her friends face and Marys parting words. The culprits were brought to justice and even though Tommy Deacon recounted everything that had happened including one of the WPCs running away, it fell upon deaf ears. After several weeks were spent on leave due to stress, Sharon finally returned to work. Her colleagues were all sympathetic but it only added to her feelings of shame and remorse. Over time, Sharon Russell with difficulty, was able to mask over what had happened but when she was awarded a medal for her courage it had made things all the more difficult to deal with. Her continued friendship with Jess had been a lifeline and she was the only person that Sharon had entrusted with the truth. Many evenings were spent with a couple of bottles of wine talking into the small hours. Sharon would be in floods of tears and Jess would always hold her until they had subsided. Suddenly Sharon was back in the present and felt a little embarrassed that she'd been ignoring her friend, after all she was here because Jess needed her and not to relive her own personal tragedies.
"Sorry about that, I was in a world of my own for a minute. Anyway Jess how are you feeling now?"
"Better for seeing you. Oh and I went round to my mum's today."
"How is your mum bless her? Is that old bastard

treating her any better?"

"Not a hope, I actually think he's getting worse. She was in tears when I got there and I could hear him shouting at her from outside on the street. I begged her to come back here but she wouldn't. I tell you Shaz I have sleepless nights about it, I really don't know how it's all going to end."

"Bless her heart, I'm sorry to hear that. Well I hate to shoot off so quickly but you know what it's like. Thanks for lunch and let's not leave it so long next time. Now you keep your chin up and if you need me then you know where I am. Jess I really want you to think about calling the police just in case things get worse."

"Oh thanks a bunch I really needed to hear that."

"Don't be daft I didn't mean they would but just to be on the safe side."

Jess said she would think about it which told her friend that she definitely wouldn't but there was really no more that Sharon Russell could do. After kissing Jess on the cheek Sharon set off for work. Marylebone Police station wasn't far away and she knew that if Jess needed her she could be back in a few minutes. Jess Metcalf spent the rest of the day alone in her flat. She didn't have a client that night and after taking a long hot bath decided to have an early night in the hope that things would seem brighter in the morning.

CHAPTER TEN

Felix Abbott had come to live in Hackney on the day of his eleventh birthday. His father had been an estate worker on a farm in Somerset and the family home came with the job. When Dick Abbott suddenly died from a heart attack Felix and his mother were treated without compassion and asked to vacate the property as soon as possible. There were no council houses in the area or family members to rely on, so Felix and Louisa Abbott boarded a train and through sheer luck, though not as far as Felix was concerned, had ended up in Hackney. His mother secured lodgings on Parkholme Road and finding herself work at the town hall, Felix knew they would now be staying in a place that he saw as nothing but the end of the earth. Back home every day had seemed like summer but here it was cold and dank and the buildings were grey and dismal and seemed to loom in on you. Being a skinny child with bucked teeth did nothing to endear him to his fellow class mates at Hackney Downs School. The old Victorian building which has since reopened as the Mossbourne Community Academy was back then, labelled the worst school in Britain. There were gangs who carried out knife attacks, bullying was accepted as the norm and the teachers did little to stop what was going on through fear for their own safety. For Felix, who had previously resided in the quiet village of Blagdon, it was a real eye opener and not one he enjoyed. He was ridiculed for his looks, his accent, in fact for anything that took the fancy of the bullies. He was not and never would be allowed to fit in by his peers. In a strange way, the day that Felix Abbott had his front teeth knocked out by Chez Maynard turned out to be a blessing in disguise. Louisa Abbott had little choice but to take her son to the dentist where front crowns were fitted along with a brace to straighten the remainder of his teeth. Chez Maynard was the hardest boy in the year and he seemed to make a beeline for Felix at every opportunity. On the last day of term before the long summer holidays it was announced that Hackney Downs would be closed for good. Most of the pupils cheered as they naively believed that it would be the end of their education. When they were all informed that places had been found at other local secondary schools the assembly room was filled with the sound of booing. As the final bell of the day rang out and everyone charged along the corridor eagerly anticipating the summer break, Chez Maynard decided to have one last pop at Felix Abbott. Sticking his foot out as the boy passed by, Chez and two of his pals laughed out loud as Felix hit the ground hard. For a moment he was stunned and just lay on the floor not attempting to get up. When a hand gently touched his arm he looked up into the most beautiful eyes he had ever seen. Jess Metcalf gave Chez a look of disgust. "You're a fucking bully Maynard. I see you've picked your mark; it would be a different story if he was as big as you wouldn't it. You're nothing but a bleeding coward."

Jess was fancied by all the lads in her year and none more so than Chez Maynard. Not wanting to argue with her he stood silently as she helped Felix Abbott to his feet. Linking her arm through his she guided him towards the main door and before exiting Jess looked over her shoulder and stuck her tongue out at Chez. Felix thought she was the bravest girl he had ever known, well for a twelve year old at least. Jess couldn't believe it when she found out her new friend lived just seven roads away from her and from then on the two became inseparable. The whole of the summer holidays were spent together and they were overjoyed when they found out that they had both been enrolled at Haggerston School on Weymouth Terrace. Jess Metcalf loved the slightly geeky boy like a brother but for Felix it was a different story. Jess was his world and he had made up his mind early on that one day he would marry her. He never told her how he felt, he was far too shy but if she ever got too friendly with any of the other boys he would go into a real strop that wouldn't end until she finished her new friendship. Felix was always a welcome visitor at the Horton Road house. Annie loved the boy dearly and could clearly see that he was besotted with her daughter.

She mentioned it a few times to Jess but was abruptly told not to be silly as they were only mates. The next four years passed quickly and with Felix's help Jess began to excel in her studies. The blackest day of Felix Abbotts life came one Friday afternoon shortly before the pair was due to leave school in search of work. Louisa Abbott had begun a friendship as she liked to call it, with Roger Fenwick who was also employed at the Town Hall. Unbeknown to Felix it was far more than a friendship and the two had secretly married a week earlier. At four in the afternoon Felix returned from school to a hallway full of suitcases, his own included and spied his mother who was dressed up to the nines, sitting on a hard chair eagerly waiting for him to come home.

"What's going on?"

"Were moving. Rogers been offered a job in France for a year."

"What's any of that got to do with me and you mum?"

"I got, I mean we got married last week so Roger is now your stepfather."

Felix was flabbergasted by what he was hearing. Oh it wasn't that he didn't like Roger, he didn't really care about the man one way or another. Roger was always polite and as long as he treated Louisa well and kept his nose out of Felix's business then they would get along fine. Starting to inch his way backwards along the hall the only thing on

Felix's mind was getting round to Jess's to talk to her about it all.

"You can go wherever you like but I aint. I'm sixteen soon and you can't make me go!"

Louisa, a normally mild unassuming woman, was up and out of her seat in seconds. Marching down the hall she grabbed hold of her sons shoulders and shook him as she spoke.

"Now you listen to me young man! You may soon be sixteen but until then you are still in my charge. Things are going good for me Felix and I don't want you to mess them up. Now you will come to France and you will put a smile on your face when Roger gets here. If you don't like it and when you reach sixteen, then if you decided to come back to this shithole that's your choice."

Less than an hour later and the new family were packed, in the car and heading for Dover. Jess Metcalf was heartbroken when she learned her friend had gone without saying goodbye. Over the next month she went from sobbing one minute to getting really angry the next and spent hours up in her room not wanting to talk to anyone. Jess couldn't believe how he could just go away without even telling her. Annie tried to console her daughter but nothing she said made any difference and it was several weeks before Jess at last came out of her shell. It took a long time but eventually she began to slowly move on and she even made other friends but she knew in her heart that she would never forget Felix Abbott.

The years passed and from time to time she would recall their friendship but it slowly faded and soon the memories weren't thought about that often. Even Annie Metcalf stopped mentioning the lad; a lad that she had been certain would one day marry her daughter. After Jess had set up her own for want of a better description, business, her old school friends had all decided to keep their distance from her. Now with more money than she knew what to do with but also a big fat zero of a social life she often got lonely. It was on one of her down days that she had opened up her laptop and set up a face book account. It didn't take her long and Jess was amazed at how easy it was to locate friends and acquaintances she hadn't seen for years. Slowly she typed in the name of Felix Abbott and although she didn't know where he now lived, decided to try London just to see if anything came up. Sure enough and within a few seconds up popped his face. He'd grown into a very handsome bloke but it was as clear as day to Jess that this was definitely her old school friend. Pressing the friends request button she sat back in her chair and was stunned when seconds later a confirm friends window came into view. It was quickly followed by a short message of Hi how are you? Not knowing what to really say she just answered with I'm fine thanks. He didn't reply immediately and when the screen remained blank she was suddenly filled with anger,

anger at how he had just disappeared all those years ago and hadn't bothered to even say goodbye. Jess began to erratically type and the message must have been one of the longest ever sent on face book. Along with a lot of other things she had issues with; she also informed him that he should be ashamed of himself and that he had caused her a lot of pain. Sitting back in her chair Jess sighed heavily as she stared at the screen. It had felt good to get it all off her chest but she now doubted very much that he would reply. She was wrong and within minutes the following message appeared.

Sorry, sorry, sorry, sorry, sorry, sorry, sorry, sorry, sorry, sorry, sorry, sorry, sorry, sorry.

The word sorry appeared so many times that in the end Jess stopped counting. It must have run into the hundreds and suddenly she began to laugh. Finally she typed in You're forgiven and placed a kiss at the end of her message. Felix asked if they could meet and within the hour Jess found herself walking into the Palm Court at the Ritz Hotel for afternoon tea. She recognised Felix straight away. Oh he was taller and had filled out but just one look at him and Jess was back in Haggerston School fourteen years ago. Out to impress, she had chosen a Stella McCartney dress and coat and her bag and shoes were Jimmy Choo. She wanted to show him just how far she had come and Jess knew that she really had achieved the look she was after. Felix's eyes never left hers for the whole time they were at

the Ritz. She thought or at least hoped that he was impressed by her dress but just as he had been all those years ago on their first meeting, Felix was mesmerised by her beauty and if Jess had chosen to wear a sack he wouldn't have noticed.
"So why didn't you tell me you were going away?"
"Please believe me, I didn't know! One minute I was coming round to see you and the next I was in a car and on my way to France. We stayed for the year and then moved back to England. Roger got a job in Middlesex and although I could have come looking for you, when it boiled down to it I didn't have the nerve. So what have you been doing with yourself girl and by the way you look good!"
Jess knew the question would arise and shed been dreading it. There was no way to sugar coat things so as always she just told him the truth.
"I'm a whore."
Felix Abbott began to choke on his tea and almost dropped the fine china cup as he did so.
"A what!"
"You heard me, a whore. I worked at Selfridges for a while and somehow just fell into it. The moneys really good and there's no strings attached. For a lot of the time I play the part of a dominatrix so I don't have sex with all of my clients. I mean you're a man of the world you must know what I'm talking about."
"Do you enjoy it?"
Felix Abbott had asked the question but looking at

her now and feeling all the old emotions begin to surface he didn't really want to hear the answer.

"Yes I do. I haven't changed Felix and if I didn't enjoy it I wouldn't do it."

For a moment Felix was stunned and his mouth hung open with shock, then he suddenly began to laugh, a real gut wrenching laugh that made the other patrons in the Palm Court turn in their seats to see what was going on.

"God I've missed you Jess! I'd forgotten how honest and brutal you can be."

"And what about you Felix, what do you do?"

"A humble carpenter by trade but I might add, a very good one."

"Well how about that! I think fate brought us back together for more than one reason."

A week later and Felix Abbott nervously pressed the intercom to Jess's flat. Over tea at the Ritz she had told him that she needed the services of a carpenter for a very special job and there was no one she would rather trust it to than him. Now downstairs and as he waited to be let in Felix could feel the onset of butterflies as they danced away in the pit of his stomach. He had gone to great lengths with his appearance and his aftershave was the best that money could buy. He was desperate for Jess to show an interest in him and as the lift moved ever closer to her home he surveyed the dozen red roses he'd bought her. When she answered the front door her face was a picture and she smiled warmly when he handed her the bouquet. After thanking him she walked through to the kitchen and laid the flowers in the sink.

"Would you like a drink of something, tea perhaps?" Felix declined; he was just too nervous and knew he was liable to spill anything she gave him to drink all down the front of his shirt.

"Right then, I might as well show you what I want." Leading him down the hall she pointed out various odd jobs that wanted doing. A few of her doors were sticking and a small piece of skirting board needed to be replaced. Felix made notes on a pad and told her that nothing would be a problem. As Jess opened the door to the dungeon she heard him gasp and the noise made her giggle as she spoke.

"What?"

"Fuck me you really did mean it."

"What that I'm a whore come dominatrix? Of course I meant it. Honestly Felix were not fourteen anymore, what did you think I was larking about or something?"

"Well yeh I suppose I did, I wasn't really sure." Gently pushing past her Felix walked into the room and making his way over to the rack picked up one of the enormous dildos.

"Fuck me!"

"I don't think you'd want me to with that!" They both began to laugh and the mood was instantly relaxed.

"So what is it you want me to do for you?"

Jess made her way into the room and pointed to the far end wall.

"Well I get most of my stuff directly from America but a seven foot cross would not only be difficult to explain to customs but also very expensive to import."

Handing Felix a brochure she pointed to the one she had set her heart on. Made from the finest oak it was highly polished and even Felix had to admit the workmanship looked second to none.

"Do you think you could make me one as nice as that?"

"Better! But it won't come cheap, I mean oak is about as expensive as you can get."

"I'm aware of that but as long as it looks like the one in the picture then I'm happy to pay. Now when can you get it finished by?"

Felix smiled, she was as impatient as ever and even after all these years she was still the same old Jess that he had loved for the whole of his life. What with his day to day work he knew it would take a couple of weeks. He would have to make it in sections and then assemble it on site, all of which Jess was happy with. Shaking hands the deal was struck and a very deep friendship from so long ago was once more rekindled. From then on Jess and Felix would spend the odd evening in each other's company but it wasn't enough as far as her friend was concerned and they would often get tetchy with each other. Jess was aware of his feeling's for her but she didn't feel the same way. Many times she had tried to broach the subject with him but he would just dismiss her words and change the topic of conversation. Finally she had given up trying and they seemed to muddle along for the next year without too much falling out. When Jess had informed Annie about her long lost friend the woman had been overjoyed. Deep down she hoped that the two would finally get it together but once again Jess had to reiterate that they were and only ever would be friends. Over recent weeks Felix seemed to be irritable and bad tempered whenever they met up. Jess could sense his unhappiness and she felt for him but just lately he was acting strange and getting more possessive than usual. Things came to a head one Saturday night when he had wanted to take her out for dinner but Jess had a client arriving at nine so she politely turned him down.

"Well that's fucking nice I must say. You'd rather spend the night with some pervert than have dinner with me!"

"Look Felix! You knew the score when we first met up again. This is my work and sometimes it has to come first. A day will come in the not too distant future, although I hope that it's not so soon, when my looks will begin to fade and I'll have to retire. Well that's unless I lower my standards and take on any weirdo that's prepared to pay me, which I'm not. I don't want that Felix, I want to get out while

I'm still young enough to have a life and to do that I need money behind me and my line of work pays extremely well."

"But you don't have to do this I can take care of you. I don't earn a bad wage and we could move away somewhere. Jess I really hate what you do, hate the thought of all those strange men laying their hands on you!"

Time was getting on and as Jess glanced at the clock, knew she would have to start getting ready soon. Still she couldn't leave things as they were and guiding her friend over to the sofa they sat down and Jess took Felix's hand in hers.

"Felix you are my best friend, you always were but you must know that is all it will ever be.
I don't want to hurt you love but you just won't leave it alone. You keep picking away at me like I'm a sore and sooner or later, just like a sore; it will spread so wide that things between us will never heal. I want you to find a woman who can love you like you deserve but I'm afraid that woman will never be me."

He didn't shout or argue; in fact Felix Abbott just stood up and walked from the flat. It was several days before Jess heard from him again but when she did it was if they had never spoken about their relationship. What Jess didn't know was that most nights he had been sleeping in his van which was parked across the road from her flat. He was constantly worried for her safety and with every client that rang her doorbell Felix Abbott became more and more angry. He just couldn't understand how she could be so intimate with complete strangers but when it came down to him she was as cold as a fish. Apart from the odd kiss Jess wouldn't allow any physical contact between them and it was driving him crazy. Six months after he began to stalk her and in effect that's exactly what he was doing, though Jess didn't know about it, his attitude towards her began to change. He still loved her, adored her in fact but now he was also angry with her. Felix saw her clients as nothing more than sad twats who needed some kind of sick kick, kicks that their wives weren't able to provide but Jess, well Jess seemed to be taunting him with it and he was starting to get pissed off. Felix would sit in the van night after night and as each client entered or exited, he found himself gripping the steering wheel so hard that his fingernails actually dug into the leather. She didn't know what she was doing to him and Felix had to make her see that she didn't need anyone but him. He couldn't eat, couldn't sleep and even though he was insane with jealousy, Felix finally realised that this couldn't go on. Jess had to be taught a lesson, taught that you couldn't mess with a person's feelings and not pay the price. He had to do something that would make her need him, really need him to such a degree that she would never want to be apart from him again.

CHAPTER ELEVEN

The following week passed without event and it was soon time to meet up with Lucy again. This time Jess was dressed in her normal designer attire and was feeling good. The women shared coffee and a light snack and for once Lucy let her new friend speak without interruption. It made a nice change and as she was so relaxed Jess just talked and talked about her life and the circumstances that surrounded her clients. When she finally finished she looked in Lucy's direction and smiled when she saw the young woman was furiously scribbling away. The table, much to the annoyance of the waitress was covered in pieces of paper and Lucy's coffee had now gone cold. Looking at her watch and seeing that it was just after two, Jess knew that she couldn't hang around for much longer. Lucy had seen Jess check the time and realised this meeting would have to come to an end soon but she was enjoying it so much that she could have stayed for hours. Sighing she placed her pen onto the table and smiled as she looked into Jess's face.
"I'm sorry I'm keeping you so long but I find your life so interesting, actually more than interesting I find it absolutely fascinating."
Jess laughed out loud, she was really starting to warm to the young girl.
"Well I suppose that's one way of putting it but I

don't think I would have chosen the word fascinating darling but then you're the writer not me."

"No, I mean you're so open and honest, it's as if nothing fazes you?"

"After ten years my lovely not much does."

"So are you still seeing your trainer client?"

Instantly the smile disappeared from Jess's face and she sighed heavily.

"To be honest Lucy I phoned him and cancelled. Suddenly he began to abuse me and it unnerved me I can tell you. I was just glad that it happened over the telephone and not face to face."

"Perhaps you need to tell me more about the man before he turns into a distant memory."

"Well after our first few meetings he started to want more and more. Sometimes I would beat him until he bled, which I wouldn't normally allow. He pleaded with me, begged in fact and then started handing me extra money far above our usual terms. Thinking about it now I can't understand why I allowed it to continue for so long. I mean I know I'm in this for the money but even I have limits and deep down I knew it was getting out of hand. Anyway, the next time I saw him he suggested trying something new, autoerotic asphyxia."

Lucy quickly picked up her pen again.

"What do you mean, go on I'm all ears."

Jess shook her head and for a moment wondered if Lucy was getting off on all the information she was providing. Having never before revealed her private life, she couldn't understand the hunger that was so apparent on the girls face. Jess studied her new found friend for a moment but finally when she decided that it wasn't anything sexual and it was purely a case of being overly enthusiastic about her work, she continued.

"He wanted to suffocate while he masturbated."

"Oh my god!"

"Don't tell me you've never heard of it? Its common practice love, especially in the world of the sadomasochist which I was quickly beginning to realise was exactly what he was all about. Anyway he wanted me to lash his arms down so that his hands were only able to touch his penis. A plastic bag was to be put over his face and I was to remove it if and when he passed out. I wouldn't do it, couldn't do it. I mean I'm used to dishing out pain but I know how far to go, this was totally different. He was a bit put out about it but cheered up when I suggested scarfing. The effect is the same but as the word suggests, a scarf is used instead of a bag and I would be more in control. I still wasn't happy about it all but he's a good payer and I didn't want to lose his business."

Lucy sat with her mouth open and the sight made Jess want to laugh.

"I told you some of my stories would make your hair curl."

"I know you did but this is just, well I don't know if

I can think of any words to describe it. I mean whatever possesses them to want to do that and what possible pleasure can they get from it?"

"A lot believe me, not that I've tried it myself. The loss of oxygen to the brain heightens the sensation when masturbating or so I've been told. Just how true it is I'm not sure but they say that the feeling is as powerful as the rush a cocaine user gets."

Jess thought for a few seconds, should she really be revealing all of this. The man was high profile and could be seen on the television most Saturday afternoons, especially if one of his horses won a race. She supposed there wasn't any such thing as client confidentiality in her game and in any case she had never mentioned his name. For some strange reason she was actually enjoying this meeting. Being able to share her life with someone had until now been impossible. It was in a strange way actually starting to feel therapeutic, so deciding that no real harm was being done she once more continued.

"On his last visit and after our session and I might add out of the blue, he began to talk about snuff movies, even reckoned he'd seen one. Now I know it's probably an urban myth and they don't exist, or so they say but he'd gone into such detail that after he left I began to worry that perhaps he wanted to make one of his own. Remember Lucy, the man is a total thrill seeker and will try anything and I mean anything in the pursuit of it. Well to tell you the truth I don't know what it is he's looking for but he certainly isn't going to find it by killing me, well at least not if I have anything to do with it."

"You don't really think he would have, do you?"

"Lucy most of the men I see, are for want of a better word, decent. Every now and again you come across a man who isn't and if your gut instinct tells you to get rid, then you get rid. The alternative doesn't bear thinking about. I can honestly say that in the whole time I've been doing this I have never felt threatened, until now that is. There was only one other occasion when I had to ask a client to leave but that wasn't through fear."

"But what if they won't go away?"

"They always go sweetheart. Remember most of them have families and high powered jobs. They would never hassle me and risk getting found out, not if they want to keep their happy little lives with their happy little families. Now I don't want to seem rude love but I really should get off now."

"Do you have a client today?"

"Yes I do, two actually. I call them the kids."

"Why?"

"Well they're two brothers and both politicians as it happens."

"So what does entertaining them entail?"

Jess knew she was now going to be held up further as she explained about the kids.

"It's the old nursery scenario. They come to me once a week and the dungeon is transformed into their

old nursery and I play the role of nanny. One of them likes to be a baby and have his nappy changed, of course I have to clean him up and apply all sorts of lotions for nappy rash etcetera."
Lucy started to giggle.
"The other brother is a naughty school boy and for him I prepare a school dinner, scold him for being a bad boy and try and teach him some manners."
"So there isn't any sex then?"
"Like I've said before Lucy, people often get the wrong idea about a dominatrix. On the other hand I often wonder what the public would think of our politicians if they knew what really went on. Anyway like I said I need to get going."
Lucy smiled as she removed her purse and pulled out two hundred and fifty pounds but immediately stopped when Jess pushed the money back in her direction.
"Do I have to say this every time we meet? You keep your cash girl or give it to charity. Sweetheart this little exercise was never about the money, maybe it's just something I needed to do and I actually think it's helping me in some kind of weird way. Now shall we say same place same time next week?"
Lucy was desperate to continue and would have been happy to meet the following day but she knew not to push things too quickly. The two women said their goodbyes and headed off in different directions. Lucy, just as she'd promised her father,

had given no indication of where she lived. Jess on the other hand had previously told the girl that her flat was in Kensington and didn't want to take the risk that she would be followed by her new admirer. Until she knew Lucy better she wouldn't be taking any chances.

Lucy opened the front door just as the hall clock was in the middle of striking four. She couldn't remember the last time she'd enjoyed herself so much and was chaffing at the bit to get started. Norma was nowhere to be seen so throwing her coat on to the hall chair Lucy ran up to her room. Now happy that she had enough research to get started she didn't want to waste a moment. Within minutes she once more descended the staircase and was now laden down with her lap top and numerous reference books. Making her way into her father's study she removed a brand new flip chart shed purchased earlier in the week but which shed hidden behind the bookcase until now. Within an hour the room was in total disarray. Her father's desk had been cleared, the laptop set up and pens and pencils now cluttered the surface. Old University books, all open on different pages, were strewn around the floor and the wastepaper basket was overflowing. Norma Sanderson had heard the girl arrive home but when Lucy hadn't ventured down into the kitchen, Norma decided to go and find out what she was up to. As she entered and saw the mess that the study was in and after she'd spent most of the morning polishing the room, she almost shouted as she spoke.

"Miss Lucy!!!!"

As usual Lucy Urquhart's hair was sticking out in all directions. Ink spots speckled her face and a leaky felt tip pen had emptied its contents on to her breast pocket. Lucy was oblivious to the fact but even if she had have noticed she wouldn't have cared less. She couldn't remember a time when she had felt more alive and eager to begin the challenge of collating all the information she had gathered and Lucy Urquhart was in no doubt that this really was going to be a challenge. Looking up from her note pad and staring doe eyed at the housekeeper got her exactly what she wanted, it always did. Norma could never stay angry at the girl for long.

"I'm sorry Norma, I know it's a mess but I really can't stop now."

"Well I don't know what Mr Urquhart will say I'm sure."

"You leave my father to me Norma, now what's for dinner I'm famished?"

Norma Sanderson shook her head but reluctantly left Lucy to her work and retreated to the kitchen to prepare the evening meal. Mr Urquhart liked to eat at seven on the dot and she was already running late. On the odd occasion when she had run over time George had never said anything but the look on his face was always indication enough that he wasn't pleased. Norma wasn't afraid of her employer, it was simply that she liked to take care of them both and pleasing him was her main priority. George Urquhart arrived home promptly at six forty five and as he made his way to the dining room he noticed a light shining from underneath the study door. When he entered he too let out a gasp.

"Lucy!!! Whatever's going on?"

"I know it's a bit of a mess but oh Daddy I've had such an amazing day and I really really need somewhere to work. Please let me use your study? I promise Ill clear away after myself."

George embraced his daughter and tenderly placed a kiss upon her cheek. He knew that it would be another of her empty promises but as long as she was happy, he couldn't deny her request. Placing his arm around her shoulder the two walked towards the door.

"Come on then, let's go and eat and you can tell me all about it."

Lucy stopped dead in her tracks and turning to look at her father her face wore a serious expression.

"Sorry Daddy but I can't do that. As much as I made a promise to you that I would keep our lives out of it and not give away any information regarding our family, I also gave a promise to the person giving me this information. You do understand don't you?"

George Urquhart again placed his arm around Lucy's shoulder and squeezed. For once she was holding up her end of the bargain and he was proud that she had respect for anyone else who was involved.

"Of course I do and I'd like to say that I'm very proud of you sweetheart."

Lucy looked up into her father's eyes and smiled. It had been years since she felt this happy.

CHAPTER TWELVE
One week later

Jess was due to meet Lucy later the next day but even now she knew she wouldn't feel like it. Falling into bed her mind whirled with thoughts of her mother and Nicky Brent and she groaned when she remembered that she also had to arrange an appointment tomorrow with a prospective new client. For a second she toyed with the idea of not bothering but the overriding factor that stopped her was that she knew the rewards would be huge. If she ever hoped to get out of this line of work and set up a new life with her mum, then she had to rake it in as much money as possible while she could. Sleep was difficult but when Jess finally managed to drift off she was jolted awake by the door bell ringing. Glancing at the bedside clock she saw that it was two am and for a moment wondered if she was dreaming. Laying her head back down, she was still staring at the ceiling a few minutes later when the bell rang again. Hauling herself from under the warmth of her duvet Jess made her way into the hall and pressed the intercom.
"Yes?"
There was no answer except for the sound of heavy breathing. Nuisance callers were not unheard of in Kensington and Jess in the past Had experienced them a few times, though none as early in the

morning as this. Irritable at having been woken she screamed into the microphone.
"Why don't you just fuck off and leave me alone you creep!"
About to return to the bedroom she was somewhat taken aback when the bell again sounded. Normally Jess would have ignored it but something made her once more press the intercom.
"What?"
The voice on the other end was muffled as if someone was trying to disguise themselves.
"I'm going to kill you bitch!"
Jess released the communication button and slumped back against the wall. She could feel her whole body tremble as she desperately tried to work out who it could be downstairs. The only thing to console her was the thought of the high tech security that the building offered. When the bell rang for a third time she could only stare at the monitor in terror. The video screen was blank but then she reasoned that whoever was trying to scare her wouldn't have shown their face. She breathed in deeply and tried to pull herself together. The bell sounded twice more but she was too scared to answer. Still in the hallway she waited for a few minutes and when nothing else happened knew that it was over. Whoever it had been couldn't get in and after double checking the lock on her front door, Jess made her way back to the bedroom but not before she'd taken a detour into the kitchen to

collect a knife. Sliding it under her pillow she once again attempted to get some sleep but for the most part it evaded her and when she did manage to nod off for a few minutes, she experienced nothing but nightmares. Jess didn't know what time she had finally drifted off but when her alarm burst into life at eight am she let out a loud sigh. It was the usual time for her to get up but Jess felt as though she had only just gone to sleep. Thinking back to last night and the bad dream shed had, Jess reached under the pillow and touched the knife shed placed there earlier. Suddenly the reality of it all struck home and she was once more scared. Now absolutely drained she wearily dragged herself out of bed and after pulling on her dressing gown went into the kitchen. Peter Lenson would be arriving at just after ten and she had to be ready. It was a fortnightly event and one Jess had never looked forward too. Out of all of her clients Peter was the one she liked the least but he was also a good payer and she wasn't about to let go of easy money just because she wasn't keen on him. He hadn't actually done anything wrong or out of the ordinary but there was just no connection and he had what Jess could only describe as a cardboard personality. Peter Lenson or whatever his real name happened to be, was a Member of Parliament or so he had told her. He wasn't repulsive to look at, was always polite and never asked for anything too kinky or overboard. So far a bit of spanking was as far as he'd asked her to go but Jess was under no illusion that it could all change in an instant as had been the case with Nicky Brent. Jess had tried over the past few months to work out what the problem was with Peter but she had never been able to come to a conclusion. Maybe it was just a mix of bad chemistry but he definitely held no attraction, unlike a lot of her clients. Still she reasoned that she didn't have to like them as it was purely business and he always paid well with a good tip on top. It wasn't her usual routine but today she showered and changed straight into her costume. Jess couldn't be bothered with the twinset and pearls shenanigans this morning and just recently she was beginning to feel like that most days. Without any doubt, that thought alone told her it was time to really start thinking seriously about getting out of this game. At ten on the dot the door bell rang out but instead of just pressing the entry button as she normally did, Jess peered into the screen. Only when she saw Peter Lenson's face did she release the lock on the street door. Standing in the hallway she checked her reflection in the mirror. After adjusting the mortarboard and straightening her gown, Jess picked up the headmasters cane from the umbrella stand. The look was topped off with a pair of clear Perspex black horn rimmed glasses that perched haughtily on the tip of her nose. As she opened up the door Peter Lenson was surprised to see that his mistress had broken their normal

routine. About to question her, he stopped when Jess whacked him on the arm with the cane.
"Go into the classroom and get changed you naughty boy!"
For whatever the reason his mistress had broken with tradition, he like it and wasn't about to complain. Peter Lenson laid his attaché case onto the console table and then scurried along the hallway in the hope of pleasing Jess. Annoyed that her table may have been scratched she picked up the case and stood it on the floor. Peter would now pay dearly for his rudeness and Jess couldn't wait to have some fun at his expense. For this morning only, the dungeon would be known as the classroom. An old fashioned school desk together with a large blackboard had been set up in the centre of the room. Jess gave the man a few minutes to change and when she entered he was wearing a school uniform complete with short trousers and a cap.
"Sit down Lenson!"
Peter did as he was told and the slightest glimmer of a smile crossed his lips when he stared up at the blackboard and saw that a large chalk penis and testicles had been drawn on it. Jess tapped the board with her cane.
"Do you find this funny Lenson?"
Peter vigorously shook his head and couldn't wait for what he knew would be coming next.
"I think you do! Further more you nasty little boy, I

know it was you who drew this disgusting image on my blackboard."

"No Mistress it wasn't me I swear!"

Jess laughed to herself, it was typical of someone in government to try and worm their way out of a situation even when it was only in role play. Her flowing black cloak was open at the front and her Basque and stockings were clearly visible. Peter stared at Jess's perfectly formed breasts as they struggled to stay in the bra and the sight caused a full scale visible erection just as shed known it would.

"Don't try to get out of it you snivelling excuse for a human being, now get up here at once!"

Peter Lenson stood up and walked over to where Jess was still pointing at the board with her cane. He knew the drill, knew what was expected of him and after hastily dropping his trousers, Peter exposed his backside to his mistress.

"Face the board and do not turn around until I tell you to. In fact, as added punishment you can clean that disgusting image off with your mouth."

Peter Lenson's tongue made contact with the board and he slowly started to lick. He knew that the dainty flicks of his tongue would annoy her and actually prayed that it would. Jess held the cane up high and bringing it down swiftly, made contact with the back of his legs. As the cane hit her clients skin he let out a loud groan and it wasn't a groan of pain. With each stroke he began to lick more

fervently with his tongue and when Jess had administered six of the best the man's legs looked as if they were on fire. Jess then placed a latex glove onto her right hand and used her left to pour a liberal amount of lubrication jelly onto her gloved fingers. Pushing the side of Peters head against the blackboard she spoke.
"Spread your legs Lenson!"
As he did what she commanded Jess cupped her hand and placed two fingers at the base of his rectum. As she slowly inserted them she could feel her clients body become tense.
"Oh oh ooooooo."
Jess started to move her fingers in and out. It was slow and gentle to begin with but she soon upped her rhythm and speed. The sight of a grown man in a school uniform with his trousers around his ankles would have been disturbing to most but for Jess Metcalf it was something she took in her stride and was all in a day's work. The pleasure for Peter Lenson was incredible and he began to masturbate.
"Stop that now Lenson, do you hear me boy?"
Peter stopped but Jess didn't and she now increased the speed. As she bent over her breasts swung freely and even with his face squashed up against the board her client could see them and his eyes were open wide with excitement. Once again he started to masturbate and this time Jess didn't say a word. She knew he wouldn't be long as sweat had begun to form on his brow. Removing her fingers

she quickly grabbed her cane and slapped it down hard onto the back of his legs again. At that precise moment Peter Lenson ejaculated all over his hand.
"Oh dear, I'm so sorry Mistress."
"You filthy little creature Lenson!"
Jess whacked him again with the cane.
"Get yourself cleaned up!"
"Yes Mistress."
Peter Lenson turned around and hung his head in shame as Jess walked from the room. When the door was closed she let out a sigh of gladness that the session was now over and the day was hers to do as she liked. Quickly changing her clothes she was standing in the hallway when Peter Lenson emerged from the dungeon dressed smartly in a three piece suit. Timidly he placed a brown envelope onto the console table before scuttling out of the flat. It was always the same scenario after one of Peters visits. He couldn't look Jess in the face and he was so full of embarrassment that he couldn't get out of the place fast enough. As the front door closed Jess picked up the envelope and checked its contents. The amount was correct and as she went to lay it on the table noticed that her client had forgotten to pick up his attaché case. If only he wasn't always in such a hurry to leave he might have remembered it. Annoyed Jess snatched it up and descended the stairs but as she went outside saw his car as it disappeared down the street. Sighing heavily she shrugged her shoulders, if it

was important he'd come back otherwise it could wait until his next visit. As Jess waited for the lift she casually opened the case and flicked through a few of the papers inside. After scanning a couple of pages and seeing some kind of logo at the top that she didn't know, she placed them back inside. Politics had never interested her and she didn't think that Peter Lenson would be dealing with anything exciting. After making herself a drink she walked into the bedroom to choose what she was going to wear for her meeting with Lucy. It again crossed her mind to cancel and just climb back into bed but that would be giving up and one thing Jess Metcalf didn't do was give up. Her need to sleep was so desperate and she reasoned that after the meeting she would be even more tired so at least sleep wouldn't evade her tonight.

On the other side of the road the man in the vacant building surveyed Peter Lenson leaving and when he saw Jess run out of the building in the hope of catching her client, he began to snap away with his camera and it was turning into a fruitful day. After the Profumo affair in the early sixties and the near collapse of the government, MI5 decided that it must never happen again. Following instructions, Silvia Gladman had put together a small group of specialised agents to follow anyone in a position of high office and who were seen to be acting strange in anyway. Peter Lenson was one of those people and over the last few weeks every visit he had made to Jess's flat had been logged. Sexual preferences were a big concern regarding security as it laid the person open to blackmail. Jess Metcalf wasn't personally deemed as a threat but her client list was so varied and because it included some unsavoury characters along with government officials, she was also being watched at all times. The man in the trilby hat now had photographs of Peter Lenson arriving at the address with the case and then leaving without it. As Peters car drove down the street he was being tailed, MI5 needed to know what was in the file and if it posed a threat to national security.

Back inside the flat, Jess pulled on her coat and set off for her meeting with Lucy. As she walked along she thought long and hard about all that had happened. A couple of weeks ago and her life had seemed almost perfect, well as perfect as it could be considering what she did for a living. Everything now felt as if it was falling apart and she didn't know what to do about it. Jess knew there was no connection and it was all just coincidence but it seemed that ever since shed been involved with Lucy Urquhart things had started to go wrong. The only problem was she liked Lucy and it wasn't as if things would miraculously be back to normal if she severed all ties with the girl. The walk seemed to take far longer than usual but Jess put that down to being so tired. She had a few sleeping tablets at the back of the medicine cabinet and knew that she

would definitely be taking a couple later. She couldn't risk not sleeping again as she had her new client to interview the next day and dark circles under her eyes would only turn the man off. At last the Patisserie Valerie came into sight but Jess could only sigh at the thought of the barrage of questions that would soon follow. After just three meetings between the two women things seemed to have fallen into a comfortable little routine, Lucy was already seated and had ordered the coffees. Looking into Jess's face she could instantly tell that something was wrong but was worried that if she asked it would seem like she was prying. Never one to hold back, she asked anyway.
"Are you alright Jess?"
"No not really but it isn't anything you can help with. Thanks for asking all the same. So where would you like to start today?"
"Any news on the trainer?"
"Why did you bring him up again? I told you that I've already finished with him."
"It's just that you said he called you all sorts of names and threatened you and well, I could see that you were really bothered and I just wondered if you'd heard anymore from him that's all."
"Thank you for your concern Lucy and as I said before he really didn't take it very well and yes he did threatened me. To be honest he was very angry and for the first time in a long time, I have to admit that I was frightened."

"I know it's no very pleasant but can we just go over what he said again?"

"Well he said he'd make me pay but it wasn't so much about his choice of words, it was more about his tone. It sounded so violent if that's possible and he scared me. That man seems to be able to switch in a second from being the kindest most gentle person into a, well to be honest I don't know what but I sure as hell wasn't about to find out."

"You remember when you told me that you weren't scared about them coming after you or causing trouble as they had families and reputations to think of?"

"Yeh."

"Well if this man is some kind of psycho, surely this time your reasoning wouldn't apply?"

Just as Norma had said, Lucy was once again putting her foot in things and what she said made Jess feel uncomfortable. A headache was slowly starting to surface and she now wished that she had just cancelled the meeting for today. Swallowing the last of her coffee she waved to the waitress who sauntered over with a refill.

"Well I don't know about that but anyway it's over and done with now so best not to dwell on things. What else would you like to know?"

"Well I was giving it some thought and I know you said our personal details should be kept private but I would really like to see your dungeon. I don't want to know anything about you or your family,

it's just that if I could see it I could get a real feel for what I'm writing about. Does that make any sense?" For a moment Jess mulled over in her mind what Lucy was asking. She wanted to weigh up the pros and cons but today her head was filled with nothing but mush and she was having difficulty in concentrating. For once Jess broke her own rules and regretted the words as soon as they'd left her mouth.
"Well to be honest I'm not really up for talking today so I suppose if you walked back with me we could kill two birds with one stone so to speak." Lucy Urquhart had never in a million years thought that Jess would agree to her request and not waiting for her to change her mind downed her cappuccino in one. Jess took a sip of her own coffee and could only smile and shake her head at the young woman's eagerness. Two minutes later Jess stood up, pulled on her coat and left the cafe with Lucy following in hot pursuit. When they reached Phillimore Place and after Jess had opened up the front door, she had expected Lucy to be impressed with her flat but the young woman made no comment. Jess Metcalf was proud of all she had achieved and the lack of a response disappointed her. She didn't have a clue about the girls own background but if she had then she would have understood that Lucy's life was lived in far superior splendour than her own. The two women walked along the hall and when Jess opened up the door

to the dungeon she heard Lucy gasp.
"Well this is it sweetheart! Help yourself while I make us both a coffee."
Lucy slowly walked around each wall of the room. She couldn't resist running her hand over the whips and canes but drew a line when it came to touching the dildos when she thought of where they might have been. When she reached the cross at the far end she took a moment to study its beauty. Used as a machine of, well torture was the only word she could think of, it was still so beautiful. Lucy was still staring up at it when Jess returned with two mugs of coffee.
"Here you are darling. Ah, like the look of that do you? Would you like to have a go on it?"
"What do you mean?"
"I'll suspend you so you know what it feels like."
Lucy thought for a moment, it wasn't that she was scared but she just hadn't expected this. Smiling she turned to Jess.
"Ok then, will it hurt?"
"Don't be so daft of course it won't. You can strip if you want too, just so that you know what it's really like."
Lucy was taking her clothes off in a second but stopped when she got down to her underwear. Jess could sense that it was as far as she was prepared to go and turning her round so that their faces almost met she gently pushed Lucy backwards. Lifting up her arms she shackled each one and then did the

same to her ankles. After asking if Lucy was comfortable she pulled on a lever and the mechanical structure slowly turned. Jess then pulled on a second lever and the bottom section of the cross split in two and separated Lucy's legs. Although Lucy Urquhart was left feeling exposed and vulnerable she was also experiencing a great deal of excitement and she sighed with anticipation. Jess rotated the cross until Lucy Urquhart was hanging upside-down. A few seconds later and Jess again pulled a lever and the girl was once again vertical. Jess picked up a riding crop and slowly she caressed it over Lucy's shoulder and then drew it slowly down between the girls breasts and across each cup of her bra. She continued down over her bare skin and stopping at Lucy's knickers Jess lingered for a second and lent in close to Lucy's face so that their lips were almost touching. Jess then smiled and as she turned and took a few steps away she winked at the girl. There was nothing sexual in it for Jess but she wanted Lucy to get the sensation and feel of what it was like. After giving Lucy a playful tap on the thigh Jess replaced the crop and turned to her new friend.
"So, how do you feel?"
"Vulnerable but it was also strangely exhilarating in a weird kind of way."
"Did it turn you on?"
Due to embarrassment, Lucy Urquhart's face was now scarlet.

"Well as much as I don't like to admit it, actually it did."
"Have you seen enough?"
Lucy nodded and within seconds she was released from the contraption. Leaving the girl to get dressed Jess walked into the kitchen where she waited for Lucy to join her. For Lucy Urquhart it had been a very worthwhile day but she still felt that there was something not quite right with Jess and the nosy side of her would really like to know what it was. Taking a seat at the table she sipped at her coffee while she thought of how to broach the subject. When nothing came to mind she just blurted it out as
she usually did.
"Are you sure you don't want to tell me what's bothering you?"
Jess placed her mug into the sink and wearing the warmest smile she could muster, turned to face the girl.
"I'm just tired darling so if you wouldn't mind, can we call it a day?"
"Of course we can and I'm sorry if I've been selfish. I could see that you weren't up to this and I still forced my will onto you."
"Babe no one ever forces their will onto me."
"Well I feel as if I did?"
"That's ok honey; after all it makes a change for someone to do it to me instead of the other way round."

The women laughed and a few moments later after arranging to meet the next day due to the shortness of this meeting Lucy Urquhart left the Phillimore place address. The man in the building opposite continued to snap away though he had no idea who the young woman was. It would take a bit of further investigating before he realised that a whole can of worms was about to be opened up.

CHAPTER THIRTEEN

The man in the trilby hat used the pedestrian walkway as he made his way across Lambeth Bridge. As much as possible he preferred to be on foot which was unusual for an investigative agent. As he turned right onto Millbank, Thames House was soon within his sights. Looking up at the massive stone building which housed the headquarters of MI5, it seemed to loom down on him and every time Harry came here he thought how grey and cold the building felt. Built by Frank Baines in nineteen twenty nine it was now grade two listed and no one could argue that it wasn't magnificent on the outside but once you entered it was boring and bland as if all the effort had been put into the exterior and by the time it came to the interior the architect had run out of steam. The whole place smelled musty, the kind of smell that a person experienced at the library and Harry Fuller found it offensive to his nostrils. He had been here more times than he cared to recall and today shouldn't have felt any different but for some reason and he didn't know what that was he wasn't comfortable. Maybe it was because he was seeing one of the top brasses; normally his only dealing with the organisation was carried out over the telephone and his orders given by some invisible face. The woman he was meeting today, even though Harry had only had a few dealings with her, was a force to be reckoned with and putting everything else aside, he didn't like taking orders from a woman. Entering through the first of three sets of double doors he stopped at the security desk. The guards who protected Thames House were all ex military and highly trained regarding terrorism threats. Most of them knew Harry Fuller on first name terms but it wouldn't be apparent to a stranger as no words of acknowledgment ever passed between the men. After informing the guard of his name and that he wished to go up to G branch on the tenth floor, Harry was politely asked to empty out the contents of his pockets before stepping through the scanner. It resembled any that could be found at airports around the world and when no alarms went off the guard proceeded to scan his body with two electronic paddles. While this was happening a second guard was inspecting Harry's possessions. A wallet, keys, phone, memory card and a camera were all being placed through a scanning machine but not just for any dangerous substances, they were also being swept for bugs and would be bagged and returned to him on leaving. He argued that he needed to take the memory card to his meeting and after the guards had thoroughly inspected it, the chip was once more in his possession. Five minutes later and when all the security had been carried out and the guards were happy that Harry Fuller wasn't a threat in any way; he was at last allowed to pass through a second set of doors. More security guards were milling about in the foyer and when Harry again stated that he would like to go to G branch on the tenth floor he was personally escorted all the way. It wasn't that he was special but just that it was normal practice for anyone who didn't work at Thames House or didn't have security clearance. Those who worked in G branch were in charge of the coordination of threat assessments and Harry's instructions had come from close to the top. Silvia Gladman was second in command to MI5s director general Sir Jonathan Evans. Silvia was a stern faced woman and a hard task mistress, she was married to her job and as far as she was concerned there wasn't any such thing as underhand tactics, not when it came down to national security. The guard knocked on the heavy oak door and when the word enter was heard he motioned for Harry to go inside. The office was large by any standards and to say it was smartly decorated was an understatement. Silvia Gladman loved her work space more than her own home and the decor reflected that.

"Ah Mr Fuller, nice to see you again. Please take a seat."

Harry Fuller was forty five years of age and for the past four years had worked for the department. Having joined the royal marines at the tender age of eighteen his abilities began to shine through and he swiftly rose through the ranks. When he reached thirty he was invited to join the elite force of the SAS where he served his Queen and country for a further ten years before retiring. Harry had been looking forward to taking things easy but within a month of leaving his unit he was head hunted by MI5. Reluctant at first, Harry had soon taken up the post when he saw the pay deal that was on offer. With all his skills it hadn't taken long before he was made the lead man in a select team of operatives. The team carried out specialised surveillance work and always except for Harry, worked in pairs. Harry Fuller was a loner and preferred solitude and he was so good at his job that no one ever argued the point. Recently he'd begun to feel unwell and for the past few weeks had been giving serious thought to calling it a day, work wise at least. Harry hated sickness and the possibility that his own illness could be serious was weighing heavily on his mind. It was probably the reason that Jess had caught a glimpse of him watching her. Always known as the invisible man to work colleagues, he was angry with himself when he realised that he'd been spotted. Harry had always told himself that if the day ever came when he got sloppy then he would hang up his hat and after this job he intended to do just that.

"So what do you have for me?"

Harry removed the small memory card from his breast pocket and inserted it into the side of Silvia's laptop. Instantly a photograph appeared and as

Harry pressed return again and again, more photographs of anyone who had visited Jess's flat in the last fifteen days filled the screen. Silvia Gladwin already knew about the so called government official who was referred to in the documents as man A and who was their primary concern but she was also interested to find out who the others were. In agitation, Silvia tapped the screen with her finger.

"Now tell me about these people."

Harry again hit the return button and as each face reappeared he began to talk.

"These are the ones I've logged coming and going to the flat and they're a mixed and varied bunch but I don't think they are a threat."

"I'll be the judge of that Harry."

"Yes Chief. Now our assignment has only visited the flat twice in that time and has no visible links to anyone except this one."

"That's interesting."

Silvia's initial brief was to find the security leak but she also knew that there could be a chance of further government embarrassment if another sex scandal should arise. Recalling her instructions from the Director General, she realised that the governments problems could be far greater than they had first thought.

"I want you to have a second Harry, just to help you out. I need someone to cover all time periods and with the best will in the world even you couldn't stay awake twenty four seven."

Harry Fuller wasn't stupid and he could read the woman's mind in an instant. He felt that Silvia didn't trust him, well not when it came down to anything of importance. Harry didn't need a second to help him he'd always worked on his own without any problems. Knowing better than to object, he simply nodded his head. Continuing to debrief Silvia, Harry watched for any change in her expression as he spoke.

"Now let me tell you a little more about this one as he could be trouble. His name is Liam Flanagan and he came over here from Northern Ireland in sixty six though you'd never know it if you heard him as he talks with a strong cockney accent. Anyway there's no direct proof that he's ever been involved with the troubles in his home land but he's been friends with a certain Pat Doherty for years. Now Doherty is a staunch nationalist and was a lifelong supporter of Bobby Sands."

"So have you seen any contact between Flanagan and man A?"

"Nothing concrete but they regularly both come and go to the girls flat. There is one other thing though."

"What's that?"

"Yesterday I saw our target enter the address with a case and when he left he was empty handed. I had him tailed and he went straight to his office. He must have realised at some point that his case was missing, unless it was done deliberately."

"Right, I will need to do some digging of my own Harry. I need to find out what was in that case, if anything. This Liam Flanagan sounds as if he could cause us some problems. I don't know why government officials have to be such kinky bastards. It would save us a lot of trouble if they were all castrated and then they could just do what they're paid to do."

Harry Fuller wasn't shocked by her remarks, he'd heard much worse and in all honesty he actually agreed with her to a point. Silvia Gladwin was silent for a moment as she thought about what action to take. If she followed protocol to get the flat bugged it would mean having to go cap in hand to the Home Secretary and it was well known within the department that Silvia hated Theresa May with a vengeance. Knowing that she could rely on the man sitting in front of her and also knowing exactly what his answer would be to the question she was about to ask, Silvia didn't have to beat about the bush.

"Obviously you are aware that our target is one of the most influential people behind the scenes in government today and any accusation, even in the slightest way would cause many people immense embarrassment. It really doesn't bear thinking about and this department will do anything to stop that happening. Harry I would like you to do me a favour. We need to be sure there are no security leaks and that the woman isn't stashing away any

evidence or important papers. I want to know exactly what's going on inside that flat."
"Ok."
"Well it isn't strictly going by the book but if we wait for clearance then it may be too late."
Harry Fuller laughed.
"I can't remember a time when you asked me to do anything that was by the book. Now what is it that you want me to do?"
"Bug the flat as soon as possible but that's strictly unofficial. If this ever gets out, then my head will well and truly be on the block."
"Leave it with me Chief and as soon as I have any news I'll get back to you and about this help you want me to have?"
"Already sorted, he's waiting for you at the front of the building and his names Josh by the way."
He knew it was futile to argue so nodding his head Harry made his way to the door but was stopped when Silvia spoke again.
"Make sure it is only me that you report back to Harry, speak to no one else. Do I make myself clear?"
Nodding his head Harry Fuller left the office and went in search of the equipment he required. Normally it would have been a case of everything being supplied from in house but that was only if a job was sanctioned. This little operation was a different kettle of fish altogether and he was out on a limb. Exiting the building Harry looked in both

directions for any sign of his new partner. The only person in the vicinity was a young man who couldn't have been more than twenty years old. Greasy hair, thick spectacles and carrying a shoulder back like students use gave the man a studious look but definitely not the look of someone who worked for MI5. Josh Hartnet had only been with the department for six months but in that time he had proved himself to such a degree that he was being earmarked for a position as a top operative. His knowledge of computers and bugging equipment was second to none and walking up to Harry Fuller he held out his hand. Harry wanted to laugh but didn't as he knew it would be embarrassing for the man.
"Pleased to meet you Josh, now we need to get a move on as time is of the essence."
Josh Hartnet didn't say a word and together the men set off on foot to a destination only Harry was privy to. A short tube journey saw the men emerge from Hammersmith station and they walked along in silence. At his home Harry had several high spec items but the rest would have to be sourced from Ray Yentob. Ray had been born in this country to Iraqi parents and was the one person that Harry and his colleagues trusted for this kind of operation. Ray lived within the Iraqi community in Hammersmith and for all intent and purpose he earned his living as a television repairman. He didn't turn away customers but he didn't encourage

them either. Working out of a small shop on Coulter Road, Ray was open for business anytime of the day or night. The shop was tucked away and its facade did little to entice anyone into the premises, which was exactly what he wanted. Harry pushed on the stiff metal door and a bell instantly rang out. Old television sets were seated on racking that covered the walls and two or three stood on the floor waiting to be collected. Large sticky labels were plastered across each of the screens with the surname of the owner written in big bold letters. Ray hated televisions almost as much as he hated the general public but he had to appear legitimate and besides the added income was always welcome as he never knew when his services would be required again by the firm as he liked to refer to MI5. As usual Ray was working in the back room but came through as soon as he heard the bell. He eyed Josh with suspicion but out of courtesy nodded in the direction of the young man. With his old acquaintance it was a different scenario.
"Hello Harry my friend, how you doing?"
Harry Fuller was a secretive man and didn't like anyone knowing who he was or where he was from but over the years he had come to trust Ray Yentob to such a degree that he had allowed the man to be on first name terms.
"Fine thanks Ray, family well?"
"Yeh fine. The old woman's still a nag, so no change there."

As Ray spoke he locked the front door and made his way into the back room. No further words passed between the men but it was an unspoken invitation for Harry to follow. The shop was swept for bugs on a daily basis so Harry knew he was free to talk without the fear of being overheard.
"So how can I help you?"
"I need a couple of pieces of bugging equipment."
"Audio, visual or both?"
"Both."
The word had been spoken by Josh Hartnet and both Harry and Ray instantly looked in the young man's direction. Harry Fuller didn't normally show any expression but today, possibly due to the fact that he wasn't feeling well, his tone spoke volumes.
"Just audio! A basic phone cable and a listen through walls device if you've got one?"
"Sure and I might just have something else you'll be interested in. Its new to the market."
Ray placed a tiny microchip into the palm of Harry's hand and at the same time Josh stepped forward to take a closer look.
"If you can gain access to a person's mobile phone, then this is a fantastic little piece of kit. Once concealed in the battery compartment it will not only transmit and record all calls but can also be switched on remotely to hear any conversations within the vicinity of the phone. Absolutely brilliant. I tell you Harry, I've been in this game for thirty years and I'm still amazed when they come

up with something new."
"It's been available for a while and has already been upgraded."
Again the two older men looked at Josh. He had a habit of butting in and saying the wrong thing and he was quickly starting to get on Harry's nerves.
"I'll take it."
A few minutes later and Harry Fuller had all that he needed. Thanking Ray he handed him a small manila envelope containing his payment. Harry had intended to go home and collect some other items but with the new piece of kit he realised that it would cover all of his needs. It was now early evening and Harry decided to take a chance and see if Jess was out.
"Where to now?"
Just the young man being here, let alone him speaking was starting to annoy Harry Fuller.
"If you want to get off that's fine by me son?"
Josh had already weighed the man up and knew that Harry liked to work alone. He wasn't that pleased to be on the operation either as he really preferred to be office based with his head glued to a computer monitor. Josh Hartnet was also astute enough to know that if he called it a day and went home, his career would be over if Silvia Gladman ever found out. Ignoring the invitation he didn't reply and continued to follow Harry into the nearest tube station. Luck was on Harry's side and as the men approached the Phillimore Place address they

saw Jess get into a taxi. It was an indication that she would probably be out for a while as she usually walked if it was only a short distance. Hopefully it would give Harry and his new partner enough time to do what they needed and after waiting a few minutes to see if she returned, Harry removed a small pouch from his jacket which held all the tools he would need to gain entry to the building. Just along from Jess's front door was the caretakers cupboard and it would be a perfect location to place the through the wall listening device. Harry had used this particular piece of equipment on several occasions and it had always been with great success. The small black box, though no bigger than the palm of your hand, was able to record conversations and any other noises through a wall of up to twelve inches thick.

"Do you know how to install one of these?" Ignoring the man, Josh treated the question with the contempt it deserved and took the device out of Harry's hand. When both men were happy with the installation Josh relocked the cupboard door. After checking that the hallway was empty Harry manipulated the lock to Jess's flat and they were inside within a few seconds. He quickly located the BT telephone cable and replaced it with the one supplied by Ray. Now with only one bugging device left to install he realised that naturally Jess would have taken her mobile phone out with her. Harry didn't know whether to forget about it and rely on what he'd already put in place or come back another time. The only problem was that he wouldn't be able to hear anything that was said outside of the flat and it could cost the department dearly if she spoke to either man A or the Irishman while she was out. Looking round Harry hoped that there would be somewhere to hide but there wasn't. Sighing heavily he then decided to wait in the building opposite and let himself back into the flat later that night. Entering the room that was to be their home for the foreseeable future, Josh surveyed the surroundings. A makeshift camp bed was situated in one corner and a tripod and camera stood at the window. Glancing round Josh spied a couple of old milk crates and placing one on top of the other he proceeded to set up his state of the art laptop.

"I will need a power source as my battery won't last indefinitely."

Harry pointed to a socket on the wall.

"The juice in this place is still on."

It turned out to be a long night as Jess had gone out to dinner with Sharon Russell and didn't return until late. Josh had fallen asleep but Harry was as vigilant as ever and remained seated at the window. At eleven fifteen the hum of the taxis diesel engine signalled that it would soon be all systems go and Harry was on his feet in seconds. As he stood up a searing pain shot through him, his legs had gone dead and he now had to vigorously rub at them to get his circulation flowing again. For a second he contemplated waking Josh but then thought better of it, the boy would be more of a hindrance than a help. Quietly Harry slipped from the building and entered the flats opposite through the street door. The corridor was empty and after getting into the cupboard he plugged a small set of headphones into the wall listening devise. Harry heard Jess go into the kitchen and put the kettle on and when he could clearly hear her start to sing, he was happy that the device was working correctly. Ten minutes later he heard Jess brushing her teeth and knew he wouldn't have to wait much longer. He allowed enough time to pass so that she would hopefully now be in a sound sleep. Once again he entered the flat but this time he had to rely on a small pair of night vision glasses that he strapped to his head and which enabled him to find his way about. Careful not to make a sound Harry scanned the front room but there was nothing. Moving into the kitchen he was relieved when he saw that she had left her phone on the counter top. As good as he was and there was no mistaking that fact, even he knew that going into Jess's bedroom without waking her would be a tall order. Within a couple of minutes the chip had been placed inside the mobiles battery compartment and Harry Fuller was once again exiting the building. Jess was woken by the sound of the front door clicking shut and now wide awake listened intently for any sounds. When none were

forthcoming she hauled herself out of bed and padded through to the hall. The door was closed, everywhere was quiet and as it should be and she laughed to herself at how paranoid she was becoming. A dream was all it was or so she told herself but still sleep was hard to accomplish for the rest of the night. Harry Fuller intended to turn in and get a few hours sleep himself but someone had to keep an eye out at all times so he woke the boy with a vigorous shake. Josh Hartnet was disorientated to begin with, not to mention the fact that he was also angry with himself when Harry explained that he had been back to the targets address and carried out the bugging as planned. "Now that you've got your beauty sleep you can do the early hours shift while I get some kip."
Josh didn't dare argue and prayed that his new partner had some humanity and wouldn't relay the fact that he'd fallen asleep to Silvia Gladman.

CHAPTER FOURTEEN

Liam Flanagan had experienced a better week profit wise than he had in months and after calling to collect a debt in Hatton Garden, he walked passed a shop and out of the corner of his eye spied a beautiful diamond pendant. It didn't take much thought before he'd gone inside and bought it as he knew that Jess, his Jess, would love it. It wasn't uncommon for him to buy her gifts though she always begged him not to. As Liam entered the jewellers he swaggered up to the counter and asked to inspect the gem. All of the Jewish owners knew who he was as most of them had borrowed money from him at one time or another. The deal was done after a certain amount of; well you couldn't call it haggling as in reality Liam already knew exactly what he would be paying. The charade was played out purely to allow the jeweller to keep face but deep down they both knew the score. With his purchase now tucked safely away in his pocket Liam set off in the direction of Kensington. His anticipation was high as he imagined her taking him in her arms and declaring her undying love. In reality he knew it wasn't going to happen in a million years but if only for a while it was nice to dream. Liam adored the ground she walked on, would have married her in a heartbeat and treated her like a princess but although Jess liked and

respected Liam, she had no deep rooted feelings for the man. At around eleven am his car pulled up outside the Phillimore Place address and Harry Fuller, who was already in situ, began to snap away with his camera. Straightening his tie and wiping a finger over his eyebrows, Liam pressed the bell.
Jess wasn't expecting any visitors and had arranged to meet Lucy at two, so when the intercom rang she was a little surprised. Looking into the monitor to see who was calling, she smiled when she saw the huge frame of a man. Pressing the entry button she put the door on the latch and went to make him a cup of tea. Cup was a bit of an understatement as Liam liked what he called a navvy mug and Jess kept one in the cupboard especially for him. Liam let himself in and walking into the kitchen planted a kiss on Jess's cheek.
"And to what do I owe this unexpected visit?"
"Do I need a reason?"
"Well I could have been entertaining a client."
Liam frowned at her words and he couldn't help but comment on what she had just said.
"Don't say that, I fucking hate it when you remind me of all the others."
Jess tenderly touched the side of his face and smiled. For all his faults and there were many, to her at least he really was a lovely man. Jess wasn't naive but she also never pried too much regarding his work. She was aware of some of what he did but in all honesty she would rather not know as

what she didn't know couldn't hurt her and there was a lot she didn't know about Liam Flanagan.
"You know the score Liam, you did when we first met and I've never tried to hide it from you."
"I know you haven't but you know how I feel about you babe, couldn't we just pretend for a bit?"
For a moment they both thought back to the beginning of their relationship. For Jess it was business pure and simple and to start with it had been just sexual gratification for Liam Flanagan. On his part at least, things had changed after their second session when he realised that he was falling for Jess big time. An hour session was soon changed for the whole of the evening and it would begin with dinner at one of her favourite restaurants. They soon became well known at Le Gavroche where a meal for two could easily run into hundreds of pounds. Liam didn't care in the least and when they returned to her flat, gone was the sordid sex of before and he now made tender love to Jess. All in all his weekly visit would set him back almost three thousand but for a few hours at least, he could pretend that she was his and that Jess loved him like he loved her. Jess sat down at the table and laughed at the same time.
"So what brings you round at this time of the day?"
Liam now took a seat opposite her and placing the small box down pushed it over in her direction. Jess knew what was coming and shook her head.
"Oh I wish you wouldn't Liam it's not fair. You pay

me for my services and that should be enough."
It was visible on his face that her words had hurt him and she wanted to apologise and take them back but that would only complicate matters and give him false hope. Slowly opening up the box Jess gasped when she saw the necklace inside.
"Oh my god Liam! It's so beautiful."
"Well what are you waiting for? Go and try it on."
Jess was on her feet in seconds and heading in the direction of the bathroom. As Liam Flanagan waited for her to return his eyes scanned the kitchen units and he soon spotted the case sitting on the counter top. Obsessed with the woman and wracked with jealousy, he wanted to know everything that was going on in her life. Finally curiosity got the better of him and walking over to the unit he flicked open the clasp and placed his hand inside. Removing the folder he began to read and by the time Jess came back he was already halfway through. She couldn't believe what she was seeing, couldn't believe his cheek. Necklace or not, he had no right to pry into her personal belongings or in this instant something belonging to of one of her clients. Storming towards him she grabbed the folder, placed it back inside the case and slammed it shut.
"What the hell do you think you're doing? That is private Liam and for starters it doesn't even belong to me."
"Sorry babe I was just being nosy that's all. I tell

you what though, I wouldn't mind meeting the person it does belong to."

"Well you can't! Liam I really can't believe you just did that? Now if you wouldn't mind leaving I have an appointment soon and I have to get ready."

"With a client?"

"No but what business it is of yours I don't know. Now I'm grateful for the gift but please don't ask me questions, we both know you're not going to like the answers."

As he made his way to the door Jess could see that he was deflated and it hurt her when she thought about all the money he must have just spent on the necklace. His smile soon reappeared when she tenderly kissed him goodbye. Staying in the hallway until the lift doors closed and he had disappeared from sight, she turned and went back inside. The man was incorrigible but she couldn't help but like him. Her mother would have called him a rough diamond but Jess knew he was a lot worse than that. Annie would have also told her daughter to hang onto him but then Annie Metcalf wasn't privy to Liam Flanagan's history, if she had have been then she would have told her girl to run a mile. Only once did Liam attempt to discuss his life with Jess and he had openly told her that violence was part and parcel of the business he was in. He also said he had a cruel streak within him that could surface at a moment's notice if violence was the only solution but Jess had silenced him by placing her finger to his lips. A clients private life was their own and she didn't want to know any details. As Liam exited the building Harry Fuller again started to snap away but thankfully for him, Liam couldn't see the man sitting behind the window blind in the building opposite. SAS or not, Liam Flanagan was a force to be reckoned with and one Harry wouldn't want to take on willingly.

At one thirty Jess was about to leave the flat when the door bell rang again. It didn't just ring whoever it was downstairs held onto the button so that it was continuous. Still cautious after the frightening episode of the other night, she once more peered into the monitor and was relieved when for the second time that day she saw a face staring back at her that she knew. Allowing him entry she was shocked when he knocked at the door in what seemed like only seconds. As Jess opened up he was leaning against the frame puffing and panting and she realised that he must have ran up the stairs. Jess walked into the kitchen and he followed her in hot pursuit but didn't give her chance to speak. As she went to hand him the attaché case he roughly grabbed her wrist.

"Did you look inside; did you read any of it?"

For a second she was taken aback and her face now wore a frown.

"I beg your pardon?"

His grip on her was beginning to hurt but as she tried to shake him off he only held on tighter. Now

as he spoke his words came out in an almost hiss and she was beginning to get a little scared.
"I said! Did you read it?"
Feeling as if once again a man was trying to take control, Jess gathered up an inner strength and shouted as she spoke.
"Nooooo I didn't now will you fucking let go of me."
Peter Lenson slowly shook his head and his eyes were wide and fierce looking. Suddenly her emotions overcame her and Jess was confused. The feeling that she had been followed, the weird call on the intercom in the middle of the night, in fact every strange thing that had happened in the last few days suddenly surfaced and the man, who only a few days ago she would have laughed off as any kind of threat, now frightened her more than she thought possible.
"You are a silly silly girl. If anyone ever found out that I left it here, well...."
"Well what?"
Peter Lenson snatched up the case and marched out of the flat. As he neared the lift Jess could be heard shouting from inside her flat.
"And don't fucking bother coming back here again. Do you hear me you creepy cunt!"
As the flat door slammed shut, Peter Lenson sighed heavily. He would undoubtedly miss his time with his mistress but retrieving the case had been far more important than losing his sex sessions. It had actually been a matter of life and death but luckily

as far as he knew, no one was privy to that fact. He had just a short time to get back to his office and replace the file before it was missed.

Jess stood in her hallway and could feel her whole body begin to tremble. God she wished shed been nicer to Liam and that he was still here. None of this would ever have happened if her dear sweet, she instantly corrected herself, Liam was a lot of things but sweet wasn't one of them. Was she becoming paranoid, for a moment Jess felt as if she was starting to lose her mind and it bothered her. Ever since she had ended it with Nicky Brent she had felt scared. Whatever was going on in her life had to stop and there was only one person who could help her. If she went down that route then there was no telling what would happen. Suddenly Jess took in a deep lungful of air; she had to get her mind right before events spiralled out of control. She decided to give it twenty four hours before she took it any further and desperately hoped that within that time things would become clearer. Pulling on her coat she left the flat and set out for her meeting with Lucy Urquhart. As Jess stepped from the building she peered in all directions making sure that Peter Lenson had gone. She was engrossed with the task and oblivious to the fact that Harry Fuller was taking picture after picture of her.

Lucy arrived at the cafe a good twenty minutes before the scheduled meeting and had already

consumed two cups of coffee when Jess entered. Instantly she could tell that the woman seemed agitated and the scenario had now happened twice in a row. Her need to ask questions was bubbling to the surface but for once Lucy didn't act on them. Giving Jess time to take a seat and compose herself, she smiled and nodded in the direction of the waitress. Jess was the first to speak and Lucy studied her face as she did so. Bare of any makeup Jess looked pale and there was just the hint of dark circles under her eyes, which Lucy took as a definite sign that Jess wasn't sleeping well. Whatever was going on must be serious and for a moment she wondered if she really wanted to get involved. Always in support of the underdog she decided that she did, so taking the bull buy the horns in a way that only Lucy Urquhart could do, she spoke.
"Are you alright Jess, only I must say you don't look it."
For a moment Jess was shocked at the girls bluntness but then replied in a joking way.
"Well thanks a bunch! I'd hate to hear you analyse me when I'm having a really bad day!"
Suddenly they both began to laugh and the mood was lightened, though Lucy knew there was a lot that the woman wasn't revealing.
"Laughter aside, are you sure you're alright?"
"No not really but it's nothing you should worry yourself about."
Lucy Urquhart suddenly grabbed Jess's hand and

looked deep into her eyes as she did so.
"Why not? If I can help you in any way then I would be glad to do it. Now please tell me what's bothering you?"
Suddenly it all came tumbling out and once she'd started Jess couldn't stop herself. She told Lucy all about Peter Lenson, Liam Flanagan, about the bell ringing in the middle of the night and well just the fact that she genuinely felt scared for the first time in her life. When she had at last finished talking she turned to Lucy who just sat staring with her mouth wide open.
"You'll catch a fly in a minute."
"Pardon?"
"Oh nothing, it's just something my old mum used to say to me when I was small. Anyway enough about my problems, what do you want to discuss today?"
"Jess you can't just dismiss this as easy as that! Do you have any idea who it is; I mean who it is that's scaring you?"
"Not really but if I had to hazard a guess then I'd have to say the trainer I told you about."
"Then you must do something! As naive as I am and I'm sure you've sussed that out by now, even I know that you can't live your life being frightened by someone. You can't tell me all this and then just brush over it like its nothing important. Jess you have to go to the police!"
"Definitely not but don't you worry your pretty little

head about things. I can take care of myself Lucy and besides I have a friend that I know will sort all of this out for me. I only have to ask him. Let me sleep on it and maybe tomorrow if I don't feel any better about it Ill contact him."

Now Jess wished she hadn't opened her big mouth but she had needed to unburden herself. This poor young girl only wanted to do some research for a book and here was Jess putting the weight of the world onto her shoulders.

"Look sweetheart, I can handle all of this and I wish now that I hadn't mentioned it. Can we just forget I ever said anything?"

"But I....."

"Please Lucy? Let's just talk about why we are here. Now what would you like to talk about today?"

Lucy thought for a moment but it was hard for her to think of anything. All that Jess had revealed was swimming around in her mind and she was finding it difficult to concentrate. Finally she said the first thing that entered her head.

"What would you say are the biggest burdens regarding your line of work or would you say that there aren't any?"

"Well to be honest, just recently it has been on my mind that a couple of my clients are becoming a bit obsessed with me or at least what they think I am. In the past there has been at least one that said he had fallen head over heels in love with me, when that happens they seem to be in their own little

world and then it's difficult to let them down."
"I can imagine."
Jess stared blankly into space as she thought about what she had just revealed but Lucy's next question brought her back to reality with a bump.
"What's the saddest tale you've ever heard?"
For a second Jess was a little shocked. She hadn't seen this coming but then this was really the reason she was here so it was just best to get on with things.
"Well, that's a difficult one. I don't mean in the sense of choice but purely down to the fact that I haven't thought about it in a very long time. I suppose it would have to be Kieran's story but I must warn you Lucy, it's a little hard to take."
"Jess if I wanted everything sugar coated then I wouldn't have chosen this topic. Believe me I can take it I'm a big girl now."
"Well here goes. I first met Kieran Gray eight years ago. I'd been in the trade for almost two years and like a lot of others, thought I knew it all. Believe me my opinion changed after our first meeting. He was about thirty years old and married to his childhood sweetheart."
"Then why would he want to use someone like you! I'm sorry that didn't come out how I meant it to."
Jess patted Lucy lightly on the hand and smiled.
"Its fine and I know what you were trying to say. He didn't as you so elegantly put it, want to use me. The man was a heartbroken wreck and didn't really

know what he wanted. Seems he and his wife had been trying to start a family for years. Eventually they managed it and a beautiful baby boy was the result. Anyway, Kieran couldn't have been happier and took to fatherhood like a duck to water. His wife, Sammy was her name, had suffered from postnatal depression since giving birth to Charlie. That was the baby's name by the way."

"I gathered that."

"Anyway, Kieran being the type of man that he was encouraged his wife to go out with her friends and enjoy herself, anything to lift her spirits. Sammy didn't worry about the baby as Kieran was such a good dad. One Saturday night when Sammy had gone out to meet some friends for a meal and when Kieran was in the middle of bathing Charlie, the phone rang. Kieran Gray made sure his son was safe in the bath seat before running downstairs to answer the call. See he only thought that he'd be a matter of seconds but it was Sammy on the other end of the phone and she was in a real state. Alcohol had exasperated her condition and she was in floods of tears. Desperate to consol her, Kieran spent a few minutes calming Sammy down and then told her to get in a taxi and come home."

"Oh no! Jess please don't say what I think you're about to?"

"I sure am! By the time Kieran went back to the bathroom Charlie was dead. The poor little mite had turned the seat over and drowned in just a few

inches of water. When Sammy came through the front door she immediately heard the wailing and instantly sobered up. Running upstairs she found her husband cradling poor little Charlie's body and sobbing uncontrollably. She phoned for an ambulance but of course it was far too late. Kieran later told me that the paramedics had to literally prise Charlie away from him and he clung to the medics leg in a desperate attempt not to lose his son. As you can imagine the couple were beyond distraught. It was the only thing that could ever come between them and it ended their marriage as they both blamed themselves. Anyway, Kieran came to me in a hell of a state. He was numb and wanted to know what his boy had gone through, feel the same terror and well you can guess what he wanted me to do."
"You didn't?"
Jess was offended and her words came out in a tone that told Lucy in no uncertain terms that she had well and truly overstepped the mark.
"Of course I didn't. Fuck me Lucy whatever do you take me for?"
"I'm sorry I shouldn't have said that."
"No you shouldn't, you really should think before you open that mouth of yours."
Visions of Norma entered Lucy's head as she recalled the house keepers earlier words.
"Where was I? Oh yes, I have a friend whose a therapist and after ringing and arranging an

appointment I got him to see Kieran that very same day. It took many sessions but finally Kieran overcame his demons and I'm happy to say that he's now married again with a couple of kids. He pops in to see me from time to time and I sometimes ask him jokingly if he ever finally got to use the services of a dominatrix."

"And Sammy?"

"Ahhh not such a happy ending I'm afraid. Depression spiralled into alcoholism and the last I heard she was sleeping rough near Victoria. I don't ask Kieran about her as I wouldn't want to upset him."

When Jess stopped talking she looked at Lucy and the girl had tears rolling down her cheeks.

"And that my love is life! Everyone judges people before they get to really know them or their stories. It's sad but like I said its life."

Lucy Urquhart dried her eyes on a napkin and took in a deep lungful of air.

"You know something Jess? I'm learning so much from you and I'm not talking about the research. So when shall we meet again?"

"Can we give it a few days? I've got a lot on at the minute and I don't mean client wise. Why don't I give you a call?"

Something about the way Jess spoke her last sentence worried Lucy but she couldn't put her finger on exactly what it was. After her last faux pas she didn't dare pry any further so agreeing to meet a week from today the women went their separate ways.

CHAPTER FIFTEEN

As Jess had headed off to meet Lucy, Harry Fuller was again on his way to Thames House and the headquarters of MI5. After the usual security checks had been carried out, he was once more shown up to the office of Silvia Gladman. Silvia had been in the middle of dictating a letter when the knock came at the door. She had contemplated carrying on with the task in hand but had then thought better of it and standing up she walked over to the window. Silvia also had, although she would never admit it, a problem with men and any authority they tried to impose upon her. Of course that wasn't the case with Harry but she still wanted to show any male she came into contact with that she wouldn't be bullied in any way and that she wouldn't let them take charge. Silvia was still looking out of the window and had her back to him as he entered the room. She didn't immediately turn around and Harry took a seat without being invited. He was chomping at the bit to reveal what he had heard on the recording and didn't want to waste time with her daft attempt at using psychology on him. For some stupid reason, at least as far as Harry Fuller was concerned, all these high flying MI5 people always had to show that they had the upper hand and were superior. Harry was doing a job pure and simple and he didn't look

kindly at being taken for a fool.   In reality Silvia was scared, scared of what she was about to hear and that she had sanctioned this operation without going through the proper channels. Finally she turned to look at him and her face appeared to be set in stone.
"Well I must say that I didn't expect to see you back here so soon Harry! I take it you have some news for me?"
Harry Fuller didn't speak and instead handed Silvia a memory stick which she inserted into her laptop. Josh had cleaned up and transferred the recordings from the bugging chip in Jess's mobile phone and Harry knew he'd done a good job. He was overly pleased with the information he'd been able to collect in such a short time and hoped that Silvia would be impressed. Every task he carried out always left him excited and he waited with baited breath for her response. Throughout the recording he tried to read Silvia Gladman's expression but it was blank until it came to the part where Jess had slammed the folder shut and put it back inside the case. Silvia's eyebrows rose only slightly but when she removed the memory stick and placed it in her desk it was enough for Harry to know that what he'd obtained was good.
"So I take it when she's having words with this Flanagan character that she means the file?"
"Well I've no photographic evidence but I can't see what else it could have been can you?"

Silvia held the bottom of her chin between her thumb and forefinger and took a second or two to think before she spoke.

"No not really, mind you with these sorts of women it could be anything. They are the dregs of our society Harry and they play on the weaknesses of a man. Any woman who sells herself for sex is the lowest of the low, well in my opinion anyway. I have never personally had or wanted to use my body to get ahead professionally."

Harry Fuller inwardly grinned at her words. True Silvia Gladman was good at her job, probably the best but she certainly wasn't anything to look at and Harry tried to imagine her plying her trade on some street corner of Soho. Silvia couldn't possibly have known what he was thinking but she still gave Harry a strange look as she continued to talk.

"I know you've told me that she's high class but when it boils down to brass tacks and pardon the pun, there really isn't any difference between what she does and a common street whore. I think we need to delve a lot deeper into all of this before we make any rash decisions."

"We?"

Silvia Gladman waved her hand in a show of dismissal and Harry knew that she was trying to appear blasé about the mess they both knew was beginning to unfold but all the same he didn't like it.

"Well you know what I mean."

Harry knew only too well, he'd seen enough over the years to recognise when someone was in a bit of a dilemma and Silvia was definitely in it up to her neck. Deciding to change tactics, he could see that she was flummoxed when he asked her a question. "Did you have any joy finding out what the file contained? I mean he wouldn't have been so angry if it wasn't important or do you see it differently Chief?"

Silvia Gladman took a few seconds before she answered and Harry studied her eyes for any sign that she was starting to lose control of the situation. "No, I see it exactly the same as you do but as for what I was able to find out? Not a lot. I do know that it has something to do with Northern Ireland and that worries me. I mean had it have been about, well let's say for arguments sake South Africa, I wouldn't have been too concerned. With this Liam Flanagan's background and with all his connections, well it could cause us problems. The government has worked tirelessly to settle things over there but recently the tension has begun to build and trouble rearing its ugly head in Northern Ireland again is the last thing that this department, let alone this country, needs."

"So what do you want me to do next?"

Silvia studied the man before she spoke. She trusted Harry Fuller, to a point at least but this did all seem to be getting out of hand. There was only one problem, without taking things further she had very little hard evidence to take to the Director General. She could just close the case but then if anything kicked off and it was ever found out that she knew, well Silvia didn't even want to contemplate that at the moment. In the past Harry Fuller had always come through for her and Silvia hoped that this time would be no different.

"We need to know for certain if there is any link between our man and Flanagan. They could be using the girl as a go between, then again it could just be a coincidence. Either way it worries me. Now I want you to take the place apart if you have to but find me the evidence I need. Make it look like a burglary but I don't need to tell you how to do that."

Harry shrugged his shoulders, compared to the things he'd been witness too in the past, things he'd actually carried out himself, this little lot paled into insignificance. There was one thing bothering him though, who would take the flack if this all went tits up and he had to ask the question.

"Not a problem but if anything should go wrong, can you guarantee me immunity? I'm far too long in the tooth to be looking at any prison time and I'm well aware that were sailing very close to the wind so to speak!"

Silvia laughed to herself, this man really was a cold hearted bastard and only cared about number one, much like herself in fact and that was exactly the reason she liked him.

"As always Harry, you know I wouldn't hang you out to dry and you're well aware of our protocol. Besides the order had to have come from somewhere now didn't it? If it did go wrong which I'm sure it won't, just sit still and keep your mouth shut. So when do you think you can get the wheels in motion?"

"I'll go over there right now. The only stumbling block is waiting for the woman to go out, that's unless you want me to go in heavy handed?"

"No no there's no need for that, well at least not at the moment. Do what I've asked and let's see what the outcome is."

Silvia Gladman sat down at her desk and as she picked up her pen and began to write, it was indication to Harry that this meeting was over. He didn't mind, after all this was the way he'd been treated for the whole of his career. Harry Fuller prided himself on doing a good job but that said he didn't really care who he worked for. If the Director General had asked him to investigate Silvia then he would have done so without a second thought. There was no such thing as loyalty in this game; a fat pay cheque at the end of the month was the only thing that mattered. When the office door closed and she was once more alone, Silvia Gladman mentally ran through all of the evidence to date and realised that whatever happened she had some very damaging stuff when it came to man A. In fact she had enough to shame him and make him do whatever she wanted. That realisation brought a smile to the thin cruel lips of a woman who would stop at nothing to get what she wanted, especially when it came down to her country.

After stopping off to collect some food Harry made his way back to Phillimore Place on foot. The night was closing in and he tried to keep in the shadows as much as possible. His training had taught him to always be on his guard and Felix Abbotts van had been parked in the same place for several days. Harry had earlier inspected it when Felix popped out for something to eat and he could tell that the man must be besotted with Jess Metcalf. Harry found it difficult to understand why anyone would do that, no woman had ever meant that much to him that he would sleep outside in a cold van just to watch over her. Making his way into the abandoned building he tapped on the door for Josh Hartnet to let him in. The young lad was bleary eyed as he opened up and Harry guessed that he'd fallen asleep again. Handing Josh a brown paper bag which contained a burger and fries, Harry then went over to the window to look out at the street.

"How did it go with the Boss?"

"Just as I expected now shut up and eat your food." Josh looked into the bag and pulled away sharply at the smell. A practicing health nut, he only ever ate organic food and hated fast food in any shape or form. He knew better than to complain, so grimacing he removed the burger and took a bite.

"Where's yours?"
"I've already eaten."
Josh raised his eyebrows in distaste, the burger tasted rancid and he would hazard a guess that whatever Harry had eaten it wasn't this kind of shit. When he couldn't stomach another bite he placed the remaining burger back in the bag and threw it into the corner of the room. Walking over to where Harry stood he looked outside to see what was holding his new partners interest. There was nothing obvious and although he didn't want to appear a fool, asked anyway.
"What are you looking at?"
Harry shook his head and it crossed his mind that if this was the sum total of what MI5 had to offer then god help this country.
"That bloke Felix Abbott, the friend or boyfriend, has his van parked over there so he could still be watching her flat."
Josh didn't have a clue what Harry was on about and in all honesty he wasn't that interested. This surveillance work wasn't all that it was made out to be and he knew after this operation he wouldn't be doing it again, at least not if he had a say in the matter. Harry was trying to work out if there was anything he could do regarding the van; this added aggravation wasn't going to make things any easier for him. Before when he'd entered the flat it had been without detection but the chance of being seen was far greater during daylight hours. Instinct told

him he had to be on his guard and take extra care. The last thing he needed was to get into any altercations that could possibly result in someone's death. Silvia Gladman would really have a field day if that happened. No, Harry would bide his time and sooner or later he would accomplish his mission but he just wished that he didn't have to accommodate the likes and dislikes of Josh Hartnet in the mean time.

CHAPTER SIXTEEN

After her meeting with Lucy concluded, Jess had felt a little deflated. She didn't know why but all the same it wasn't an emotion she was comfortable with. Walking back to Phillimore Place she had suddenly decided to give Sharon Russell a call and see if her friend fancied getting together later for a bite to eat. Sharon was over the moon to hear from Jess so soon after their last encounter and the women arranged to meet up at Carluccio's Restaurant on Kensington High Street an hour later. Jess had just enough time to go home and freshen up before she set off for her dinner date. As she left through the main door Harry Fuller laid down his camera and turned to Josh.

"I'm going to follow her and see where she goes then I'll come back and do what I have to. Make sure you keep tracking her mobile and let me know if she's on her way back"

With that Harry was out of the building in seconds and kept a discrete distance behind Jess so as not to be seen. When he saw Jess greet her friend with a kiss on the cheek and when the two had entered the restaurant, Harry reasoned that he had at least a couple of hours grace. He quickly made his way back to Phillimore Place and was annoyed when he saw that Felix's van was still in situ. Pulling his hat brim down and his coat collar up high so that his face was mostly hidden, he confidently walked towards Jess's building. His clothing was nondescript and to anyone including Felix, he appeared like a normal visitor calling on one of the other residents. Just as before he let himself into the flat but this time set about meticulously going through each room. After spending far more time than he would have liked searching every nook and cranny, Harry Fuller had come up with a big fat zero, there was absolutely nothing to report back to Silvia Gladman. Anger and frustration started to build up and seconds later he seemed to explode as he totally trashed the place. Harry always carried a combat knife and removing it he ripped at the sofa then upturned the side tables and toppled over lamps. By the time he'd finished the flat had been trashed and taking one last look at the destruction he'd caused, Harry Fuller sneered as he kicked in the front door from outside. It had to look like a burglary but now through the noise he'd created, there was a chance of being heard by a neighbour. Swiftly he ran down the stairwell and reaching the ground floor, casually strolled out of the building. Jess Metcalf had enjoyed a wonderful evening with her old friend and a little the worse for wear, had decided to walk back. After letting herself into her flat she suddenly sobered up when she saw the carnage that just a few hours earlier had been her cosy little home. Suddenly she felt scared; scared that whoever had done this could still be inside.

Not waiting for the lift she descended the stairs as quickly as she could and as soon as the front door swung open, she began to run. Felix Abbott, who was still keeping watch from his van, was by her side in seconds.

"Jess! Jess! Whatever's the matter?"

"I've been burgled."

"What?"

"I've just got home and my flats been ransacked and anyway how come you're here?"

Felix was now embarrassed. He knew he had to come clean as there were no more lame excuses to use, or at least none that she would believe.

"I've been keeping an eye on you, well since you had that scare the other night I....."

Suddenly Jess lost it, lost all of her etiquette and decorum as she turned on her oldest friend.

"Keeping a fucking eye on me? What are you some kind of bleeding stalker?"

"Look let's not go into all of this now. Come on I'll go back with you and we can see what's what."

Jess didn't argue she suddenly felt as if the stuffing had been well and truly knocked out of her. Inside she surveyed all the damage and felt like crying. Photographs of her mum were smashed and the beautiful china statues that shed begun to collect since she'd started to make any real money were now lying on the floor
shattered into a hundred pieces. Suddenly she couldn't hold back any longer and the tears started

to fall.

"Look at my beautiful things! It's all gone. Everything I worked so damn hard for. Whoever would want to do this to me?"

Immediately Felix could feel her eyes as they bore into him and he responded in a way that was hostile but which also told her he was terribly hurt.

"Don't fucking go there Jess! If you think for one moment that I had anything to do with this then you're out of fucking order."

"Did I say that?"

"You didn't have to; your face says it all."

"Well if you've been keeping an eye on me like you say you have then you must have seen who it was!"

"I'm sorry but I didn't. There were a couple of people who came and went after you left but no one who looked suspicious and I couldn't give you a description of them if I tried."

"Well I'm glad you aint a fucking detective because you're useless at it!"

As usual when it came down to Felix Jess felt guilty but he didn't seem too bothered by her remarks and was now inspecting the door that Harry had this time forced open in an attempt to make it look like a burglary. When Felix went to retrieve some tools from his van he also called the police. He knew Jess would be angry with him but he didn't care, this had to stop and his friend needed help whether she admitted it or not. Before he'd had time to complete a makeshift repair to Jess's front door, two uniformed officers announced their visit on the intercom and were now exiting the lift. After they all introduced themselves the Officers, accompanied by Felix, walked into the flat. Jess had no alternative but to let them in but as soon as she saw them she gave her friend a look of daggers.

"I'm afraid you've wasted your time officers. My friend had no right to call you and I apologise for your wasted journey at this late hour."

PC Dave Gillam looked around at the chaos that had once been, from the look of the decor and furnishings, a very nice home. Frowning he turned to Jess and spoke in a calm and comforting tone.

"I understand you must be upset Miss but we need to stop this happening to someone else, now if I could just ask you a few questions? I know it's difficult but can you tell me if there is anything missing?"

Jess held up her hands in a sign of submission. She was mentally exhausted and really couldn't be bothered to argue any further.

"Look officer, I'm not going to beat about the bush so I'll just come straight out with it. I'm a whore, a dominatrix and this was probably a disgruntled client."

Jess looked for any glimmer of a smile on the man's lips but there was none. His next sentence, as far as Jess was concerned, came out of the blue and surprised her more than a little.

"Miss Metcalf what you choose to do in the privacy

of your own home is your business. Nobody has the right to do this to another person regardless of what that person does for a living. A crime has been committed and we will do our best to bring the culprit to book. Now if you could take a few minutes to look around and see if any items have been taken?"

Doing as shed been asked Jess made her way into the bedroom but everything, albeit in a mess, seemed to be there. It was the same in the dungeon and spare room, in fact she was starting to wonder what the point of this burglary had been as nothing was missing. Finally she made her way back to where the two policemen stood in the kitchen. Shrugging her shoulders she told them everything was still here, right down to the whisky jar that was full of one pound coins shed been saving for over a year.

"So Miss Metcalf, do you think it could be one of your clients after all?"

Jess walked over to the upturned brass table lamp and peeling back the green felt base placed her hand inside. Removing what could only be described as a printed sheet of black and white images, she handed it to the police officer.

"This is everyone whose called here in, well I'd say probably the last month, at least anyone who pressed my intercom that is. Shortly after I moved in and strictly for safety purposes, I hired a firm to install a security device."

Jess pointed with her finger to a small printer that now lay upside down in the doorway.

"I only printed these off yesterday. When anyone presses my bell a hidden camera takes a photograph. Nobody knows and its purely for my own safety. You'll even find several snaps of Felix amongst them."

At the mention of his name Felix Abbott appeared from the hallway.

"All done Jess, at least for tonight. I'll come back tomorrow and do a more permanent job but for now it's safe."

The officers took a short statement from Jess and Felix and told them both that they would return in the morning with a scene of crimes officer who would then check for prints. Jess was informed that it would be best if she tried not to touch anything until then.

"No worries on that score, all I want to do is crawl into bed and try and forget this night ever happened."

Felix saw the officers to the front door and when he returned he told Jess in no uncertain terms that he would spend the remainder of the night in the spare room. Now too tired to argue she just waved her hand and then headed for her bedroom. Harry Fuller took a few final photographs as the policemen left and then instructed Josh to clean the place thoroughly. As far as Harry was concerned, once he'd reported back to Silvia this little operation was now over. By the look on Josh Hartnet's face Harry could see that the young man wasn't happy with his order but he wouldn't complain as he knew he'd been little better than useless for the entire time he'd been here.

The two policemen didn't study the photographs until they got back to the station but when they finally did, Dave let out a loud gasp. None of the faces were recognised except the one of Deputy Chief Inspector Sharon Russell but that one was enough to cause shock. PC Gillam had been a constable for ten years and had never had any real desires to rise in the ranks. Most new rookies were assigned to him until they had been evaluated and at the moment his charge was PC Simon Long. Simon had joined the force six months earlier and still desperate to make a good impression, hung on Dave Gilliam's every word.

"Wow Dave look at this!"

Dave had already recognised the face of Sharon Russell but he wasn't sure if the young officer had. Desperate to keep things under wraps, at least until he'd informed a superior, he looked at the young policeman and his expression was stern as he spoke.

"If you know what's good for you lad you won't breath a word about this to anyone."

"But I....."

"I said anyone! A career can be made or broken with the scrawl of a pen and what we have here is serious stuff. First thing in the morning I will take this up to the Chief Inspector. For now as far as you are concerned at least, you've never seen it. Do I make myself clear?"

Simon Long nodded his head. He knew that he couldn't breathe a word because if it became common knowledge then it would be obvious where the leak had come from. Soon after, the men signed off from their shift and there was nothing more said about the matter.

The next day and one hour before he was due on duty, PC Dave Gillam sat outside the office of Chief Inspector Raymond Banks. The Inspectors secretary Sue Handley was annoyed when the man still took a seat in the corridor after she'd told him the Inspector had a very busy schedule that day. Although she sighed from time to time which didn't go unnoticed by PC Gillam, she still knew better than to ask him to leave. At nine on the dot the Inspector walked towards his office but was prematurely stopped when Sue Handley got up from her desk and quickly approached him. As she spoke Chief Banks looked over her shoulder in PC Gilliam's direction. It was highly unusual for a street plod to come directly to him so the Chief knew that whatever it concerned was serious. As he walked into his office he told Dave to follow and close the door behind him.

"So PC Gillam, what's so important that you couldn't go through the proper channels?"

"Well Sir, along with one of the young juniors

assigned to me, we came across something last night that concerned me. I realise I've disregarded protocol by coming straight to you but I knew that if I'd gone through the proper channels then there would be a lot more people privy to this information."

The Chief Inspector nodded sagely and asked the policeman to continue. Dave recounted everything that had happened last night and left nothing out. Finally when he'd finished speaking he removed the paper which contained the photographs and laid it onto the table. The Inspector studied each one and although he spent a few seconds longer looking at Sharon Russell's, he did recognise one of the others as being high profile.

"Leave this with me and from now on mum's the word, do you understand me Officer Gillam?"

"Yes Sir."

"Good! Oh and Gillam, I can see you put a lot of thought into this matter, you're just the sort of man that the force needs."

The Inspector told Dave to go about his duties and as soon as the office door was once again closed, Raymond Banks picked up the telephone and placed a call to Hugo Barrow-Laws, the Commissioner. A few minutes later and as Sue Handley protested that he had a very busy day, he calmly told her to cancel any appointments for this morning and then left the station. Just as he'd imagined the Commissioner of the Met was very

interested in the information and informed Banks that he would look into the matter personally. Chief Banks, hopeful of getting a pat on the back for his astuteness, was also informed that the case was now closed and as far as the victim was concerned, she was to be informed that there was no further evidence to go on. Fifteen minutes later and the Commissioner entered the front foyer of MI5. He was treated no differently to any other visitor and after passing the security checks was shown up to Silvia Gladman's office. The two went way back and even though the Commissioner was happily married there had always been chemistry between the two that neither could deny.
"Hello Hugo! Why I haven't seen you in ages. Come on in and take a seat, coffee?"
"I'm sorry to say this isn't a social visit Silvia. I think there may be a potential security problem."
Recounting what he'd been told, the Commissioner then handed her the photographs. Silvia tried desperately not to show any expression when she saw the man's picture but she didn't do a very good job.
"I thought you'd find them interesting."
Shaking her head Silvia opened up the drawer to her desk and placed the pictures inside.
"Are these the only copies?"
"As far as I'm aware. Apart from the Officers who attended the scene, no one else knows anything about it."

"I would be grateful if it stayed that way Hugo."
"You have my word Silvia. As far as the Met is concerned in any of this, I have instructed my officers that we have nothing to go on. The obligatory visit by scene of crimes will be carried out today but I can assure you that it will be logged as breaking and entry which was possibly carried out by a disgruntled punter. I'm aware that whatever problems you are having here could cause embarrassment but believe you me, my department would be up for ridicule if vice ever got wind that one of my senior officers is associated with a known prostitute but obviously that pales into insignificance as far as your department are concerned. I could ride the storm without too much flack but for you the involvement of high ranking government officials is a different matter altogether."

Silvia smiled as she nodded her head in agreement, she also knew that the problem would be far easier for him to smooth over than it would be for her. Placing a kiss on her cheek, the commissioner walked from the office. He was glad that he'd carried out this task just as protocol demanded. He was also glad that as far as he was concerned at least, the matter was now closed. This could all turn out to be very messy if the shit hit the fan and it always seemed to with this type of scandal. Back in her office Silvia Gladman was pacing the floor. Man A was in over his head and as far as she knew the stupid bugger didn't even know it. Where to go from here she really didn't have a clue, the one thing she did know was that this wasn't over by a long way.

CHAPTER SEVENTEEN

After a surprisingly good night Jess woke feeling refreshed and for a few seconds thought she'd dreamt the nightmare burglary. Sitting up in bed she stared around at all the destruction that now cluttered her bedroom floor and it suddenly hit her that it hadn't been a dream after all. Tension began to build in the back of her neck and when she heard a loud bang in the kitchen she almost jumped out of her skin. Quickly pulling on her dressing gown, she grabbed the knife that she had placed under her mattress a few nights ago when someone had been ringing the door bell. Creeping along the hall she peered around the kitchen doorframe and let out a sigh of relief when she spied Felix making a cup of tea. Jess opened a unit drawer and put the knife inside but she wasn't quick enough and he saw her.
"I hope that wasn't for me?"
She instantly felt her face flush red with embarrassment.
"Don't be so stupid!"
Walking over to where she stood Felix placed a steaming hot mug in her hands.
"Lighten up will you, I was only having a laugh."
"Sorry but I haven't got much of a sense of humour at the moment."
"Did the Old Bill say what time they were coming back?"

Jess wearily took a seat at the table.
"Sometime today but I'm not waiting for them Felix, I've got to tidy up soon or I'll go round the bend with all this mess. I doubt they'll even find any fingerprints, I mean it might have been different if they were druggies but then my money jar would have gone for sure and it's still sitting there."
Jess pointed to the glass unit on which sat a giant whisky bottle filled to the brim with coins.
"I don't care what anyone says, someone's trying to frighten me."
Felix Abbott felt so sorry for Jess but he was also angry with himself that after keeping an eye on her for nearly two weeks, he hadn't seen the person that had done all this. True he hadn't been here twenty four hours a day as he had to work but her flat was broken into at night and he should have been more alert. Finishing his tea he went down to the van and collected a new door lock. Jess was still at the table when he returned but she didn't speak as he set about carrying out a permanent repair to the door. Thirty minutes later and with the job complete he made sure she was alright and then set off for work.
A few minutes later the intercom rang. Wearily Jess walked into the hall to see who it was and spying a policeman and a woman in plain clothes, she buzzed them up. The scene of crimes officer, along with the help of the policeman, dusted for prints but as Jess watched them from the kitchen she couldn't help but think they seemed to be going about it half

heartedly. Sometime later when the officer informed her that they couldn't find anything she slowly shook her head. Seeing them to the door Jess once more took a seat at the table and must have remained there for over an hour as she went through everything in her mind. Finally she came to a decision and picking up her phone dialled Liam Flanagan's number.

"Hello Princess how are you?"

"Liam I need your help."

"Say no more, I'll be over as quick as I can."

With that the call ended and Jess set about trying to tidy up the front room. She wasn't very successful as the place was in such a mess and when Liam Flanagan pressed the intercom she let him in and was standing in the hallway still holding one of the ripped sofa cushions as he came through the door. One look at her drawn face and seeing her for the first time without makeup, told him that something bad had happened. Removing the cushion from her arms he tenderly took hold of Jess's hand and led her back through to the kitchen.

"Now you sit down sweetheart and I'll make us some coffee, after that you can tell me all about it."

When Jess had revealed not only the burglary but her fears about being followed and the late night stranger who had scared her by pressing the intercom, she turned to look at Liam and he could see that her beautiful eyes were full of tears and desperation. Anger raced through his veins and he felt like taking on the world single handed if it would ease her suffering. He also knew that rage was the last thing she needed to see at the moment and made sure his tone was soft as he spoke.

"So babe, have you any idea who it was?"

"I've racked my brains over and over and the only name I can think of, the only person that might really want to hurt me is Nicky Brent."

"Who?"

"A bloke I saw for a short time but I ended it when he started to ask for really kinky stuff."

What she said cut Liam Flanagan like a knife. He thought of her as his girl and when she talked of other men, not to mention kinky sex, it gutted him. Jess could see the pain that her words were causing but she had to be honest if she wanted his help.

"Nicky Brent? I know that name. You mean the horse trainer?"

"Yeah and I have to admit he frightened me Liam. Do you think you could have a word and warn him off. I'm scared and its starting to get to me."

Liam Flanagan stood up and walked around the table to where Jess sat. He expected nothing in return and after cupping her cheeks in his hands gently kissed her lips.

"You know how I feel about you darling and before you say another word, no I don't want anything in a way of thanks. Leave it with me and I'll have a word and I promise you this Brent bloke won't bother you again. Now is there anything else, do

you want me to help you tidy up a bit?"
Jess laughed out loud. Of all the images she had of Liam Flanagan and there were many, wearing an apron and a set of rubber gloves wasn't one of them. "Its fine I can manage. Liam I've known you almost since the day I started out in this game and a better friend I couldn't wish for, thank you."
Liam pulled on his coat and winked at Jess before leaving the flat. Once outside on the street anger cursed through his veins, anger that anyone had dared to scare the woman he loved. Back at the Hercules Tavern Liam summoned two of his most trusted men. Jack Owen and Frank Bennett had been with Liam since the day he'd left the Richardson firm and there wasn't anything he felt uncomfortable asking them to do. The men were instructed to dress up smartly and then drive over to Brentford in search of Nicky Brent. When they had located the man they were told to arrange a meeting and to inform Mr Brent that their boss was interested in purchasing and stabling a racehorse at the man's yard. Jack and Frank did a good job and as with all greedy men Nicky Brent fell for the ruse hook line and sinker as soon as they told him that money wasn't a problem. The meeting was set for two days time at The George public house in Brentford. Set close to his home, Nicky was confident that everything was as it should be but nothing could be further from the truth. Liam had carried out a spot of business in the pub a few

months earlier and though not on overly friendly terms with the landlord, a bloke by the name of Ralph Vaughn, Liam knew he wasn't the type to call the Old Bill at the first sign of any trouble.
Hopefully everything would go smoothly and there wouldn't be a problem, if things didn't pan out then Liam just hoped that his men could keep any aggro well out of view of the regulars.
At eight pm on the day of the meeting, Jack and Frank met up with Nicky Brent as agreed and straight away made their apologies for their boss's absence. Frank informed Nicky that Liam was stuck in a business meeting that he couldn't get out of but would join them as soon as possible and that they should have a few drinks and a bite to eat while they waited. The tab of course would be picked up by Mr Flanagan as an apology for his lateness. Over steak and chips and a bottle of wine Frank and Jack talked nonstop about how successful their boss was and that when it came down to investments money was no object. The three seemed to get on like a house on fire and after the food had been eaten another bottle of wine was ordered. It didn't take long before Nicky started to feel a little the worse for wear. Frank Bennett then went over to the bar and ordered three brandies. A few minutes later and Nicky Brent could feel his head begin to swim and making his excuses headed in the direction of the toilets. Splashing his face several times with water, Nicky tried to shake off

the effects of the alcohol. He was angry with himself for getting in this state before he'd even got to meet his new investor. Entering the bar area he noticed that Jack Owen was on his mobile and as he reached the table Jack covered the mouthpiece with his hand.

"It's the Boss. Yeah Mr Flanagan I'm still here, ok well be waiting."

Replacing the mobile into his pocket Jack looked at Nicky Brent and smiled.

"Once again Mr Flanagan sends his apologies and asked me to tell you that he's on his way and will pick us up in five minutes. He would like to take you on to a Lap dancing club. It's all arranged VIP area the works, of course that's only if you'd like to go? My boss says you can relax and talk about business at the same time. Mind you if you see the beauties that work there I doubt you'll get much business sorted tonight, aint that right Frank?"

Frank Bennett laughed out loud as he vigorously nodded his head. Jack took a few moments to go into great detail about the girls and by the time he'd finished Nicky was almost salivating.

"That sounds great, I just love Lap dancing clubs don't you boys?"

Just as the men finished their drinks Liam's brand new top of the range Jaguar pulled up a short walk away from the pub and Jacks phone rang out. He didn't answer as he already knew who the caller was and it was only confirmation from his boss that

it was now time to leave. Frank, Jack and Nicky Brent walked the short distance and just as Nicky was becoming concerned Frank pointed out his boss's car, which was slightly parked in the shadows and well away from any street lamps. Looking into the rear view mirror Liam saw them approach and got out of the Jag to greet Nicky.
"Hello Mr Brent I'm Liam. I've heard a lot about you and I'm very pleased to meet you in person at last. Please forgive me for earlier and I promise I'm going to make it up to you, now shall we get off as I have something rather special planned. Frank you drive, me and Nicky I mean Mr Brent will sit in the back and make ourselves comfortable."
"Please call me Nicky Mr Flanagan and I'll call you Liam if that's ok, no need for formalities is there?"
As the car glided away from the curb the men began to chat.
"Well then Nicky, do you have any good propositions for me. I fancy a nice little filly, maybe a contender for the Guineas or the Oaks, now that would be nice. I've always preferred the female gender."
"Me too. Actually there's a sale at Tattersall's coming up in the next two weeks if you're interested. I know for a fact there's a very desirable little filly with an excellent pedigree that should go at a reasonable price; then again you can never be sure."
"How much do you think shell fetch? I won't hold

you too it but just to give me a bit of an idea you know?"

"Well I would like to think that a hundred thousand should secure her, that's guineas of course."

Liam slowly nodded his head. He wanted the man to think that he was giving the proposition some serious thought.

"So we're talking around a hundred and five grand. That sounds about right and your fees would be what?"

"Approximately twenty thousand a year, of course that doesn't include entries and transport etcetera. Believe you me, for a horse of that breeding it's not much. I mean if you were to get a classic winner it would be money well spent. I would need to have the cash made available to me as soon as possible though."

"Nicky the moneys no problem at all. In fact I can let you have a deposit tonight, just to show you how serious I really am. Frank, take a detour and well go and pick some cash up at Benny's."

When Nicky heard the word cash he thought all of his Christmases had come at once. He couldn't believe his luck, what a night of opportunities this was turning out to be.

"So Nicky, tell me how many horses do you have in training at the moment?"

"Seventy six but I'm hoping to get that number up to around a hundred by the beginning of the next season."

"Well I can safely say that I'd be looking at about a string of ten, of course in my colours!"
"Really?"
"Definitely."
As the car pulled up outside a set of steel gates Jack got out and unlocked them. Pushing hard on one so that the car had enough room to pass through he then closed and locked the gates to Benny's scrap yard before getting back inside. The place was vast and after they had driven for a few seconds Nicky Brent started to get suspicious.
"What's all this about Liam?"
"Relax my friend there's no problem. This is where I keep my undeclared wonga that's all. I own fifty percent of this place and it's an ideal front. Now I just need to get some cash from the safe and well be off ok? It won't take a minute."
The Jaguar drove into the middle of the yard and stopped outside a small brick office. Liam, Frank and Jack got out of the vehicle and Nicky Brent began to feel nervous. Deciding to get out of the car as he would feel safer out in the open, Nicky stepped onto the muddy ground. Looking up at the piles of cars that were stacked at least four high, they seemed to surround the men and Nicky had a gut feeling that he should run. There was just one problem; there was nowhere to run to. Liam walked to the back of the Jag and invited Nicky to join him.
"You might be interested in this Nicky."

Curiosity and a need to keep on the man's good side saw Nicky Brent walk to the rear of the car. Liam bent over and opening up a blanket revealed two razor sharp short swords which made Nicky gasp out loud. Liam picked up one in each hand and it was a signal to his men that things were about to kick off.

"Grab him boys!"

Instantly Frank and Jack both got hold of Nicky's arms. Pulling him outstretched they then placed a foot on each of the man's feet rendering him unable to move. Standing spread eagled in front of Liam, Nicky Brent couldn't for the life of him understand what was going on.

"Well done lads, now don't let go of him until I tell you to."

By now Nicky had gone way beyond panic and his words came out in a high pitched feminine tone.

"What's going on? What's all this about?"

Liam didn't answer the man and with his left arm he plunged the sword he was holding straight into Nicky's gut and out through his back.

"Oh my god!!!! Fucking hell what are you doing! Arghhhhh."

Liam Flanagan let go of the sword which was still plunged into Nicky Brent's body.

"Ok lads, you can let go now. I can't see the cunt running off anywhere can you?"

Frank and Jack laughed as they stepped to one side and Nicky Brent fell to his knees gasping.

"Arrrgh!"
Blood oozed from the vicious wounds and as he coughed, more blood spluttered from Nicky's mouth when he tried to speak. Liam wasn't content with the damage he'd already inflicted and stepping forward he raised the other sword in his right hand and brought it down directly between the man's shoulder and neck. The razor sharp blade cut deep into Nicky's chest and his head lopped to one side. A gaping wound was now visible and as blood gushed freely Liam pulled out the sword and with as much force as he could muster, swiftly brought it back down on the other side of the man's neck. Nicky Brent's head was cut clean off and fell to the floor as his body slumped to the ground. Liam Flanagan walked over to the corpse and after removing the first sword from Nicky's body, proceeded to plunge it into the dismembered head. Holding it up high like a trophy he resembled some ancient warrior and with his next sentence, even for Frank Bennett and Jack Owen it was a little too much to take.
"Get a photo of this will you boys?"
Jack Owen was now feeling nervous and words tumbled from his mouth that he quickly regretted.
"Is that for your face book Boss?"
Frank laughed at Jacks words but when their boss didn't join in, Jack went silent and now feared he'd said something out of turn. Liam Flanagan's mood

could turn in an instant and Jack didn't fancy meeting the same fate as the poor bastard lying on the dirt in front of him. Finally Liam decided that he'd had enough enjoyment for one night and Nicky Brent's body along with his dismembered head was placed into the boot of one of the cars that was due to be crushed the following morning. The blood on the floor was scuffed into the ground by Frank Bennett and in no time at all it was as if this despicably cruel act had never taken place. For all intent and purpose Nicky Brent would become part of a metal cube, never to be heard of again and as far as Liam Flanagan was concerned it was a job well done. With the deed finalised Liam smiled at his two accomplices.

His men hadn't visibly shown any kind of shock at the level of violence that had been dished out but Frank Bennett was still intrigued.

"Fuck me Boss, that cunt must have really pissed you off?"

Liam didn't want to go into any details about Jess. As far as he was concerned she was his and the matter was private. Somehow he felt that just the mention of her name would taint Jess with all the dirt and violence that his life consisted of and to Liam she was a pure goddess.

"Not me but someone I really care about. Needless to say the wanker will never do it again."

Frank knew that his Boss's words put an end to the matter and that to pry any further would be considered rude. Liam Flanagan was a fair man, as far as he could be in this line of work but to stick your nose into his personal business, no matter who you were, could only end badly for the person doing the prying.

CHAPTER EIGHTEEN

Two days after Jess's flat had been burgled all hell broke loose in Northern Ireland. MI5 had been closely monitoring the planned parade to mark the centenary of the Ulster covenant. The march had begun in central Belfast and was due to end at Stormont. It was the biggest police operation that Ireland had seen in over twenty years. When the covenant had been signed back in nineteen twelve it had divided a nation. Citizens who signed wanted to remain under the rule of the United Kingdom but the nationalist wanted home rule and the result was a country divided in two. This caused and continued to be a bone of contention and when the IRA was formed and their fight for home rule began, a bloody war erupted that would last for the best part of eighty years. Now the British government thought that they had everything under control but it didn't stop those at the top from being nervous. A file had been put together detailing exactly who of note would be attending the march and Aidan Brody was at the top of the list. In the late seventies and into the early eighties Aidan had been a thorn in the side of the IRA. He had fiercely protested against home rule and being a protestant to boot, was and would always be a high profile target. MI5 had received information that the man would be attending the centenary celebration and it was a red alert for the British government. For the last twenty five years Aiden Brody had been in a witness protection programme but his unannounced return to Irish soil three days earlier had set alarm bells ringing. Now with the march underway all eyes were on the procession. The government had men posted all along the route, some were even taking part in the march and as yet no one had reported any problems. Calm seemed to be the order of the day until the centenary men reached the Prince of Wales Road. Suddenly a man fell to the ground outside O'Leary's pub and several people ran screaming and shouting into the crowds. There was so much noise from the bands and the amount of people in attendance that the incident passed without much notice except for the few eyes that had been following the prime target. The entire display was being monitored via a satellite link screened directly to Thames House and when the shooting occurred, staff could be seen running around the department like headless chickens. Somehow a group of renegade nationalists that called themselves the new IRA had received information regarding Aiden's attendance. The assassin had used a high powered rifle with silencer so as not to draw too much attention and the man hadn't stood a chance. Aidan Brody was now lying on the pavement with a hole through the centre of his head and blood oozing from the fatal wound. Within seconds a small crowd that had witnessed the event and who were now all fearful for their own safety, dispersed. One of MI5s on the ground agents threw his coat over the body and informed anyone who inquired that the man had drunk too much of the black stuff, was sleeping it off and that an ambulance was on its way. Due to it being a Sunday, Silvia had left a deputy to run things in her absence. She was away for the weekend and had seen fit to leave Layton Hansen in charge, a choice she would soon come to regret. Layton was twenty nine years of age and although he'd been with the department for eight years, had no real experience of emergency high profile situations. Silvia had been convinced that there wouldn't be any problems and now Layton was being bombarded with questions that he didn't know the answers to. Beads of sweat stood out on his forehead and he could feel the onset of a panic attack and knew he had to do the one thing that would, through no fault of his own, put a black mark on his otherwise exemplary record. Sliding open his phone, he took a deep breath before proceeding to telephone Silvia Gladman. Layton knew that she would be far from happy about being disturbed but he also knew, or at least hoped, that once he explained the situation the woman would be back at Millbank as soon as was humanly possible.

When the call came through Silvia was stretching out her arms and had been in the middle of enjoying her first lie in for months. Snatching up her phone she huffed with annoyance as she answered.

"Whoever you are, this had better be good!"

"Its Layton Hansen Ms Gladman and we've got a real problem here."

Layton relayed the events, which had yet to reach the news and the colour drained from Silvia's face.

"I'm at my holiday home in Dorset so send a helicopter to collect me. I want a complete media blackout on this Layton, do you hear me?"

"Yes Chief and would you like me to call the Director General for you?"

"Noooooooo! If you value your career you will do nothing until I get there, do you understand?"

Her voice was so shrill that Layton Hansen had to pull the receiver away from his ear. About to speak again he realised that the line had already gone dead and even though he'd done nothing wrong, felt that he was truly in deep shit. Layton had learnt within his first few weeks in the department that his boss could instil the fear of god into a person and would blame anyone in the vicinity rather than take the flack herself if something went wrong. Well today things had gone very wrong and he knew he would be made to face the proverbial firing squad when she arrived. In less than an hour Silvia Gladman made her entrance into the offices of MI5. Her face was full of anger as she marched in and everyone in the department seemed to suddenly

look in the direction of the floor as she passed.
"Layton, in my office now!"
Taking a seat behind her desk she waited for Layton Hansen to close the door.
"Right! I want a complete breakdown of what's happened."
Nervously Layton relayed every detail from when the march began right up until the shooting and as he spoke he couldn't help but notice the colour drain from his boss's face. When he had finished speaking Silvia waved in the direction of the door and Layton scuttled out as quickly as he could. Inhaling deeply, she picked up the telephone and tapped in the number for Whitehall. Silvia wasn't in the least bit nervous and her action was carried out in an attempt to calm herself and nothing more. Screaming down the receiver wasn't professional conduct but it would take all of her resolve not to do it. Instead of going through to the switchboard Silvia had the direct line numbers of all the departments and the Foreign Office was the one she was now calling. When the line wasn't answered she slapped at her brow as she remembered it was Sunday. Flicking through her address book, Silvia found the man's home number and redialled. The Under-Secretary of State for Foreign Affairs and the person who handled the day to day business at Whitehall answered within seconds.
"Hello?"
"It's me."

The man instantly recognised her voice and didn't bother with polite formality. The short conversation began and ended without any niceties.

"I need to see you now!"

"My dear, I don't know if you realise it but it's a Sunday."

Silvia was now standing up and she placed a hand onto the desk to support herself. Her rage was such, that if she could have reached down the line and throttled the man then she would have.

"I know what fucking day it is you moron! I want you in my office within the hour to sort out the dreadful mess you have caused."

"What on earth are you talking about woman?"

"I suggest you get over here now if you want to salvage any of your dignity let alone your career!"

With that the line went dead and Sylvia sat back down to wait. She wasn't in any doubt that the man would do as he'd been told; he wouldn't dare do anything else. Silvia only had to wait twenty minutes and as her office door opened, she was conscious of her posture and sat bolt upright. The man was tall and he had such an air of arrogance about him that she felt like standing up and slapping his face. She had never liked him and never would. They had met a few times at various government functions but never socially and this was the first time she had ever summoned him to her office. The abrupt phone call hadn't got the two off to a very good start but in all honesty Silvia

couldn't have cared less. The only thing she was bothered about was how she could end the sorry mess that he had caused.
"Take a seat."
"I'd rather stand if you don't mind."
Silvia could tell by his expression that he wasn't happy.
"Now what is all this about and I would be grateful if you could get to the point as I have a roast dinner waiting for me."
Something about the way he spoke grated on Silvia Gladman and standing up she placed her palms flat onto the desk and leaned forward.
"A fucking roast dinner! I really don't think you realise the gravity of the situation."
"No I do not so could you please enlighten me?"
Removing a memory stick from her desk drawer, Silvia pushed it into her laptop and hit return. Turning the screen around so that it now faced the man, she studied his face. There wasn't much of a reaction but when she hit return again and a taped conversation of Jess and Liam arguing could be heard, his face
visibly drained of colour.
"Where did you get that?"
"You know full well where I got it but what were you doing leaving highly secret information in the flat of a whore. This particular whore I might add, also entertains a London villain who just happens to originate from Northern Ireland and is an IRA

sympathiser."
As Silvia Gladman continued to talk she left the screen facing towards the man so that he could see a rerun of Aiden Broody assassination. Not knowing what to expect she wasn't surprised when the man's face remained expressionless and void of any emotion.
"The information was leaked and it could only have come from you. This I am sad to say is the result."
His gaze was intently fixed on the footage playing in front of him and when it finished he looked from the screen into Silvia's eyes. Now she could see some emotion as his face wore a look of terror but it wasn't for the victim, it was purely for him and the effect it would have on his career.
"I didn't know, I swear I didn't know."
"Maybe you didn't but that's not really the problem now is it? National security has been breached and all because you couldn't keep your dick in your pants. If the media gets hold of this they will have a field day. The government will be made to look like fools and I hasten to add, your career will be well and truly over. Good god man, can you imagine if it became public knowledge that there was a leak from the British government, well I don't even want to think what the consequences would be."
The man ran his hands through his hair and Silvia knew that he was desperately wracking his brains as he tried to think of what else he could say or do to make things right. With eyes that unlike a few

minutes ago, now looked old and tired, he seemed to stare into space and then he looked up at her.
"Now what?"
"It never ceases to amaze me how you people drop everyone else in it from a great height and them ask for help to put things right. A man has lost his life because of you and you ask me now what? Just think about it for a moment, regardless of your negligence which I might add was a major contributory factor in all of this, who do you, see is to blame?"
The man only took a second before he answered. It wasn't a surprise to Silvia, she expected nothing less. Members of the government not only had a reputation for blaming anyone but themselves, they actually believed they were whiter than white.
"My Mistress, I mean Jess Metcalf. The bitch should have kept my things private."
"And what do you think needs to be done about all of this?"
The man knew that it was all going to come back on him and he started to get angry.
"You can stop right there with all your psycho babble Sylvia. I know exactly what you're trying to do."
"And what might that be?"
Silvia had read the signs but she wasn't about to tread carefully. When it came down to cold hard facts, the only person responsible was the idiot standing in front of her. As far as she was

concerned he had made the mess and he could damn well clear it up.

"If you think for one moment that I'm trying to psyche you out then you are wrong. This could have been leaked and I could have let the media take a free hand with the story. By tonight it would have gone viral. Thankfully for you I love my country too much and that is why I'm giving you a chance to put this right."

"But how, I don't understand?"

"Shut the bitch up; make sure that she and the perverts, who use her services, never put this government in jeopardy again."

The man was beginning to sweat, he knew she was referring to him when she said perverts but he didn't protest. Raising his hand to wipe his brow, he spoke.

"Now just hold on a minute Silvia! Are you saying I have to kill the woman?"

Silvia Gladman feigned shock and placed her hand to her chest as she spoke.

"I can assure you I have said no such thing nor would I ever suggest it. All I am saying is that this cannot be allowed to continue. Now what you choose to do about the situation, regardless of the damage that it will do to your reputation, is entirely up to you. Here at MI5 we cannot be seen to instruct you but we can give you our opinion into damage limitation."

"I couldn't possibly hurt someone, well at least not

physically. Is there any way you could sort it all out? Please help me out here."
Silvia laughed in a sarcastic way.
"This is your mess and you will have to sort it out. Off the record I do know of someone but I can only give you a number, the rest will be up to you."
Her final words told the man in no uncertain terms what she meant, he also knew that he had Hobson's choice in the matter if he wanted to continue with his career and get out of this mess unscathed. Taking a step forward, he could only shake his head in show of defeat as he snatched a small scrap of paper from Silvia Gladman containing a telephone number. He knew what was expected of him but the thought of what he was required to do, had to do in fact, still weighed heavily on his mind. He had never physically hurt anyone in his life least of all a woman and he didn't know if he would even be able to ask someone else to do it for him. Sighing heavily he finally accepted that if he wanted to hold onto his life as he knew it, he had no choice at all.
Before the man had even left the building Silvia Gladman was removing a mobile from her handbag. It was only used when the conversation had to remain totally confidential and untraceable. Dialling the number she waited for Harry Fuller to answer. Harry didn't know who was calling as the number was withheld and was a little surprised when he heard her voice. Silvia relayed the conversation she had just had and told Harry that

when the man arranged to meet up with him she wanted every word recorded.

"I don't think I have to tell you what he wants doing and any decision you decide upon is entirely up to you."

"So this isn't MI5 sanctioned then?"

"Good god man no! I will warn you of one thing Harry, he's a slippery bastard. He also has far more money than sense so I'm sure you won't lose out in all of this if you play your cards right and take him up on the offer, an offer I'm positive he will make in the next few hours."

Harry Fuller thanked her, though he didn't once mention her name. Taking a seat in his armchair he waited for the call, a call he knew was imminent from a man filled with nothing but desperation.

CHAPTER NINETEEN

After spending the day at home, a home which was almost back to normal due to the hours that had been spent clearing up, Jess was feeling bored. She hadn't arranged a meeting with Lucy until the day after tomorrow and was now at a loss as to how to fill her time. Dressing down in jeans and a sweatshirt she pulled on her coat and decided to pay her mum an unscheduled visit. It was almost four o'clock and as she stepped from the taxi, hoped her father had already left for his early doors pint down at the local pub. Pressing the bell, Jess could soon make out her mother's form as she came down the hallway to answer the door. Not expecting her daughter, Annie Metcalf's face was a picture of joy as she opened up.

"Well bless my soul, this is starting to become a habit darling and what a lovely habit it is."

Jess stepped inside and embraced her mother as she did so.

"It isn't a problem is it mum? You know me turning up unannounced?"

Annie tenderly touched the side of her daughters face and as she did so Jess held her mother tight giving her the warmest embrace she could.

"Never in a million years my darling, now come through to the back and after I put the kettle on you can tell me all about it."

"About what?"
Annie smiled and shook her head.
"Sweetheart never forget you're my baby and there aint nothing you can hide from me. Oh I might not always say anything but it doesn't mean that I don't notice when there's something wrong."
Annie led the way down the hall and through into the back room. When she was sure that her daughter had followed her she went into the kitchen. As Jess waited for her mother to return she stood at the fireplace and stared into the over mantle mirror trying to see whatever it was that her mother had seen. Pulling down the skin under her eyes and after examining her eyeballs she was still at a loss. Jess had to admit that she looked a bit tired, drawn even but there was nothing else she was sure of it. A few minutes later and Annie entered. Placing the mugs of tea onto the table she took a seat and beckoned for her daughter to do the same.
"So then! What's all this about?"
"Mum I really don't know what......"
Annie Metcalf grabbed her daughters hand and squeezed it tightly.
"Don't try and fool me please. Your fathers been doing it all our married life and I don't need you to do the same, now what's up?"
Jess sighed but knew she couldn't hold back, her mother was a wise woman and would know if Jess wasn't being honest.

"I've been having a bit of bother that's all; it's nothing to worry about. Just some leery bastard trying to frighten me but I've got it all under control now."

Annie's brow furrowed and Jess instantly knew that no matter what she said, her mother was still worried.

"You sure?"

"Positive. Now enough about me how are you? Is the old bastard treating you any better?"

"About the same but I mustn't grumble. There's a lot worse off than me."

"You always say that mum and yes there are a lot worse off but they aint you and they aint my mum. Well maybe this will cheer you up a bit. I've got a meeting set up and if it comes off I will have enough money what with my other savings to set us both up in a new life far away from London."

Annie arched her eyebrows but smiled as she did so.

"Really? What is it?"

"Well someone I met a while back, someone I don't see any more, well he knows this Arab who is willing to pay me a lot of money for a few days work. I've got to meet him tomorrow afternoon at the Savoy."

Annie Metcalf again grabbed her daughters hands only this time as she held them Jess could feel her mother shaking. It wasn't through fear but purely down to happiness.

"I had to come and tell you mum, please say you'll come with me?"
Jess expected her mother to make all the excuses under the sun just as she always did, so Annie's next sentence shocked her but also made her whoop for joy at the same time.
"You try bloody stopping me girl!"
In unison the two women began to laugh and cry both at the same time. They spent a few minutes chatting and making plans about their future before Jess decided that she had better make a move. After hugging her mother close she set of on her journey home. It was the first time for a while that she'd felt this happy and as Jess walked along she seemed to have a real spring in her step. After reaching the main road she hailed a taxi and wore a smile on her face for the entire journey but just as the cab was about to turn off from Kensington High Street Jess had a change of heart.
"Actually, can you drop me here please?"
Her happiness had brought about a sudden hunger and right at this moment she felt as though she could eat a horse. Walking into Gems traditional fish and chip shop she ordered a large cod and chips with lashings of salt and vinegar.
"Put a few scraps on if you've got any love and don't bother wrapping them as I'm going to eat them on my way home".
"That's just what I like to do darling mind you it aint the same since they stopped wrapping them in

newspaper but that's progress I suppose."
Jess laughed and after handing over payment began the short walk to her flat. The night was getting chilly and the steam and vinegar aroma wafted up as she hungrily pulled at the crispy batter on the fish. From Kensington High Street Jess turned into Phillimore Gardens. She was really enjoying the food and smiled to herself as she thought back to the many times as a teenager when she had experienced this same pleasure on nights out with Felix. Passing Stafford Terrace and the Essex Villas she realised that the road was almost deserted. Screwing up the paper she looked round for a bin and noticed a man standing on the pavement a couple of hundred yards behind her. He seemed to be staring intently, whether or not she was being paranoid really didn't come into it and when he didn't move Jess instantly felt threatened. Dropping the chip papers onto the pavement she turned and began to run. By the time she reached Phillimore Place she was panting heavily and dinner reappeared down the toilet pan. Jess Metcalf stayed on the bathroom floor for a short while and when she at last managed to haul herself to her feet, knew this all had to stop. Walking into the kitchen she switched on the television as Nicky Brent's face appeared on the screen. Turning up the volume she was just in time to hear the newsreaders report. 'Renowned racehorse trainer, Nicky Brent is missing. Police were informed today by Mr Brent's

stable manager Shamus O'Dowd that the trainer has not been seen for over twenty four hours and had failed to attend a scheduled meeting. When contacted by our news team Mr O'Dowd told our reporter that Mr Brent was always reachable by telephone but for some reason he now wasn't answering any calls. Mr O'Dowd also added that his employer never let anyone down without contacting them in advance and his no show at the yard was totally out of character. A detective working on the case told ITN that it was still too early to speculate but they did have concerns regarding Mr Brent's safety.'

Jess gripped the edge of the worktop and at the same time could feel the colour drain from her face. She didn't have a clue what was going on but a bad feeling was starting to build in the pit of her stomach. She had to see Liam face to face and find out what had gone on. Grabbing her coat Jess ran from the flat. Walking at a fast pace her eyes darted in all directions in case the man from a short while ago was still lurking about. Reaching the High Street she headed to the underground. Jess knew Liam frequented a pub on Holloway Road but not the name as shed never been that interested in his life and where he went. Still she reasoned that he was a known face so he shouldn't be that difficult to track down. It was starting to get dark as Jess emerged from the station and taking a right turn she entered the first pub she came to. The Lord

Palmerston was dark and dingy and the few old men who were in the middle of putting the world to rights, stopped talking mid sentence when Jess walked in. A few seconds looking around told her she definitely wouldn't find Liam here. Moving on to The Lamb and then The Horatia it was a similar story and she was starting to worry that she wouldn't find him. Telephoning wasn't an option at the moment as she wanted to surprise him and not give Liam time to invent a story just to placate her. Jess was now in dire need of a drink and walking into The Coronet she ordered a vodka and coke then took a seat to rest for a while. The pub was owned by Wetherspoon's so she knew she wouldn't find him here but Jess needed a few minutes to regain her composure and think of what to do next. The place was busy and she had to share a table with two men. One was propped up in a wheelchair, the kind that had a neck brace to stop the person from slumping over. Every couple of minutes the man sitting beside her would lean forward and offer up a straw so that the man in the wheelchair could take a sip of his drink. Jess soon learned that Solly Rabin was a carer and that he had looked after the man, who he went on to introduce as Desmond McKeon, for the last ten years. Jess smiled and nodded in Desmond's direction but there was no response and Desmond's eyes appeared glassy as if he was just staring right through her.
"I wouldn't waste your time love."

Jess frowned and Solly could see that she was a compassionate sort and felt sad for his charge. "Don't fret your pretty little head over it love, he don't know any different. He can manage basic skills such as eating, drinking and shitting and believe me he does plenty of the latter but anything else, well it's like the lights are on but no one's at home."

"Has he always been this way?"

"What Desmond? Nah, a few years ago he was as able bodied as you or I. One of the best pick pockets in the area was our Desmond that's until that cunt, pardon my French love, Liam Flanagan got hold of him. The bastard burnt the soles of his feet out with some kind of gas torch. The poor bastard then got hit on the head with something, hence the state he's in today but no one knows exactly what happened. You see people round here don't get involved and never see a fucking thing, the wankers."

Jess could feel her whole body tense at the mention of Liam's name and deep inside she now knew that something terrible must have
happened to Nicky Brent. After finishing up her drink she decided to call it a day and return home. Maybe in the light of things a telephone call would be best after all.

Back in Kensington Jess closed the door to her flat and leant against the cold paintwork. Sighing heavily she wondered just how much Liam would tell her. She wanted it all, wanted every last detail because she was desperate to hear that she'd got things all wrong and that she hadn't been responsible for a man's death. Maybe Liam had just kidnapped Nicky and had him stashed away somewhere, the only trouble was, that after listening to Solly's story she knew it was a distinct possibility that Nicky was dead. Picking up her mobile phone she scrolled down to Liam Flanagan's number and then pressed call. As usual he answered in seconds but Jess wasn't friendly when she spoke.

"Liam I need to see you. I haven't got a clue what's going on but I'd be grateful if you could come round to mine as soon as you can and explain things to me."

Without giving him a chance to reply Jess ended the call.

Fifteen minutes later and Liam Flanagan pressed the intercom. Jess checked the screen and after opening the front door stood waiting in the hall as he emerged from the lift.

"Please tell me this hasn't got anything to do with you?"

"Has what got anything to do with me?"

Suddenly Jess was angry and her eyes bore into Liam in a way that he'd never seen before. Strangely, even after all shed heard earlier she still wasn't frightened of him. Liam knew her too well and that she would see straight through any bullshit he tried to tell her. This wasn't a time for lies, not if he wanted to keep her friendship, so he decided to admit to the bare minimum.

"Look that wanker was full of himself and I got a bit carried away that's all."

"A bit carried away! What exactly did you do to him Liam?"

For a moment Liam Flanagan didn't speak and Jess knew that he was trying to think of what to say. It told her that whatever had gone on was bad but still she remained rooted to the spot, desperate not to hear what she knew deep down he was going to say next.

"Believe me you don't want to hear all the gruesome details; needless to say Brent won't be bothering you again."

"You mean he's dead?"

Liam just nodded his head.

"Oh no, dear god in heaven no! It wasn't him Liam or at least I'm not sure it was him! For fucks sake I only asked you to have a word with him!"

Jess walked from the hall and began to pace up and down in the kitchen. She racked her brains trying to think of a reason not to feel this terrible guilt and she ran her fingers through her hair wildly as she did so. An innocent man had lost his life and shed had a hand in it. For a moment she contemplated telephoning Sharon Russell but then thought better of it. Sharon was a good friend but even she couldn't sort this mess out. Liam stepped forward and tried to take her hands but Jess shrugged him away.

"Don't you dare touch me; you disgust me Liam I never want to see you again. Now get out of my fucking life and my home and don't ever come back do you hear? You bastard!"

Again he stepped forward but the look she gave him told him in no uncertain terms that she meant every word. Liam was a face, a villain like no other but when it came down to Jess Metcalf he was a puppy and her words broke his heart. Liam didn't feel guilty about Brent, it was part of the job and went with the territory so to speak but it did bother him what Jess thought of him. Knowing her well enough he didn't argue and as he turned to leave his shoulders were slumped over in a defeated manner. Although Jess didn't see it, there were tears in his eyes and crying was something Liam definitely hadn't allowed himself to do for many years. Liam Flanagan had jumped into a cab the minute Jess had phoned him and now he would have to walk to the High Street to find a taxi back to Holloway. Turning out of Phillimore Place and after passing Essex Villas, Liam decided to cross over the road and that one small decision would be the worst decision of his life. Halfway across he saw a cars headlights and suddenly the vehicle accelerated. Liam Flanagan, like a rabbit in the glare of a spotlight was rooted to the spot. The car was travelling at over sixty miles and hour when it made contact with him and Liam never stood a chance. His body was thrown upwards and Liam's legs rotated as he did a summersault in the air. His face smashed into the top of the roof but the car didn't stop and as it picked up momentum his body bounced along the roof like a ragdoll. The sound as his flesh and bones hit the metal panels was a clear indication to anyone that he was badly injured. Liam slid down the back of the car's rear windscreen and landed with a thud on the tarmac. Only then did the car screech to a halt. Liam Flanagan's crumpled body was now twitching on the road and somehow in a desperate attempt to survive, he raised himself onto his elbows and mustering every last piece of energy he had lifted his body so that he was now kneeling. The car's engine was still running as a lone figure remained seated behind the wheel, a figure that had no intention of getting out to see what condition his victim was in. Liam heard the car rev up its engine and as he slowly turned his head, saw it spin in the road. The wheels screeched and smoke came from the rubber tyres as the car once more accelerated in his direction. In that split second Liam Flanagan knew that his time on this earth was up. The car hit him full on but this time he didn't bounce and instead went straight underneath. Now unconscious and near to death Liam didn't see the car begin to reverse and the driver manoeuvre the wheels so that they would make contact with Liam's head. The vehicle slightly lifted from the road as it squashed Liam Flanagan's scull. With his task now complete the driver pulled away slowly and disappeared around the corner into the next road. The impact was heard by a Mr and Mrs Selby who resided in the house directly in front of the collision but by the time the elderly couple had made their way outside the car was long gone. Mrs Selby knelt on the floor but she could see that the man was already dead. Out of respect the couple waited until the police came but they weren't able to give much of a statement as they hadn't seen anything. The driver of the patrol car searched Liam's pockets and pulling out a wallet he looked inside. Liam Flanagan was known throughout most of London and realising who the victim was, the policeman rolled his eyes and shook his head in a gesture that said it all. Calling in the accident he informed the emergency services that any attempt at resuscitation would be futile. Liam's injuries were so severe that half of his head was missing and Mrs Selby, after a request by the policeman, went to get a blanket from the house to cover the body. Within minutes sirens and flashing lights were going off in the road but it was an everyday occurrence to people living in London. As Liam's body was removed, the area was cordoned off and signs were put in place asking anyone who had been witness to the accident to come forward, of course no one did.

Oblivious to all that had happened, Jess was

hunched on the floor of her kitchen. She sobbed her heart out at the loss of Nicky Brent, not because she had any feeling for him but purely due to the fact that she felt responsible. In just a few days her life had turned into a nightmare and she didn't have the first idea what she was going to do to get out of it.

CHAPTER TWENTY

Jess didn't sleep a wink as thoughts of Nicky Brent invaded her mind. Finally at six am she couldn't stand it any longer and went into the kitchen. By seven am and after calming her nerves with a coffee she dialled Sharon Russell's number. Her friend was in the middle of getting ready for work and was annoyed at being interrupted. Her tone was curt as she answered and for a moment it took Jess by surprise.

"Hello!"

"Oh hi Sharon, sorry to disturb you but I'm in trouble or at least I think I am. Is there any chance you could pop round and see me?"

Sharon glanced at the bedroom clock and knew she had a spare hour. Late last night she had received a telephone call from the secretary to the Commissioner of the Met asking her to attend an appointment the following day at Scotland Yard. She didn't have a clue what it was concerning but it didn't sound too good. No one was ever summoned to the Yard unless there was a problem and Sharon was worried sick. She'd spent most of the previous night racking her brains trying to work out if she'd said or done anything wrong but nothing came to mind and it was driving her crazy not knowing or being able to prepare herself. Even though she had received a rapid rise through the ranks in the last couple of years, Sharon knew that this wasn't the usual procedure so it had nothing to do with her career advancement. The next few hours were spent in turmoil and her sleep that night had been as nonexistent as Jess's. She didn't need to be at the Yard until ten so there was plenty of time and maybe someone else's problems would take her mind off her forthcoming meeting with the Commissioner.

"Of course I can. I have to be at work by ten but I can call in at yours in an hour or so if that's any good?"

"That would be great and thanks Shaz."

"Don't be daft. Now will you be ok until I get there?"

"Yeah of course I will, see you later then."

With that Jess hung up and Sharon Russell continued to get dressed. Walking into the bathroom Jess switched on the shower and at the same time could feel the first onset of tears, life had been so good up until a couple of weeks ago and she wished with all her heart she could just turn the clock back. At just before eight the bell to Jess's flat rang out and even though it wasn't overly loud, the sound still made her jump. Checking that it was her old friend downstairs, she pressed the entry button. Sharon Russell looked smart and it didn't go unnoticed. It wasn't the case that she didn't always look good but today she appeared to have gone the extra mile and it showed.

"You look very smart."
"Thanks. I've got a meeting with the big Chief today though what it's all about god above only knows."
Jess suddenly felt guilty and knew she would now have to explain every detail to her friend. Deciding not to wait she came straight out with it.
"I think I might know a bit about it."
Sharon Russell furrowed her brow at her friends words and for a second wondered if Jess had been on the sherry.
"You? Don't be daft however could you?"
One look at Jess's face told Sharon in no uncertain terms that her friend meant every word she was saying.
"Let's go into the kitchen, I think you'll need to sit down for this. I'll make us a coffee and then we can talk, I just hope that when I've finished were still friends."
Confused was an understatement, Sharon Russell didn't have a clue what her friend was talking about but then Jess wasn't one to exaggerate so she knew that whatever it was it wouldn't be good. When the coffees were placed on the table and Jess had taken a seat opposite her friend, she finally plucked up the courage to begin.
"This all started quite a while ago."
"What did?"
"Please Sharon just let me get it all off my chest, its difficult enough without you asking questions."

Sharon held up her hand and smiled. She could see that Jess was struggling with whatever it was she wanted to say. Looking up at the wall clock that faced Jess's back she could see it was already eight thirty and time was moving fast. There was still her journey to the Yard to make and with the rush hour commuters it wouldn't be a quick one. Staying silent would be the best policy if her friend was ever to spit out what she had to say.

"When I first moved here I had a small camera installed into the intercom. It was only a security measure but every time someone calls a picture is taken. Every couple of days the pictures are printed out and I hide them away for safekeeping. I know it sounds a bit over the top but believe you me, from time to time over the last few years I've had the displeasure of meeting some unsavoury characters. Anyway, when I got burgled the police came and searched the flat. They said I had to tell them anything I could to help with their inquiries so I handed over the recent photographs. Your picture was among them."

"So that's why I've been called to the Yard!"

"It doesn't end there I'm afraid. There were also photographs of Nicky Brent."

"The missing trainer?"

"There were several of Liam Flanagan as well and it gets worse. I thought Brent was following me, trying to scare me so I asked Liam to have a word with him. Only trouble is I now believe he did a lot more than have a word and oh Sharon I'm at my wits end about all this and I don't know what to do."

Jess began to cry but Sharon didn't get up to comfort her old friend. She was in too much shock herself and was desperately trying to work out how all this would affect her and her career.

"Fuck me! What a mess."

When the tears had stopped the two women sat in silence for several seconds and it was finally Sharon who spoke first.

"Look, let me go to my meeting and find out what's going on and I promise I'll come back later and fill you in."

Sharon's words brought Jess a little relief and after walking her to the door, Jess kissed her dear friend on the cheek and the Policewoman set off for her meeting. When Sharon arrived at the flat she had a long overcoat draped over her arm as shed decided that her best route of travel to the Yard would be via the underground and she didn't want to attract any unwanted attention by showing her uniform. Worried about what was to come, the last thing she needed was someone causing a scene because of what she did for a living. After making her way to the tube station on Kensington High Street, she purchased a ticket and boarded the circle line. The journey took less than fifteen minutes and when she emerged at St James Park turned left onto Broadway. The building that housed Scotland Yard was situated on her left and Sharon could feel the onset of stress in the pit of her stomach. The Commissioners office was located on the top floor and as she entered the lift she suddenly felt nauseous. There was no going back now, not if she valued her career and as she walked along the corridor she rubbed at her palms when she felt them begin to sweat. Met by Arlene Lacy, secretary to the top man for the last five years, Sharon was politely asked to take a seat. Thankfully she was told to go in within a few minutes of her arrival. The Commissioner, Hugo Barrow-Laws was seated behind a large mahogany desk and Sharon was expecting the man to be dismissive in his address. She couldn't have been more off the mark and the Commissioner greeted her with a warm friendly smile, at least to begin with.

"Please take a seat Deputy Chief Inspector and thank you for coming at such short notice. I know it can be a bind but I always find its best to clear these matters up as quickly as possible."

Sharon did as she was asked and even though the man's approach was friendly, it did nothing to help her relax.

"Do you know why I have summoned you here today Inspector?"

Sharon Russell shook her head. "No Sir."

"It seems we have a security problem or at least MI5 do and you are inadvertently involved. The Met are in possession of some photographs of you."

"Yes Sir and I can explain if..."

"Please don't interrupt me Deputy Chief Inspector!" Suddenly the man's tone had turned from friendly to austere and Sharon knew she was well and truly in the shit. God, she'd worked so hard to get where she was and now it looked as though shed be back pounding the beat through no fault of her own. Sharon knew she'd done nothing wrong but no matter how you looked at it, the photographs didn't paint a very pretty picture.

"Inspector, whom you chose to be friends with, is none of my concern. What does concern me is the fact that the inhabitant of the address you frequently visit also entertains a high ranking member of the government not to mention a known IRA supporter. MI5 believe that somehow information has been passed on from within that flat to the IRA which resulted in the assassination of a well known loyalist paramilitary supporter. Now do you know anything about this?"

For a minute Sharon was in shock and didn't know how to answer. She could feel the Commissioner staring at her and knew she had to answer quickly if she was to appear innocent which of course she was.

"No Sir."

"I didn't think so. I have also been informed this morning that only a few hours ago this so called IRA supporter, a man by the name of Liam Flanagan, was killed in a hit and run accident not far from the address. Miss Russell you have an exemplary record and there is no reason for any of this to affect your future within the Metropolitan police force but I would advise you to end all contact with the inhabitant at that address. Of course what you choose to do is entirely up to you and I would like you to see me as an advisor who only has your best interests at heart."

Sharon knew exactly what she was being asked to do. She loved Jess but her whole life had been about the force and she couldn't give it up now, no matter what the cost. Sharon thanked the Commissioner and after assuring him that she would do the right thing for all concerned, she left the Yard and had never been so glad to be out in the fresh air. Remembering her promise to Jess and feeling honour bound to carry out that promise to her friend, at least one last time, Sharon entered the underground and once again made her way over to Phillimore Place. The carriage was heaving with people but Sharon was too deep in thought to look at anyone. She was grateful that there had been no mention of Nicky Brent by the Commissioner but then she supposed in the grand scale of things he was of no interest. The underground journey seemed to take forever even though in reality it was no longer than on her arrival. Sharon's mind was racing, not only with worry but also sadness that her next visit would probably be the last time she would ever see her friend.

Jess had been on tender hooks for the last couple of hours. Trying to occupy herself shed cleaned out the kitchen cupboards, scrubbed the bathroom and was in the middle of vigorously polishing the hall mirror when the bell rang. Spying her friends face in the monitor she smiled and pressed the entry. As soon as she saw Sharon's expression she knew there was a problem.

"Hi babe! I'll make us both a coffee and you can tell me all about it."

Sharon quickly walked into the kitchen ahead of Jess.

"Thanks but no coffee for me if you don't mind. I can't stop long; in all honesty this will be my last visit. Jess you mean the world to me you know that and that's why I've come back today but from now on, well I won't be coming here again."

"Why? Oh Shaz whatever's happened? Have I done something to offend you?"

Jess was stunned she hadn't expected this in a million years. The two went way back and she had thought that they would be friends for life. Everything was falling apart and Jess didn't have a clue what she had done to deserve it. Taking a seat she waited for her friend, or at least up until now that's what she had thought Sharon was, to continue.

"Jess you really have got yourself into a very deep hole and I can't, as much as it hurts me babe, I can't be seen to associate with you anymore. Its only

because of our friendship and the promise I made to you that I've come back here at all. You've been seeing someone from the government haven't you?"
"Yes a politician named Peter Lenson."
"He's not a politician and his names not Lenson though he is high up and I do mean very high up in the government. You've also been seeing Liam Flanagan?"
"Well yes you know I have. None of that's a secret, well at least not as far as I'm concerned. Liam's been a client of mine for a long time now but I can't see what any of that has to do....."
"Stop Jess, just stop alright! Whether you know it or not Liam Flanagan has ties to the IRA and somehow information has been passed over to Ireland. It could only have come from one person and one place, this flat!"
"Oh no! Sharon I swear I had nothing to do with it. I caught him looking in a brief case a while back but I was only out of the room for a short time so he couldn't have seen that much. You
wait till I see Liam; he's going to get a piece of my mind I can tell you."
"That won't happen."
"Why, what do you mean?"
Sharon Russell walked over to her friend and tenderly touched her shoulder.
"I'm sorry but Liam Flanagan was involved in a hit and run last night, he didn't survive."
From out of nowhere Jess began to wail. She had

always denied any feelings for the man, god he was old enough to be her father but hearing the news that he was dead suddenly felt as if she'd been hit by a sledge hammer. In times of need he had always been her rock and Jess didn't know what she would do without him. Suddenly she realised that if she hadn't made him leave then he would still be alive.

"Oh god! This is all my fault."

"Don't be so stupid, how can it be?"

"Because Liam was here last night and we had an argument. I told him to go and that I never wanted to see him again. I didn't really mean it, I was just so angry with him and now he's dead and it's all because of me."

The sound of deep racking sobs tore at Sharon's heart strings and she took her friend into her arms and allowed Jess to cry. When she felt that the crying was at last beginning to subside, Sharon lifted up her friends face and wiped away the tears.

"Now can you understand why I have to cut off all ties with you?"

Jess Metcalf could only nod her head as a fresh set of tears rolled down her cheeks. Sharon Russell picked up her coat and as she headed in the direction of the door she stopped and turned to face her friend one last time.

"My darling I couldn't help you out of this mess even if I wanted to but I can offer you one piece of advice. Now whether you decide to take it is entirely up to you but I'm going to give it regardless. Get out of London as quickly as possible."

With those parting words Sharon Russell walked out of the flat and out of Jess Metcalf's life. For the remainder of the day Jess busied herself with cleaning and at the same time attempted to work out what to do with her life. Liam's death had hit her far harder than she would ever have thought possible and she desperately tried to put it to the back of her mind. That was easier said than done but thankfully, even though it took her hours, Jess finally came up with a plan.

CHAPTER TWENTY ONE

After all the upset of the previous day, Jess hadn't expected to get any sleep but putting her life in order, mentally at least, she had surprisingly achieved a good night. When her alarm burst into life at seven thirty she woke feeling relaxed, fresh and ready to take on the world. Liam's death still weighed heavily but the meeting with her hopefully newest client which had been arranged for eleven am was upmost in her thoughts. Unlike her normal practice, she had been asked to meet him at a hotel. If it wasn't for his status Jess would have flatly refused but it wasn't everyday that a Sheik requested your company. Savouring her coffee, Jess again thought about all that had happened. She didn't want to keep thinking about it but somehow her mind seemed to be doing its own thing and wouldn't let her move on. Vigorously shaking her head she decided that even after everything she was still looking forward to the meeting. Aware of what kind of money these people had she knew that this would, if things went well, be her and her mother's ticket out of London and a life she was slowly starting to hate. Whatever happened she was going to leave London and take Annie with her. Her mum definitely needed something or someone to give her back the life that had been stolen by her husband. Jess Metcalf wasn't poor by any standards, quite the opposite in fact but to continue living in the style to which she had become accustomed she needed a large bank balance. Jess wanted to give her mother everything her heart desired and that would cost but if luck was on her side today might just provide that. The flat on Phillimore Place was almost paid for and with London prices so high she knew when it was eventually sold she would reap a handsome profit. Jess had always fancied a little white villa on one of the Greek islands and she knew that Annie would absolutely adore it as the furthest she had ever travelled was Clacton and that was years ago. Even then it had only been a day trip, back when Jess's father had still been a reasonable man. Jess took her time dressing and removing three suits from the wardrobe chose the fitted black Channel. Aware that she had to appear very respectable she had also opted for the one with the longest hemline. Topping off the outfit with high court shoes and a matching clutch bag she stood back to admire herself in the mirror. As she combed her hair she thought back to the telephone call that had happened just five days ago regarding the Sheik. To begin with the man's accent had been hard to understand but after taking things slowly she finally understood that it wasn't a pervert on the other end but a foreign employee who was working hard to learn the English language. There were no real details given, those she would learn today and she prayed that it would be a success and that the man, whoever he was, would ask for her services. Her scheduled meeting with Lucy Urquhart wasn't until two so with plenty of time Jess set off on her journey. At the top of the road she hailed a cab and when it pulled up outside The Savoy Hotel Jess looked up at the tall building. In all her years working in the trade as she liked to call it, she had never been inside this particular establishment. The doorman opened up the taxis door and Jess Metcalf stepped out into the glorious sunshine. She had taught herself to walk, talk and act the part of a sophisticated lady and she was now receiving admiring glances. Reaching the reception desk Jess informed the young woman on duty that she had a business meeting with Sheik Mohamed Halabi. Within a few minutes she was approached by the sheiks aide.

"Miss Metcalf?"

Jess offered her hand and the man accepted it graciously. It was obvious that he knew why she was here but not once did he show her anything but the utmost courtesy and respect.

"If you would like to follow me, my employer is waiting for you upstairs."

The ride up to the penthouse suite was taken in silence which did nothing to put her at ease. Jess was unusually nervous and it wasn't anything to do with her luxurious surroundings or the person she was about to meet. If she was going to put her plan

into action then Jess needed this client like never before. She was shown into a large opulent sitting room and a minute or two later Mohamed Halabi emerged from the bedroom. The sexual attraction was instant on both sides and Jess immediately relaxed. After tea and polite conversation the so called business meeting finally got under way.
"So Miss Metcalf."
"Please call me Jess."
The Arab smiled to reveal the most brilliant set of white teeth Jess had ever seen. It never ceased to amaze her just what money could buy and this man had it in barrel loads. The Sheik explained that he was in London for ten days and for the next week would like to hire her services. Jess would be required to stay in the suite and be available twenty four hours a day. She would not be allowed to leave or speak to another living soul during her stay but in return she would be paid the sum of one hundred
thousand pounds for her services and discretion. Jess had mentally prepared herself to barter but when the amount was mentioned, didn't feel she could. With the money she already had, the sale of her flat and now this, well it would be enough to set her and her mother up for life.
"I would like to explain my circumstances to you Jess."
"That really won't be necessary."
"Maybe not but I am a man of honour, though some

in my country would see what I am doing as a disgrace. I have four wives Jess, all of whom I love dearly but all of my marriages were arranged from childhood. My wives are excellent mothers and tend to my every need in all but the bedroom department. Women are viewed as objects in my country, vessels to carry heirs. They have a duty to carry out and that is all. I have tried over the years to feel close and be intimate with them but to no avail. I need to feel that closeness with a woman and that is why I have approached you. I do not see it as being unfaithful nor do I look upon you with any less respect than that which I have for my wives."

Jess politely held up her hand to stop him, today of all days she really didn't need to hear this.

"Please Mohamed you really don't need to explain. This is purely a financial arrangement and if I took offence that easily, then I would be in the wrong business. Your terms are very agreeable so can we just leave it at that?"

Mohamed Halabi smiled but at the same time he saw a coldness in the woman, almost as if she was detached from any emotional feeling. He wondered if all western women were like this or if it was just down to the line of work that Jess had chosen. All the same he agreed with her and after shaking on the deal Jess arranged to start work the following day. As she travelled back down in the lift she recalled the conversation and realised that she must have come over as quite hard in her manner which wasn't the case but Jess Metcalf didn't have time nor want to hear about another man's sorry tale. Exiting the hotel she set off for Covent Garden to see Lucy Urquhart.

By the time she reached Patisserie Valerie it had begun to rain and the place was heaving with people all trying to get out of the wet. Straining her neck, she thought, no actually hoped for a moment that Lucy hadn't turned up but suddenly she saw the mop of unruly hair that belonged to her friend. Lucy was tucked away in the back corner and as usual was scribbling away on a piece of paper. As Jess took her seat she waved in the direction of the waitress and due to the two women's regularity, it was a signal to bring over a coffee.

"You look busy sweetheart."

Lucy glanced up and smiled.

"Just notes, I love to people watch and there are so many colourful characters to describe."

Lucy stopped writing for a few seconds and looked Jess up and down.

"You look nice, not that you don't usually but I must say today you're exceptionally smart. That didn't sound at all right, you always look really lovely."

Jess laughed as her friend tried to back pedal for fear that what she'd just said might offend.

"I went to meet a new client."

"Really! Who? Oh sorry, I know I can be a nosey cow at times but your life is so interesting."

"You haven't got a clue sweetheart. It was an Arab if you must know so I had to appear very respectable. Lucy we need to have a talk love."
"Well of course we do that's why we're here isn't it?"
The waitress placed the coffee onto the table but didn't hang about. Normally she would spend a few minutes making small talk with Jess but today she was run off her feet and Jess was grateful for that fact.
"No I mean I have something to tell you. I'm in a lot of trouble and after the next few days, which will be spent with the Arab, well I won't be around again as I'm leaving London."
Lucy immediately went into panic mode and her eyes were pleading as she spoke.
"Won't be around again! But what about me, what about all my research. Jess you told me you would help me and I haven't got nearly enough. Oh please don't go I'm sure whatever it is you can sort it out, can I do anything to help?"
For a split second an image of Liam appeared in Jess's mind and she momentarily wanted to cry. Taking in a deep lungful or air she stopped herself and smiled.
"No darling you can't but thanks for asking all the same. Look let's just make the most of today shall we?"
It wasn't turning out to be as simple as she had hoped. Her friend wouldn't be brushed aside as easily as Jess had thought and seconds later the

barrage of questions began but they weren't questions regarding research.

"I don't want to; I want to know why you are leaving. Is it the trainer, is he frightening you again because if it is you need to go to the....."

Jess grabbed Lucy by the arm and at the same time shook her head in despair at the girl.

"No it isn't the trainer. Look love, I can't discuss it and it's not because I don't want to. I think that anyone I confide in could end up being in danger and that's not something I want on my conscience. I have to leave London Lucy, I don't have a choice. There is something you can do for me though."

Jess rifled through her bag and retrieved a small black notebook. Tearing a page from the back she handed it to Lucy.

"What's this?"

"You know I've been scared lately, that I thought someone was following me?"

"Yes, the trainer."

"Well I don't know if it was him, actually no, I'm sure it wasn't but I was being stalked or followed by someone and I need to get away as soon as possible. This is the phone number of who I now think it might be. While I'm with the Arab I will phone you every day, in fact Ill phone you every day until I move just so that you know I'm safe. If you don't hear from me, well I want you to take that piece of paper to the police and tell them all that I've told you."

Lucy now looked confused, she really didn't have a clue what was going on.
"But you haven't really told me anything Jess?"
"Sweetheart, believe me when I say that I've told you enough, enough to keep you safe at least."
Jess knew that to remain in the coffee shop any longer would be a mistake. Lucy was like a dog with a bone and would never leave things alone. Jess could see that there would be no research done so it would all be a waste of her time.
"Now I really need to get going so take care of yourself and maybe you'll send me a copy of that book one day. When I get settled I'll let you know where I am."
In reality that was the last thing Jess had planned. Once she'd earned her money from the Arab she just wanted to disappear, vanish from the face of the earth if that was what it would take to feel safe again. Bending down she placed a kiss on Lucy Urquhart's head and with a warm smile walked from the cafe. Lucy sat in stunned silence, when she'd left home today this was the last thing she imagined would happen. Focusing on the torn page Lucy scanned the number but it meant nothing to her so folding it in half she slipped it into her purse. Exiting the cafe she was at least grateful that the rain had subsided but it did nothing to lighten her mood. Deciding not to go straight home Lucy spent a while walking the streets of Covent Garden and Soho. Normally she loved the hustle and bustle of

China Town but today it seemed overcrowded, noisy and just downright sad. Trying to understand what Jess had been talking about she went over it all a dozen times in her head but it still didn't make any sense. True there had been a couple of times when shed known that the woman had something on her mind and was worried but Jess had now told her that she didn't think it was the trainer. Whoever or whatever the problem was it had never seemed so bad that it would make her up and leave her home. Pulling her coat tightly around her she felt lost and realised that sometimes London could seem like the loneliest place on earth. Suddenly she wanted to get away from here and back to the safety and warmth of Manor Lodge. By the time Lucy pushed her key into the lock it was six forty five and her father's car pulled up just as she opened the door. From the expression on her face George Urquhart could see that there was something bothering his daughter but then there was always something bothering Lucy. She tried to take the weight of the world on her shoulders and fight every cause that upset her. George wondered to himself if she would ever learn to just live her own life and stop fretting so much about other people. Placing his hat and coat on the rack he made his way into the study only to find his daughter sitting behind his desk staring out of the window.
"Penny for them?"
"Oh I suppose it's nothing really Daddy. It's just

that I've lost my source of research for the book"
George walked over to Lucy and placed his hand on her shoulder.
"Never mind darling. I'm sure it won't be that difficult to find someone else to help you."
Lucy now felt angry as if her father wasn't taking her seriously and was almost mocking her.
Roughly she pushed his hand from her shoulder as she spoke.
"What a stupid remark, of course it will!"
Her curt tone shocked George. Oh his daughter could be as mad as hell sometimes but she never spoke to him in a sharp way no matter what the problem. Lucy saw the hurt on her father's face but for once she didn't apologise, he had to learn that she was a grown up now and with that came adult problems that you couldn't just brush over.
"Don't be like that with me Lucy; I'm only concerned about you. Now if you'd like to explain to me why you've lost this so called source, maybe I can be of help?"
"I doubt that very much!"
Again her remarks were cutting and George Urquhart didn't like it.
"I really don't know what's got into you today Lucy but I didn't raise you to be so rude. Now please have the common courtesy to speak to me properly and in a civil manner."
Lucy Urquhart sighed heavily but deep down it wasn't aimed towards her father but purely out of

frustration at circumstances that were out of her control.

"The woman's in some kind of trouble and she's leaving London. Well not before she's spent a week with some Arab but after that she's going. Things were working out and she made a promise to help me, well not actually a promise but you know what I mean."

Lucy knew she was betraying Jess by revealing her business and she suddenly felt guilty. Anger had engulfed her, she was lashing out and Jess was the target, a target that definitely didn't deserve it. Now she wished she could take back what she'd said.

"Sometimes my darling you just have to accept things and move on."

Studying her father for a moment she realised he wasn't that interested and probably hadn't really heard or understood a word shed said. Frustration engulfed her, no one seemed to understand the impact this was all having on her. George Urquhart had now opened up the times and was now trying to answer the one crossword question that he hadn't been able to solve and which had annoyed him all day. Lucy knew she was wasting her breath and her father's dismissal was really starting to get under her skin.

"I'm going up to my room; I'll see you at dinner."

"That's a good idea Darling and don't worry, I'm sure everything will sort itself......"

Lucy didn't hear the last words her father said as she slammed the study door on her way out.

CHAPTER TWENTY TWO

Just as Jess was in the middle of packing a case for the week ahead her mobile began to ring. Looking through her most expensive and sexiest underwear she was having difficulty deciding which to include, so for a moment she gave up and answered the call.
"Hi Jess its Felix. I wondered if you fancied going for a coffee sometime later today."
"Well hello there stranger, I thought you'd disappeared off the face of the earth?"
"No just working hard, anyway how about that coffee?"
"I'd love to Felix but I'm now on my way out. I have to go away to work for a week but I'll be back next Tuesday night. Why don't you pop round then and we can get a takeaway and have a nice long chat?"
Felix Abbott could feel his mouth go dry. He hated her seeing other men but knew better than to say anything. After their last meeting when he'd worn his heart on his sleeve their friendship had become a bit strained to say the least. Jess asking him round for a meal was a sign that the ice was thawing and he didn't want to go and upset the applecart again.
"Ok what time?"
"Well I should be home around five, so shall we say seven?"
Felix told her that would be great and they both then ended the call. Every word of the conversation

was being transmitted via the device in Jess's mobile phone to Harry Fuller in the vacant building across the road. He decided to follow Jess and see where she was going but as far as Harry was concerned he now had one weeks grace before he had to fulfil his contract. As Jess finished her packing she had time for a quick coffee before she left. Sitting at the kitchen table she thought back to the conversation with Felix and smiled. He was a good friend and after the last couple of days when the few friends she had seemed to be disappearing from her life like rats on a sinking ship, she was glad that he was still onboard. Her mind then wandered to thoughts of Liam Flanagan but she wouldn't allow herself to get upset and she wiped a solitary tear from her cheek. Sniffing loudly Jess went back into the bedroom and selected several pieces of underwear and placed them into her trolley case. After checking her makeup in the mirror and satisfied that her mascara hadn't run, she grabbed her case and set off for The Savoy Hotel. That evening Mohamed went to great lengths to make Jess feel comfortable, the finest wine and an intimate dinner had been arranged in the suite just as if it was a proper date. It was something that hadn't happened for a long time and Jess found she was really enjoying herself. Mornings started with the most sumptuous breakfast followed by a long soak in the bath and at ten o'clock a personal masseuse would arrive to give her a complete body massage. Evenings were spent with Mohamed and after dinner they would sit and talk about anything and everything. The Arab was not only drop dead handsome he seemed to have a way about him, he was able to make Jess fell as though she was the most important woman in the world. When it came down to sex it was like a fairytale, he was tender and attentive and Jess now knew what real lovemaking felt like. Mohamed had no inhibitions as he'd been instructed in the art of sex from a very young age and knew exactly what a woman wanted and how to please her. Sometimes it would be Jess who took charge and he would just lie back and enjoy every part of her. When they kissed it was pure passion, more passion than Jess had never experienced with a man before. Early on in her career she had set herself a rule to never allow herself to get attached to a client especially if she was attracted to them. Until now she had followed that rule to the letter but there was something different about Mohamed. Jess didn't know if it was because she was feeling vulnerable or just down to the fact that after all these years she had finally found someone she truly wanted to be with. Whatever the reason, Jess Metcalf couldn't help herself and knew that she was falling in love. Most evenings they would make love two or three times and each time the passion was as intense as the first. It was ironic that when she had finally met the man of her dreams nothing could ever come of it and Jess now had an inkling of how some of her clients must feel. In the daylight hours she was left to her own devices but wasn't allowed to leave the penthouse. It didn't worry Jess as it allowed her to catch up on all her paperwork, make plans and surf the net on her laptop looking for places to buy in Greece. As the week drew to a close she was sad at the thought of not seeing Mohamed again but she was also excited at the prospect of leaving London and starting out fresh with Annie. Even though she had been instructed not to have any contact with the outside world, Jess still phoned Lucy everyday just to check in and let her know that she was safe. The conversations were short and to the point but at least she had contact with someone. The day before her contract with Mohamed Halabi was due to end; Jess woke and made her way through to the sitting room. A brown envelope lay on the coffee table containing a short note which had obviously been written by the man's aide. It explained that Mr Halabi had been called away unexpectedly and that her services would no longer be required. The aide thanked Jess and said that the Sheik would very much like to see her again on his next visit to England. Jess screwed the paper up and threw it into the bin. What really interested her was the small leather case that sat beside the letter and whether she had been deducted a day's pay. Opening it up and after fifteen minutes of counting, Jess knew that she needn't have worried as the case contained two thousand brand new crisp fifty pound notes. She felt like throwing it in the air in celebration but then changed her mind at the thought of having to pick it all up. After quickly showering, Jess hastily packed and was in the back of a taxi and heading home within the hour. Back in the flat and feeling the need to relax she changed into jeans and a t-shirt. The mail had piled up while shed been gone and it took quite a while to open everything. Most of the post was junk but one letter in a quality envelope looked interesting and she placed it in the letter rack to read later. After unpacking and tidying the flat she popped to the shop around four to collect a few groceries. Fleetingly she contemplated calling Felix and bringing their dinner date forward by a day but then decided against it. He would only bombard her with questions and she wasn't really in the mood today. A bottle of wine and a nice quiet night in would do her just fine.

By ten o'clock the wine and food had been consumed and Jess felt tired. She decided on an early night as she had a lot to do the following day and going to see her mother was top of the list. Sleep came easily and the next morning Jess was enjoying a lay in when she was suddenly woken by a strange tapping sound. At first she ignored it and after checking the bedside clock and seeing that it was only eight thirty she turned over and tried to go back to sleep but the tapping continued. Climbing out of bed she walked through to the front room and then into the kitchen. The curtains were closed and the only light from the window came via a small gap in the centre of the material. Fear began to build and her body suddenly felt cold but when she couldn't see anything she scolded herself for being so silly. As she padded along the hallway desperate to climb back into her nice warm bed she heard the tapping begin again as she passed the dungeon. Pushing open the door she walked inside and as the door closed shut behind her Jess spun round.

"Who the hell are you and how did you get into my home? Now get out before I call the police!"

Harry Fuller grinned.

"I'm here on business and not the sort of business that usually takes place in this room."

"I don't care what business you're on, now what the fuck do you want?"

"To shut you up, you see you've turned into what's called a liability. I'm afraid you know too much."

Jess went to grab the handle of the door but was stopped when the man clasped her wrist and dragged her into the middle of the room. No coward by any means, Jess Metcalf lashed out with her hands as she desperately fought for release. The glint of a knife stopped her dead in her tracks and looking into his face she saw a menacing look that spoke volumes.

"I have cash, lots of cash if that's what you're after?"

"Money! You really think this is about money?

The person I'm working for has more than he could ever spend you stupid bitch!"
Now realising that he hadn't come to rob her Jess really started to get scared.
With the tip of the knife Harry pointed over to the cross. Jess walked backwards, she didn't dare drop her gaze from his for fear that he might plunge the blade straight into her stomach. When she could feel the wood of the cross pressing into her spine she again spoke though a tremble could now be heard in her voice.
"Now what?"
"Why, you are going to get onto it of course!"
"No I'm fucking not!"
Harry Fuller swiftly pressed the blade against Jess's neck and without any further argument she placed her wrist onto the cross and he secured the shackle. Confident with the knowledge that she couldn't go anywhere he then shackled her other wrist and then her feet. Walking over to where Jess kept all of her accessories he selected a leather strap that had a rubber ball in the centre. As he made his way back over to the cross he could see that Jess's eyes were wide open with terror. This was Jess's worst nightmare as ever since childhood shed had a fear of choking and the thought of her mouth being covered made her go into panic mode.
"Please no! Whatever you want me to do I'll do but please don't cover my mouth."
He ignored her words as he placed the device into

her mouth just as she tried to scream. Jess Metcalf was instantly silenced and her assailant smiled with pleasure as he secured the strap behind her head. Now he would be able to do exactly as he liked without any verbal interference. Here for only one reason, to silence her for good, he was beginning to get excited. He hadn't imagined this would happen but now that it had he saw it as an added bonus. Harry laid the knife on the floor and removed a syringe and small medical vial from his coat pocket. Puncturing the foil cap he used the syringe to siphon out the Diacetylmorphine otherwise known as clinical Heroin. Holding it up to the light he flicked the top as he pressed the plunger to release any air that had been trapped. As Harry held it in front of Jess's face her eyes were silently pleading with him. Beads of sweat stood out on her forehead and she violently struggled to free herself from the shackles but it was
useless.
"Now if you keep fighting it will make things difficult for me and I might add, very painful for you."
Harry gripped Jess's right arm and slapped it hard in the hope of raising her veins.
"Now please don't fret, this won't take long and then you'll have a nice long sleep."
Harry slowly brought the syringe towards Jess's arm and she once again began to violently struggle from side to side. It was ironic but her cross, the

beautiful cross that had given so many people pleasure and brought her so much wealth was now being used to ensure her demise. As the needle pierced her skin Jess whimpered from behind the gag and tears formed in her eyes. The liquid filled her veins and in seconds her eyelids became heavy and she was overcome with drowsiness. Jess had fallen unconscious but Harry hadn't given her quite enough to kill her. Releasing the shackles on her feet and then wrists he lifted Jess's body from the cross and placed it over his shoulder. Her dead weight was heavy as he walked slowly along the hall and into the bedroom. Harry laid her gently onto the bed being careful not to be heavy handed as he didn't want to bruise her skin. It had to look like an overdose or there would be all sorts of questions asked and this case had been dirty and messy enough already. After removing the gag, Harry was happy that everything was as it should be and when he'd arranged her body on the bed he couldn't help but feel desire start to fill his body. She really was a looker and Harry couldn't control himself as he raised her top and exposed her breasts. He gasped at how perfect they were and slowly ran his hands over her skin. Bending onto the bed he placed his mouth over her nipple and gently sucked. Pushing his hand down her pyjama bottoms he pushed his fingers inside and was aroused even more. Something inside his head clicked and he stood up. This was not how he conducted himself and momentarily he felt shame at allowing himself to get carried away. Walking into the kitchen Harry removed a glass from the cabinet and a bottle of whisky from the holdall that he'd brought with him. Pouring a liberal measure into the glass he placed a small amount of the liquid into Jess's open mouth and then stood the bottle onto the bedside table. For the whole time Harry had worn latex gloves so as not to leave any evidence and his hands inside were starting to sweat but he knew better than to take them off. Once more fishing inside his pocket, he removed the empty syringe and placed it back into Jess's arm. Straightening her clothing he stood back to admire his handwork and thought that he would be sad not come here again. Over the last three weeks it had felt like he had come to know the woman, if only from a distance. Satisfied that he'd succeeded in doing exactly as he'd been instructed by MI5 or at least on Silvia Gladman's recommendation, Harry was about to finish what he had started when the intercom suddenly burst into life. For a moment he panicked as it had never been his intention to leave Jess as she was, he had in fact planned to suffocate her. As with so many overdoses the user will often struggle for breath so it wouldn't appear to be anything out of the ordinary and by suffocating her he would be able to make sure she was dead. Now his plans were in tatters as to stay around would leave him vulnerable to capture and that was something Harry Fuller wouldn't let happen. Walking into the hall he peered into the monitor and saw Felix and Lucy standing outside the street door. After the bell rang again Harry Fuller noticed Felix remove a key from his pocket and place it into the door lock. He was now in trouble and needed to get out fast. Frantically he ran from room to room to make sure he hadn't left any evidence. He couldn't see anything obvious but there was no time left to look further and switching off the lights, Harry let himself out of the apartment. Putting on his trademark trilby hat and after pulling the collar of his overcoat up high around his neck, he knew it would be impossible for anyone to get a good look at his face. Choosing the stairs he was just about to enter the foyer when he heard voices talking as they waited for the lift. For a few seconds he held back in the stairwell until the two people were safely inside the lift and had begun there ascent. Not until he reached the High Street did Jess's assailant remove his latex gloves. After screwing them into a ball Harry threw them into one of the many litter bins that lined the street. Things hadn't gone to plan and it troubled Harry Fuller enormously. Knowing he would have to report all that had occurred to Silvia Gladman he headed towards Millbank. One way or another, this mess had to be sorted out but just how he didn't quite know at this precise moment. He had kidded himself earlier about retiring and now knew it would never happen. This sort of operation was in his blood and he was sure that he'd die doing it. As for Jess Metcalf, well if the drugs hadn't already killed her then she would keep for another day. He wanted the fifty grand that had been promised to him but that wouldn't materialise until the woman was dead and buried.

CHAPTER TWENTY THREE
(2 Hours earlier that day)

Lucy had felt lost for the past week. It wasn't that she saw Jess everyday but with her new friend being off of the scene she couldn't seem to muster up any real interest or enthusiasm in anything. Norma had tidied up the study four days ago and as yet Lucy hadn't even ventured in there let alone created a mess. All she seemed to do was wait around all day for Jess to make her daily call. Once Lucy knew that Jess was safe, then and only then could she relax, except the scenario would begin all over again the following day. When Tuesday had at last arrived Lucy was grateful that tonight Jess would be back in her flat and she hoped to be able to talk her out of leaving London. After breakfast she sat in the kitchen watching Norma Sanderson prepare lunch and seemed to be forever glancing at the wall clock and it didn't go unnoticed.
"Whatever's the matter Miss Lucy? You're as jumpy as a cat on hot coals!"
"Sorry Norma, I'm waiting for someone to ring me. Actually it probably won't be until later but oh I don't know, for some strange reason I've suddenly got a bad feeling. I didn't hear from her yesterday but I put it down to the fact that she was probably busy. I just wish she would hurry up and call and put my mind at rest."

"People do have lives of their own you know. Maybe this person can't get to a telephone or something?"
"No it's not that, you don't understand Norma she's...."
Lucy stopped herself from going further when she realised she was about to reveal Jess's private affairs again. Standing up she smiled at the housekeeper and walked from the kitchen.
"Now where are you off to?"
Lucy was already halfway up the back stairs and didn't answer. In the privacy of her room she paced the floor but when her bedside clock showed nine thirty, she did the one thing Jess had asked her not to do. Scanning her list of contacts she pressed connect when Jess's number came into view. Her friends mobile rang six times and then went to voicemail. Lucy Urquhart tried again and the exact same thing happened. Maybe it was a woman's intuition, she wasn't sure but she had a strange feeling that something was wrong. Phoning over and over again Lucy must have called a dozen times and left a message on every occasion but Jess never got back to her. Running down the stairs she almost bumped into Norma as she emerged from the downstairs kitchen.
"And now where are you off to? Will you be back for lunch or not?"
Again Lucy didn't answer and grabbing her coat she ran from the house and hailed the first taxi that

came into view. Jess hadn't told her where she was meeting the Arab so Lucy only had one option; she asked the cabbie to take her over to Phillimore Place in Kensington. Felix Abbott had set off for work early but when the job had been delayed because of a shortage of materials, he had returned and parked his van on the side of the street. He looked towards the street door of Jess's flat and knowing that she wasn't due home until later, toyed with the idea of letting himself inside. It was something he'd done many times before, often when Jess was out he would go in and just walk from room to room and to a stranger it would have seemed perverted but it wasn't anything like that. It was just that he liked to smell her perfume or hold her clothes next to his skin. Felix adored Jess Metcalf, worshiped the ground she walked on in fact and he knew this was the closest he could or would ever get to her. About to get out of his van he stopped when he noticed a young woman approach the main door of the building. Lucy Urquhart rang the bell several times and kept glancing up at Jess's windows. Deciding to find out just who she was and what she wanted Felix locked the van and walked over.

"Excuse me Miss, can I help you?"

For a moment Lucy was on her guard. She didn't know the man and was wondering why he was asking to help her but with Felix's next sentence she instantly relaxed.

"It is Jess you're looking for?"

"Yes but who are you?"

"I'm a friend of hers. Felix Abbott pleased to make your acquaintance."

Felix held out his hand and the two smiled at each other as they shook.

"She's mentioned you many times Mr Abbott and I'm Lucy, Lucy Urquhart."

Felix didn't recognise the name and he was sure Jess hadn't ever spoken to him about the woman but as far as he was concerned it didn't make any difference as she obviously wanted Jess for something.

"I'm afraid she's away for a few days but she'll be back later tonight if you'd like me to give her a message?"

"That's just it, I know she's away but she's been phoning me every day to let me know she's safe. I haven't heard a thing since the day before yesterday and I'm starting to get worried, what with all the problems she's been having. I take it you know she's been followed a couple of times?"

Neither of them was aware that Jess had returned a day early and Felix did think the young woman was being overly cautious. Still when he thought back to the night that Jess had ran home and was scared out of her wits when he touched her shoulder and then there was the burglary, suddenly it did make him feel uneasy.

"Well she did mention it but I'm sure there's nothing to worry about and in all honesty it is still early.

I know Jess and she wouldn't normally be up until now let alone be making phone calls. Wherever she is I'm sure she's fine and......"

Lucy cut Felix off mid sentence and she once again glanced up at the windows.

"If she's been gone almost a week then why are all the lights on or do you thing she left them on for a reason?"

Felix followed the woman's gaze and then swallowed hard. He'd been busy last night and hadn't parked up until late. Knowing that Jess was away he had turned straight in but there were definitely no lights on then and he couldn't recall seeing them on early this morning when he'd left for work.

"That's odd I think we need to check things out just to be on the safe side. Were probably worrying over nothing but I do have a spare set of keys for emergencies so we can at least have a look."

Felix opened the street door and was about to invite Lucy to join him but she was already standing close behind. The two made their way to Jess's flat and as Felix opened the front door he suddenly had a bad feeling. For some strange reason he didn't want to go inside but knew that he had to as telling the young woman that he was scared would make him look stupid.

"I'll check the front room and kitchen and you do the bedroom and bathroom."

"Ok but have you noticed something?"

"What's that?"
"The lights are off now."
With a look that told Lucy he didn't believe her Felix stared into the front room.
"Bloody hell they are as well, something's definitely not right here."
Lucy nodded her head and doing as shed been asked briskly walked along the hallway. Deciding to have a quick look in the dungeon she popped her head around the door but there was no one there and no sign of anything wrong. Checking the bathroom and finding it empty she was about to continue down the hall when she stopped dead in her tracks. The faintest groan was coming from behind the closed bedroom door. It was almost inaudible but Lucy was sure that she had heard something. Slowly turning the handle she pushed open the door and the sight that greeted her on the other side made her instantly scream. Rooted to the spot Lucy could only look on in horror when she saw her friend lying motionless on the bed. It wouldn't normally appear strange especially if Jess was still asleep but Lucy could see that wasn't the case. Jess's chin rested on her chest and there appeared to be some kind of white foam around her mouth. If Jess had any strength left in her it wasn't enough to raise her head though she was conscious of someone being in the room. Hearing Lucy scream Felix flew out of the kitchen and ran along the hallway. Pushing Lucy aside he ran over to Jess

and gently cradled her in his arms.

"Babe? Honey please speak to me, oh god!"

Felix now heard her groan and spinning round told Lucy, who stood motionless in shock, to call for an ambulance. At first glance he had thought she was dead and then the noise she emitted had made him jump. As quickly but as gently as he could Felix removed the syringe from her arm.

"Ok sweetheart I'm here now. The ambulance won't be long and then we'll get you to the hospital."

"Is she going to die?"

"I don't know but it doesn't look good!"

Felix could see that she was in a bad way but he had to say something, had to at least try and comfort Jess. Gently he pushed her fringe to one side and stroked the side of her face.

"Don't you worry well get you ship shape in no time sweetheart."

As he held her his eyes moved around the room and he soon spied the whisky bottle and realised that she must have got drunk. That was a scenario he could easily accept but injecting herself? Whatever Jess was going through he knew she would never do something like this. As Lucy reappeared he told her to fetch more blankets from the cupboard and together they carefully laid them on top of Jess's frail body. The ambulance seemed to take an age getting to the flat and twice Felix questioned Lucy to make sure she had actually called them. It annoyed her but she didn't say anything as she was too worried about her friend and to hear an argument was the last thing Jess needed. Finally two paramedics entered the flat and took over but as Felix stepped back and placed his arm around Lucy's shoulder he could see that things were far from good. Remembering that she had private medical care Felix informed the medics but they were too busy trying to save the woman's life and weren't in the least bit interested.

"Sorry mate but we aint got time for all that. We need to get her seen by a doctor as soon as possible. Quick Steve she's gone into cardiac arrest!"

Felix was starting to panic and when the second paramedic opened up the defibrillator the colour drained from Felix's face. Lucy, who had been watching the man and could see how much Jess meant to him, moved her arm around Felix's waist and squeezed him tightly. The paramedic shouted clear as he placed the paddles onto Jess's chest. As electricity surged through her body it seemed to momentarily lift her off of the bed. Lucy and Felix held their breath and didn't exhale until they heard the words she's back.

"Right Sir, we need to move her quickly. Would one of you like to travel in the ambulance with her?"

Felix shook his head, he couldn't bear it if her heart stopped again and Lucy was too scared to go with them so she just said Well follow you. Jess was swiftly lifted onto a stretcher and a few minutes later she was in the back of the ambulance which

was speeding towards the emergency department of the Chelsea and Westminster hospital. Felix locked the door to Jess's flat and the pair made their way out onto the street. Once outside they just stared at each other in shock and it was Lucy who broke the silence.
"Come on well get a taxi and follow them to the hospital."
"It's ok my vans parked over there on the street."
"Are you sure you're alright to drive?"
Felix Abbott glared at the girl and his look was enough to silence her. On route to the hospital Lucy asked only one question but it was a rhetorical one.
"This all seems strange, I mean it's not that I know Jess that well but I have come to realise how strong she is and I find it hard to believe that she tried to kill herself. Nothing can be so bad that a person would take their life over it surely?"
The van screeched to a halt and Felix Abbott slammed his palms onto the steering wheel.
"How dare you! If you knew Jess then you wouldn't even ask such a stupid fucking question. That woman has a heart of gold but she's also made of steel. People might piss her off, scare her even but there's no way she would ever do something like this willingly."
"Ok I'm sorry! I shouldn't have asked."
"No you bloody well shouldn't."
The rest of the drive was taken in silence. Lucy felt far too uncomfortable to strike up any sort of a

conversation and Felix was still seething over Lucy's earlier remark. At the casualty department the sad looking pair waited for news. Fifty minutes later they were approached by a doctor who informed them that Jess was still unconscious and that it would be hours before he would be able to tell them anything further. Felix glanced at Lucy and sighing loudly began to speak.
"Let me take you home."
"But what if she comes round and there's no one here? I couldn't bare it if she woke up all alone."
"That won't happen. I promise as soon as I've dropped you off I will come back and wait and I don't care if it takes all night. Now let me have your mobile number and as soon as there's any news I'll call you."
"Promise?"
"Cross my heart and hope to die, now come on let's get you home."
Felix really didn't have a clue who the woman was but in the short space of time that he had known her and seen how upset she was over Jess, well he'd come to like her and somehow knew that she could be trusted. On the drive over to Holland Park Lucy could sense that he wanted to ask her something but when nothing was forthcoming as per usual she went in like a bull at a gate.
"I can see you've got something on your mind. I suppose you're wondering how I know Jess?"
Felix felt embarrassed and for a moment he didn't

know what to say. Glancing at the woman sitting beside him he could see that she was the type not to give up so after a few seconds he at last spoke.
"Ok! So how exactly do you know Jess?"
Lucy breathed in deeply, this was going to be interesting.
"Well I put an advert in the Evening Standard newspaper. You see I'm hoping to write a book about sex workers, their lives, their clients and why they choose to live the lives they do."
Lucy could visibly see Felix cringe and momentarily regretted her choice of words. Still he had asked and she wasn't about to lie. Lucy Urquhart was a straight talker and couldn't do with beating around the bush. It was a complete waste of time to sugar coat things as you always ended up having to reveal the cold hard facts in the end so what was the point.
"I know it doesn't sound too good but you wanted to know. Anyway Jess applied and it went from there really. After our initial meeting we agreed to meet up once a week and she tells me about her life and some of the stories she's come across. I can tell you that she's very discreet and never mentions anyone's names or not their real ones if that's what you're worried about?"
Felix laughed out loud. The young woman was funny even if she wasn't trying to be and he could imagine Jess having a few good chuckles every time they got together.
"Not in the least. I'm not one of her clients if that's

what you're thinking."
Lucy was now embarrassed and she could feel her cheeks begin to flush.
"No I know you're not. Jess has told me all about you, though I could tell by your expression earlier that she hasn't mentioned me to you. No worries, anyway I did offer to pay her for her time but she wouldn't hear of it."
"That's my Jess."
"Yeh I know what you mean. She's a good person really kind, that's why I've been so worried. I could tell straight away that she was also a very strong woman and when she said she was being followed and that she thought someone might be out to hurt her, well I believed her without question."
"She actually said that, actually said that someone was out to hurt her?"
"Basically yes but that wasn't until our last meeting almost a week ago. Have you got any idea who it could be?"
As the van turned into Abbotsbury Road Felix shook his head as he replied.
"Not a clue but if I could get my hands on the bastard well Id...."
"Just here thanks."
Felix pulled into the curb and looked up at the large imposing house.
"Impressive!"
"Do you think so? To be honest it doesn't really mean that much to me. A house is just a house, I

mean you can only be in one room at a time whether you've got two or twenty."

Again Felix wanted to laugh as this posh young woman who had befriended his Jess. Glancing at the huge front window he saw a man and a woman staring intently at them.

"Who are they? Mum and Dad?"

Lucy reached for the door handle to let herself out and looked towards her home at the same time.

"Oh that's just my father and our housekeeper and I expect I'm in for an ear bashing as to who you are and what I'm doing with you."

"Servants as well hey?"

Lucy gave Felix a strange look as she got out of the van as if to say whatever are you talking about but she didn't quiz him about his remark. Running into the house Lucy closed the front door and breathing in deeply was now ready for the roasting that she knew was definitely on the cards from either her father or Norma Sanderson. Just as he had told her he would, Felix returned to the hospital and spent the rest of the day waiting for some positive news on Jess.

CHAPTER TWENTY FOUR

Keeping to his word Felix had phoned Lucy from the hospital with updates on Jess's progress, in fact he called her daily and after three days the news they were both hoping for finally came through. After numerous psychological reports had been carried out by the mental health department and an attempt at group counselling that Jess wouldn't take part in, she was now deemed fit and could receive short visits from family and friends. The police had come to the hospital to interview Jess regarding the drugs but she told them that she couldn't remember anything so there was nothing more they could do. She had decided to remain silent about the attack because if she tried to explain, then she would have to tell them about Liam and Nicky Brent and that would open up a whole can of worms and bring more problems. As much as it went against the grain Jess decided to let the matter drop and prayed that it was all over but deep down she had a nagging doubt. As soon as she saw him, Jess had asked Felix if her mother knew that she was in hospital. When he informed her that he'd decided not to tell Annie Jess had let out a sigh of relief. It wasn't unusual for her to go a week without visiting her mother and Jess knew she could get away with using the excuse that the Arab had asked her to stay for a few extra days. Asking for a telephone to be brought to her bedside Jess Metcalf called her mother and told her what a wonderful time she was having and that she would try and pop round in the next couple of days. Annie Metcalf was over the moon to hear from her daughter and she now knew that Jess's plan was really happening and that soon the two of them could leave London.

Over in Holland Park it had taken all of Lucy's resolve not to talk about what had happened regarding her friend. It would have helped her if she could have unburdened herself to Norma Sanderson and tell the woman all her fears and worries but Lucy knew that she must not breath a word. The fact that she had made a promise, unlike the shallow ones she usually made to her father and the realisation that this one was really important kept her on her guard. A real chatter box, she would normally run away at the mouth and it would all just tumble out but this time she accepted that she couldn't speak about it to anyone. It seemed that finally Lucy Urquhart was growing up. She was aware that she was a gossip at the best of times so to avoid saying anything she shouldn't, had spent the last few days holed up in her room. George Urquhart was so busy with work that he hadn't really noticed his daughters absence but it was a different matter when it came down to Norma Sanderson. The bubbly brash girl that she had loved for years had suddenly disappeared and was replaced with a quiet moody stranger who

Norma was very worried about. Making her way upstairs Norma Sanderson gently tapped on Lucy's door. When there was no answer, just as there hadn't been over the last few days, she was about to walk away when she heard the faintest reply.
"Come in."
Norma made the sign of the cross over her chest and opening the door wore the happiest smile she could muster.
"Hello darling how are you feeling today?"
Lucy knew Norma meant well, she also knew that the woman was desperate to find out what the problem was.
"Honestly I'm fine."
"Well I know that isn't the whole truth but as you well know I've never been one to pry. If you need to talk then you know where I am sweetheart."
Lucy Urquhart smiled and after Norma had spent longer than usual tidying up the room and when she knew that the girl wasn't going to offer up any explanation for her quietness, she went back down stairs and busied herself with the day to day chores of running the house. Lucy hated keeping things from Norma; after all since her own mother had passed away Norma had been the one person she had always turned to. Dragging herself up off of the bed she changed into fresh clothes and made her way downstairs. Hopefully Jess would be glad to see her or at least she prayed that would be the case. Her new found friend, had on a daily basis, been

seeing a psychiatrist and Lucy knew that wasn't a good thing but she was unaware that with all attempted suicides and that was exactly what Jess was being treated for, it was standard practice. Pulling on her coat she stood in the hall and waited for her cab to arrive. Normally Lucy Urquhart walked everywhere but today she felt emotionally drained. Felix had arranged for them to visit on a rota basis and as his turn wasn't until this evening Lucy had agreed to do the afternoon shift. Norma didn't hear her leave and the girl was glad of that as contrary to what she'd said upstairs, Lucy knew the housekeeper would only question her further and she was still too upset about it all and feared she would break down and that it would all come tumbling out. The driver from the private hire company she had telephoned spoke little English, which suited Lucy perfectly. Originally Jess had been taken to the Chelsea and Westminster NHS hospital but as soon as she was out of danger, both physically and mentally, she had been moved to the private Cromwell hospital. It couldn't be proven that she had definitely tried to take her own life, so her private admission had been logged as rest due to an accidental overdose. When Jess first started her career shed made sure that she had private healthcare, though she never expected to need it like she did now. Lucy's taxi pulled up on Cromwell road and the building resembled a five star hotel more than it did a hospital. After giving her name to the receptionist and informing the woman that she was here to visit Jess Metcalf, Lucy was personally shown up to room two one three. As Lucy Urquhart tapped on the door and walked in she was surprised to see Jess sitting up in bed and the smile she received instantly put her at her ease. Almost running over to the bed Lucy grabbed her friends hand as she clumsily sat down on the edge of the mattress.

"Oh Jess! You don't know how glad I am to see you, I've been so worried. You know we thought you wouldn't make it?"

Same old Lucy always putting her foot in it but her words still brought a smile to Jess's face.

"Well hello to you too Lucy! How are you doing?"

"How am I doing? I think it's me who should be asking you that. God you were in such a state Jess, I was so scared."

"Lucy stop! I'm fine honestly."

"So why did you do it, you must have been in turmoil? If you'd phoned I would have come round in an instant. I would never have let you take drugs no matter how you were feeling."

"I didn't."

"Sorry?"

"I didn't take drugs. Some man broke into my flat, held me down and stuck a needle into my arm. They wanted it to look like suicide and from your reaction they seem to have succeeded."

Lucy's eyes opened wide, this was all so intriguing

and for a moment she was overcome with guilt at the thought of how much she was enjoying it all.
"There was more than one then?"
"No, when I said they I meant he must have been paid by someone to get rid of me."
"Oh my god! You have to tell someone Jess, you have to phone the police and..."
Jess placed a finger to her lips which instantly silenced Lucy. At the same time she half-heartedly laughed but as she did so she also began to cry. Since her attack she didn't seem able to control her emotions and cried at the least little thing. Felix had told her it was a good thing like a release valve but Jess didn't like it. She hated showing any sign of weakness and to Jess Metcalf crying was definitely a weakness. Lightly tapping the bed clothes she beckoned for Lucy to move in a little closer.
"Now promise you're not going to do anything silly like go to the police on my behalf? I'm so tired and right now I know I couldn't deal with it."
"Ok I promise I won't and I'm sorry to be nosey but I just can't believe what I saw. I haven't been able to eat or sleep but I promise I haven't breathed a word to anyone. Poor Felix has been at his wits end, you know he really does love you and......""
Jess furrowed her brow and Lucy lowered her gaze. Jess smiled, she liked the young girl and although at the beginning she had her doubts, now she knew that trust was something Lucy didn't take lightly.
"Enough about Felix Abbott and I'm well aware

how he feels about me thank you very much. Lucy I need to ask you to do something for me."

"Just ask Jess, if I can do anything to help I will."

"It's good of you to offer but it's no great task or anything like that. Remember our last meeting when I gave you a piece of paper with a phone number on it?"

"Of course I do but I think now you should be talking to the police about him and..."

"Noooooo! Lucy you said a minute ago that you wouldn't so promise me you won't, please please promise me?"

Lucy was taken aback by the way Jess was almost pleading with her and she reached out and touched the woman's hand in an attempt to calm her.

"Ok ok I won't if that's what you want, though I really don't understand why you wouldn't want to find out...."

Jess cut Lucy off mid sentence. She knew she had to try and explain but where to begin or just how much she should tell the girl was a worry. Jess could be brutally honest but she knew the outcome would cause even more trouble. The problem with holding back was that Lucy Urquhart was a bright girl and would be able to tell in an instant if Jess was trying to pull the wool over her eyes. Deciding the best line of action would be to reveal only the bare minimum, she began to speak.

"Look that number was, well I guess it was who I thought might be hassling me. Now things are getting out of hand and I just want to forget about it all and move on."

"But why?"

"Honey I really can't go there but needless to say, if I value my life then that piece of paper you're holding for safe keeping needs to be destroyed. I now know the persons real name and what he represents. I really need you to tear that piece of paper into shreds and throw it away. Promise me that you'll do what I ask darling please?"

Lucy Urquhart couldn't believe what she was hearing but at the same time she didn't want Jess upset anymore than she already was. Crossing her heart with her finger just as shed done as a child she promised that when she got back home she would get rid of the piece of paper and with Lucy's words Jess let out a sigh of relief.

"Good girl and I thank you from the bottom of my heart. Now how's that novel coming along? I hope you're working hard on it; I don't want to have gone through all of this for nothing babe. To see your name in print would be well worth me telling my story."

Lucy thought that Jess's last sentence was strange, maybe it was all the medication she was on but still Lucy couldn't help but ask.

"What do you mean all that you've gone through?"

Jess Metcalf realised that she had said too much and tried to back pedal but her words didn't cut it with the young girl. Lucy had already made up her mind that one way or another she would make it her business to find out exactly what had happened to her friend. It might take her a while but justice had to be done and the culprit caught no matter what.

"Oh take no notice of me sweetheart, my heads all over the place. I just meant all of our meetings and stuff. Look when I get out of here we need to have a few intense get-togethers because I've not changed my mind about getting out of this game once and for all and you still need research for your book. I have never been one to renege on a deal so I will tell you all that you need to know then I am going to disappear for good."

"But why? I mean you have a good life or at least a profitable one. Why do you want to disappear? Oh Jess I really wish you would tell me what's going on?"

"Look sweetheart, you can only last a certain amount of time in this game. It takes its toll on your looks not to mention your mind. I have loved my career and believe me I wouldn't have changed it for the world but when it's over its over. I just want to relax and take care of my mum for a change. She's had a hard life with my bastard of a father and deserves to be looked after for once. What with how things have been for the last few weeks and now this, well to tell you the truth I'm drained love. I really need to chill for a bit and get my head together."

Jess hoped she sounded convincing and that Lucy would now let the matter drop.

"I'm not sure I understand what's going on Jess?"

"You don't need to Lucy. Now I'm not being rude sweetheart but I'm really tired. What say I give you a call once I'm discharged and we can meet up somewhere?"

Lucy knew when she was being given the brush off but she didn't say anymore and standing up placed a kiss onto Jess's forehead before walking to the door. About to open it she was stopped when her friend gave her one last reminder.

"Remember what I said about that phone number Lucy, destroy it!"

Lucy Urquhart nodded and then walked from the room. Jess wasn't that tired but she knew that if she didn't get rid of the girl then Lucy would only continue to question her. As yet no one was privy to what had gone on; well only her attacker and she couldn't see him saying anything. Jess was sure that if the only thing linking her to the culprit was destroyed and that she disappeared, then it should all be over with, or at least she hoped it would be.

Lucy slowly walked home and thought about everything on the way. It was all a mess and nothing made sense. Letting herself into the house she slipped into the study without being seen by Norma. Her father was still at work so Lucy had a good couple of hours to begin her investigations. Wiping the board in her father's study Lucy set about making a list of suspects. Going back over her old notes she wrote down the names of Peter Lenson, Nicky Brent, Morris Granger, Sharon Russell, Liam Flanagan, the Arab, the Kids and many more, she even included Felix on the list. Standing back to look at her handy work Lucy realised that there was just one problem but it was a major one. She didn't have a clue if any of these names were the peoples real names and that included Felix. It was a dead end, how could you even begin to search for a person when you didn't even know what they were called. Slumping down in her father's chair she bit on the tip of her pen while she thought of what to do next. There was one other thing she could try but she knew that if she did it then Jess would be really angry with her. Still Lucy hoped she would also be pleased if her attacker was eventually caught. Removing the folded piece of paper from her purse she inspected the numbers. The right thing to do would be to take it straight round to the police but as far as they were concerned it was an attempted suicide and they wouldn't be interested. Even if they were, as far as Lucy's involvement was concerned it would all be over and Lucy didn't want it to be over. She wanted to personally help her friend and in doing so somehow tie Jess to her. Not able to restrain herself she lifted the receiver of the desk phone and slowly tapped in the numbers. Suddenly she could hear a mobile ringing and for a moment it didn't really register but when it finally hit home that the sound was coming from within the desk she was sitting at, Lucy ended the call. Replacing the receiver she tried to open the drawer but it was locked. Picking up the handset she redialled the number and again ringing could be heard coming from inside the desk. Now very anxious Lucy grabbed her father's long steel letter opener. Forcing the tip of the opener on the rim of the drawer she began to furiously wiggle it. Somehow it worked and Lucy suddenly heard the lock click down. Slowly pulling the drawer open, the first thing that came into view was a mobile phone which was still ringing; when she replaced the handset into its cradle the mobile fell silent. Moving her hand around in the drawer she felt something smooth and opening it further she looked down and saw a pile of magazines. Lifting one out Lucy studied it and realised they were fetish magazines and about as hard core as you could get. Now feeling physically sick, she had to swallow hard to stop herself from vomiting. This didn't make sense, none of it. Slowly she realised that it all made perfect sense, Peter Lenson was in fact her father. Lucy again felt sick rise into her throat, her head was pounding and she couldn't think straight. Not able to stop herself she once more tapped in the number Jess had given her into the desk phone and the mobile started to ring. Lucy dropped both telephones and crossing her arms onto the desk she lowered her head and began to

sob, heart wrenching sobs that made her whole body tremble. Five minutes later when there were no more tears left she at last lifted her head.
By the time George Urquhart came home Lucy had composed herself. Still sitting behind her father's desk her face now wore a cold hard expression. As George turned the handle to the study door he let out a gasp. The row of antique bookcases that lined the wall were covered in page after page of sadomasochistic scenes. It had taken Lucy quite a while to glue them all on but she was so angry and disgusted that she wouldn't allow herself to stop until she had completed the task.
"What the hell's going on here?"
"You know fine well what this is about daddy dearest! Did you think by locking away your dirty little secret I wouldn't find out?"
George took a step further into the room but Lucy held her palm out in his direction.
"Darling it's not what you think, I was..."
Lucy stood up and walking around the desk, stopped a few feet away from her father.
"Don't try and worm your way out of this. Your sexual preferences are your own business but trying to kill someone is a different matter."
"I didn't I..."
Lucy Urquhart stood up and walked towards her father.
"Don't fucking lie to me! Jess was my friend and you or someone you employed, tried to kill her.

Why daddy, why did you do it?"
George went to touch his daughter but she stepped sideways and shrugged away his arm. The thought of any physical contact with her father repulsed Lucy.
"Look things got out of hand and she knew too much. Darling you don't understand the world that I live in, believe me I had no choice in the matter."
"You had every choice and you know the saddest thing of all? Whatever it was you were trying to cover up, I don't think Jess knew anything about it. Whatever you think she knew, you were wrong but you didn't bother to find that out did you? I shall be leaving in the morning and I swear to you on my mother's grave that you will never see me again. I can't bear to look at you anymore, you absolutely disgust me."
With those parting words Lucy ran from the study and into the hall. Almost bumping into Norma, the woman couldn't be off seeing the look of anger and tears in Lucy's eyes.
"Whatever's the matter darling?"
Lucy didn't reply and grabbing her coat she ran towards the front door as Norma called after her.
"Now where are you going, dinner won't be long and you know your father doesn't like you to be late."
Lucy Urquhart had just two words to say Fuck him! As George emerged from the study Norma was standing in the hall open mouthed and totally

flabbergasted at Lucy's words.
"Oh Mr Urquhart, whatever's the matter?"
George didn't try to explain and ignoring his housekeeper continued to walk on and made his way outside. The last couple of weeks had taken their toll on George Urquhart, far more than anyone could ever have known. Every night he'd had horrific nightmares about what had happened to Jess and now that his daughter had found out about his secret life, well there was nothing left but to end it all. There was no one he could talk to or share his burden with and he knew his daughter well enough to know that she would never forgive him. It had taken every ounce of strength he had just to carry on after his wife had died but Lucy had given him a reason to continue, without her George felt his life wasn't worth living. Entering the garage he removed a few packing cases before he found what he was looking for. The roll of thick rope had once been used for towing but had lain redundant for years until now. Hauling it over his shoulder he once again entered the house. The hall was empty and he guessed that Norma was downstairs in the kitchen. George was glad of that fact; he had always liked the woman and wouldn't have wanted her to witness his action. In a robotic way as if he was void of all feeling, George climbed the stairs and secured one end of the rope to the banister. After making a noose with the other he swiftly placed it around his neck, climbed up onto the

handrail and jumped. Lucy sat on the green a few yards from the house. It was cold and the bench was hard but she was oblivious to the discomfort. After mulling everything over in her mind she came to the conclusion that she had two choices, go to the police regarding what her father had done or keep her mouth shut. In the short time she had known her Lucy had come too really like Jess Metcalf but when all was said and done, she wasn't family, it wasn't Jess's blood that flowed through Lucy Urquhart's veins. There and then Lucy made up her mind. As much as it would hurt her, she would end all contact with Jess and stay loyal to her father, though even mentally referring to him as her father now seemed to leave a bitter taste in her mouth. Standing in the darkness Lucy stared up at the sky and swore on her mother's grave that one day she would make the bastard pay for what he'd done. Lucy was drained and her eyelids felt heavy, there was nowhere to go so reluctantly she headed home. The hallway was now in darkness and after switching on the light she hadn't got more than four or five steps when she saw a moving shadow in the stairwell. Norma Sanderson was in the process of removing a meat pie from the oven when she heard the terrible piercing screams. The pie fell to the floor and smashed as she raced up the stone stairs. The sight that greeted her was horrific. The lifeless body of George Urquhart was swinging in the stairwell and Lucy was on her knees wailing and

rocking back and forth. Grabbing the telephone Norma dialled the emergency services and after quickly relaying what had happened she then went to comfort Lucy. Kneeling on the floor she took the girl into her arms and held her close. Lucy's entire body shook with every heartbreaking sob that wracked through her tiny frame. Everything seemed to happen in slow motion but in reality it was less than ten minutes before help arrived. As Georges body was cut down by the police and paramedics Norma led Lucy into the sitting room. The girl was inconsolable and no matter what Norma said or did it made little difference. With Norma by her side Lucy answered as many question as she could but in the end the detectives said they would return at a later date. The family doctor was called and after Lucy was sedated Norma helped her up the stairs. Sitting on the side of the bed she waited for the girl to drift off to sleep but it took longer than expected as Lucy fought against the drug and was desperate for answers.
"Why Norma, why did he do it?"
"I don't know sweetheart."
Suddenly the sobbing resumed and the sound broke Norma Sanderson's heart. Her beautiful bubbly girl seemed to be fading before her eyes and there was nothing Norma could do about it.
"It's all my fault."
"Don't be so silly, how could it be?"
"You don't understand Norma, it really is all my

fault and I'll never forgive myself, I'll never be able to hug my daddy and tell him that I love him no matter what he did."

Lucy relayed everything and when she'd finished she looked at Norma as if she was pleading for an answer. The housekeeper didn't offer any but she also didn't seem shocked.

"Please don't tell me that you knew?"

"About your father? I didn't know anything about this Jess woman if that's what you mean but I did have my suspicions regarding the fetish business."

Suddenly Lucy sat bolt upright.

"Then why in god's name didn't you tell me Norma, I could have..."

Norma cut Lucy off mid sentence.

"No you couldn't have stopped it if that's what you were about to say. Darling how people choose to live their lives is up to them. Your father loved you more than life itself but his sex life was nothing to do with you. Now I don't know anything about what you've told me but please don't let that tarnish your memories of him. Your father was a good man and it seems to me that he was out of his depth and didn't know what else to do. You can let this eat you up and ruin the rest of your life or you can let it go but either way you're never going to change things."

Norma reached into the pocket of her apron and removed a white envelope.

"I found this in the study when the paramedics were

here. I didn't want the police to see it and I don't know if I'm doing the right thing by giving it to you now but there's something in here that he obviously wanted you to read."
Norma slowly handed over the letter and as Lucy began to tear open the envelope her hands were shaking terribly. Taking in a deep breath she began to read.

My beautiful darling daughter
I am so sorry for the hurt that I have caused and the pain you must be feeling right at this moment. I know you said I had a choice but at the time I didn't think so. With hindsight you were right but I'm unable to turn the clock back. What I am about to do will have a terrible impact on you and once again I do have a choice but this one is far easier. After your mother passed away I didn't think I could go on but with Norma's help and having you to raise I had a reason to continue. That is no longer the case and to live without you in my life is unbearable. I know you hate me and deep down I don't blame you but I was lost darling and had nowhere to turn. Soon I will be at peace and once more reunited with your mother. Never blame yourself my princess, this was all my doing. Be strong, live your life and remember that I will love you for all time. Begging your forgiveness.
Daddy xxx

Lucy laid the letter onto the duvet and the sobbing

began all over again but finally she couldn't struggle any longer and laying her head down, drifted off to sleep. Norma Sanderson wearily went down stairs to the kitchen and made herself a cup of hot sweet tea. Sitting down at the table, her eyes surveyed the mess on the floor. The pie and broken dish still lay in pieces but for once she couldn't be bothered to sort it out. Her mind went over everything that Lucy had told her but still she couldn't seem to get her head around it. In the space of a couple of months her happy little family, for that's how she looked upon the Urquhart's, had fallen to pieces. A lone tear dropped onto the scrubbed pine as she recalled a promise she had made to George shortly after Sonia's death. She had sworn to help raise and care for Lucy as if she were her own. Now more than ever she had to keep that promise and staring upwards she prayed to god for help.

THE END

EPILOGUE

The funeral of George Urquhart was a dismal affair but not through the lack of people attending. The church was filled to capacity with government officials and even a few politicians but apart from Norma there was no one there that really liked the man or knew how Lucy was feeling. In honour of her father, Lucy had played her part well but when the service was finally over she went straight back to the house with Norma and locked the front door. The subject of Jess Metcalf was never again mentioned by Norma Sanderson, who thought it best to let sleeping dogs lie. Lucy would never see or speak to Jess again; it would have been too painful not to mention embarrassing. For the first six months after her father's death Lucy wouldn't leave the house. The once happy home now seemed soulless, it broke Norma's heart and she knew she had to do something. Finally, after much pressure from the house keeper, Lucy began to get to grips with life. Deciding to go travelling and after promising Norma that she would only stay in the best hotels and keep in regular contact, Lucy set off on a journey that would last for several months. On her return she was the old Lucy, bubbly, funny and happy. It had taken her a long time but she had at last accepted that her father was gone, that none of it was her fault and that no matter what, she would always love him. To date Lucy Urquhart's book remains unfinished.

Harry Fuller never received his fifty thousand pounds payment and was informed by Silvia Gladman that no further action would be required regarding Jess Metcalf. Maybe she was going soft in her old age or maybe it was just the fact that she had gotten too mixed up in all of this without following protocol. Either way, her decision meant that for the foreseeable future Jess would be allowed to live and Harry was glad about it as he quite liked the young woman. When a few weeks later he was summoned to Millbank and told that his services would no longer be required by MI5, he had taken it upon himself to write up a dossier regarding all that had happened and who had been involved. Doing as he'd been instructed Harry Fuller left London but not before he'd deposited the dossier with a solicitor and had written a letter to Silvia. Harry wanted to make sure that she was in no doubt, should anything suspicious ever happen to him, then the file would be passed on to the press so that it could be made public knowledge. For a while his threat bothered Silvia Gladman but she reasoned that as long as Harry remained safe then she had little to worry about.

As for Jess, a short spell of recuperation had been spent at the Savoy Hotel all courtesy of Mohamed the Arab. He had returned unexpectedly to London and on hearing of her plight had offered the use of his penthouse. Jess didn't argue and in all honesty she and Annie had enjoyed a whale of a time, especially when it came to Annie ordering room service, something shed never experienced in her life before. When Jess received news of Georges demise she had contemplated telephoning Lucy but it only took her a few seconds to realise that it wouldn't be a good idea.

Prior to taking up residence in the Savoy, Jess had made a quick visit back to her flat to collect some clothes. She was too scared to go alone so had asked Felix to accompany her. About to leave, Jess spied the letter that shed placed in the rack just over a week ago and snatching it up she shoved it into her handbag. Later that day just after shed taken a bath Jess suddenly remembered the letter and removing it, slowly unfolded the paper. When she read that it was from a firm of solicitors and Liam's name was mentioned on the top line Jess was intrigued and as she read on couldn't believe what she was seeing. Jess was to inherit the whole of Liam Flanagan's business concerns and it took a few minutes for the news to sink in. It was a nice surprise but not a total shock as Jess was well aware of his feelings for her but she hadn't realised just how wealthy he was. When she felt well enough she had quickly sold off all of Liam's properties and businesses and was now a woman of means and one who would never have to work again. Six months later she finally sold her own flat and along with Annie had moved to a beautiful whitewashed villa on the island of Crete. Her days were spent either lounging in the sun or leisurely passing the time browsing the local markets. Annie Metcalf was a new woman. Her hair had grown and was now a classy shade of blonde and her clothes all came from high end boutiques. It had taken several months before Jess could stop herself from smiling at the transformation every time she looked at her mother. Bob Metcalf never did learn where his wife had disappeared to. He had arrived home from the pub one Friday night and the house was empty. A white envelope was propped up on the fireplace and a single sheet of paper contained just two words Fuck you! Slightly inebriated Bob had ransacked the two bed terrace from top to bottom in a desperate attempt to find out where she'd gone but it was a futile attempt that resulted in nothing. A few months later Jess received a message from Felix informing her that her father had suffered a stroke and was now in a nursing home. When Jess sat her mother down and gently told her, Annie had just shrugged her shoulders and went back to her gardening. Felix Abbott would visit every couple of months or so but his relationship with Jess would never be anything more than platonic. It took a while but in the end he accepted it, had to accept it as he would rather have her in his life as a friend than not to have her at all. Two years after the move Jess strangely started to get restless for her old life. She wasn't ungrateful for the money and all the trappings it brought but there was only so much shopping and sunbathing a person could do before it got boring. It had taken her a while but she finally came to realise that as much as her clients needed her she needed them more. The day that things would change had started off normally enough. Annie had cooked them both breakfast and had been heading in the direction of the garden when she was stopped by the sound of her daughters voice. She wouldn't call it eves dropping as all the doorways were open arched but she still hovered a little longer than was necessary so she could listen in on the conversation.

"Hello is that Morris? This is your Mistress calling. I shall be back in London within a couple of months and I demand that you call on me. That's a good boy Morris, see you soon."

Annie Metcalf smiled to herself, Jess was going back to what she knew and loved best and Annie couldn't have been happier. Jess had no intention of selling the villa or asking her mother to return with her and Annie instinctively knew the topic would never arise. Her own life had changed so much and she could never envisage going back to London. In Crete all the locals loved her and no one knew of her past and the unhappiness she had experienced. Annie was never forced to explain herself to anyone and as far as she was concerned it was going to stay that way. It was agreed that Jess would visit whenever she could and having a bolt hole, a little place for her to relax in, would do her good. All in all and even after she'd finally learnt what Jess had gone through at the hands of Harry Fuller, Annie

Metcalf had to admit that life was turning out well for her daughter not to mention herself.

Printed in Great Britain
by Amazon